THE RELATIONSHIP PACT

KINGS OF FOOTBALL

ADRIANA LOCKE

The Relationship Pact

Cover Designer: Letitia Hasser, RBA Designs

Content Editor: Marion Making Manuscripts

Copy Editor: Editing 4 Indies, Jenny Sims

Proofreader: Michele Ficht

Umbrella Publishing

This book is dedicated to Aunt Judy. I'm working on the firetrucks.

SYNOPSIS

How hard can it be?

That was the question rolling around Larissa Mason's mind just before she asked Hollis Hudson to be her fake boyfriend.

It was only supposed to be for five minutes, after all.

Granted, that was also before she felt his hand on the small of her back as he charmed the heck out of her family.

And it was *definitely* before she saw the football god shirtless. Otherwise, she would've had an idea of just how hard *some things* could be.

It turns out that pretending to be in love with a crazily handsome, somewhat enigmatic, and absolutely unforgettable tight end (who has an amazing tight end) is easy.

Reminding herself that just because opposites attract doesn't mean they're forever is much harder.

What they have isn't love—it's a relationship pact. *Right?*

PROLOGUE

See those three boys over there?

Yeah, the kings of football?

The ones with their heads in their hands, drinking their beers and trying to figure out what the hell happened to their season?

They choked.

That's right. These all-Americans became the biggest upset in college football and a complete embarrassment to their town.

Can it really be that bad?

Yes.

Former national champions, Braxton College was annihilated this year.

No, not just annihilated—completely and utterly destroyed.

Three games.

That's it.

They won three games all season.

Interceptions. Dropped balls. Missed blocks. Fumbles. You name it, they did it.

First, there's Hollis Hudson, the mysterious tight end who keeps everything locked down. He couldn't run a route to save his life this year.

Next is Crew Smith, the protective one. Once an NFL hopeful, he now holds the record for the most interceptions in a season for a quarterback.

And rounding out the trifecta of crap is River Tate, the popular frat boy. He's supposed to be a superstar wide receiver but dropped more passes than he caught.

Guys wanted to be them.

Girls wanted their hearts.

But at this point, not sure anyone would touch them with a ten-foot pole.

The truth is, they've screwed up their prospective NFL careers.

Maybe their entire lives.

There are three stories to be told…

This is Hollis's.

ONE
HOLLIS

Me: My abs are still impressive.

I hit send on the text message and drop my phone to the bed.

The sky is dark outside my hotel room window. I yank the curtains closed before resuming getting dressed. The black sweater I borrowed from River's closet before I left campus sits snugly over my aforementioned abdominal muscles. I slip on a pair of sneakers—also borrowed from River because he has a better wardrobe than I do—and take a quick look in the mirror.

"Not too shabby," I say to my reflection.

I'm reaching for my wallet next to the mini-fridge when my phone dings, so I grab it instead.

River: Oh, thank God. I was getting worried. <sarcastic emoji>

Crew: What kind of status update is this, Hollis? Your abs? Really?

I grin as I type out my response.

Me: Would you rather I had given you the weather?

As soon as I type that out, I know what's coming. My eyes shoot to the ceiling, and I brace for the flurry of incoming texts undoubtedly on their way.

Crew: The weatherman Hollis Hudson!

River: Only if you jump up and down for two minutes while you recite it.

Crew: You should bring that back.

River: Totally.

Flashbacks of my freshman year pledge for Kappa—the weather pledge—come floating back.

The fraternity officers were trying to embarrass me with that whole thing. I had to wake up at the ass crack of dawn and post myself reading the weather report on social media.

For a year.

On top of that, if anyone asked me the weather—which, naturally, everyone did—I had to recite it on the spot while jumping up and down.

For two minutes.

It was a hassle and a pain in the ass, as designed. The joke was on them, though. I got so much freaking attention from the female body of Braxton College without even having to try that I should've sent the officers a thank-you note.

Because the weather report my freshman year? It was raining women.

Crew: We're just screwing with you. Did you make it to Savannah?

Me: I just got here a little bit ago. Hotel is fucking niiiiiiice.

River: It better be. Lincoln Landry is a baseball legend. He can afford to put you up in nice digs.

My whole body tenses. I sit on the edge of one of the two queen-sized beds with the softest blankets I've ever felt and let my elbows rest on my knees.

It's been three months since I received the letter requesting my presence at the Catching-A-Care awards banquet, a nonprofit ran by future Hall of Fame baseball player for the Tennessee Arrows, Lincoln Landry. I'm as shocked now as the day I opened the envelope.

How the charity found out about the time I quietly spend with a foster group home on the weekends is beyond me. It's not something I advertise or talk about during interviews. It's a talking point I hide from the media.

It's not for them. I don't want it exploited as some mindless chatter while camera operators zoom in on a play.

It's my thing. It's the *one thing* I have all to myself. It's the only thing not jaded by my position on campus or the fact that I'm an athlete or that my abs are awesome.

But, somehow, the board of directors got my name, and here I am.

A part of me was a little pissed off about the whole thing. I went back and forth with the directors for a long time—me saying, "Thanks but no thanks" and them saying, "But we'd really like to do this." Eventually, they promised not to name the city I volunteer in or the organization, and I agreed to attend. I think they labeled me as being "difficult," but whatever. I don't want the kids feeling like I was spending time there for any other reason than I care.

The Board put me up in this kick-ass hotel—even covering it for an extra week because I mentioned I was coming in early. As much as I hate to admit it, it's a pretty good distraction from life at the moment.

River: What are you doing tonight?

Crew: Don't you mean WHO he's doing tonight?

River: Excellent point.

I roll my eyes.

Me: Oh, come on.

Crew: Dude. Don't try to lie to us. We know you.

River: The real you.

Crew: And we like you anyway. Go figure.

River: Most of the time. Easy with your generalizations there, Hollywood.

Crew: I stand corrected. However, do you have a name yet?

My laughter fills the room.

Me: While I'm honored you think I can work that fast, I haven't.

River: We don't think. We know. We've seen you in action.

I scoff.

Me: Like you're any better, asshole.

Crew: Hey, I'm really feeling the love, but I gotta go. I'm in the middle of something. Thanks for checking in, Hollis, even if it was super random and slightly weird.

Me: You asked for check-ins. I'm giving them to you. Be careful what you wish for.

Crew: Noted.

River: A redhead.

Me: ?

Crew: He's totally going with a blonde.

Me: I thought you were gone.

Crew: Bye.

River: I'm gone too.

Me: Later.

Tossing my phone on the bed, I look up. My reflection is smiling back at me.

I sit and stare at myself for a while, taking in the strangeness of seeing something other than a grimace on my face. Between royally fucking up our football season, ruining any chance I had at the pros—however small that chance might've been—and now the holidays, life has been more piss than posies.

But when is it not, really?

Get your shit together. Crazy Carl's words filter through my mind. The late-sixties alien hunter from our favorite bar, The Truth is Out There, gave River, Crew, and me that wise piece of advice after we lost our last game … and ended the season with an interception.

Somehow, it seemed fitting.

I grab my wallet, shove it in my pocket, and head for the door.

"You know you're screwed when Crazy Carl makes sense," I grumble, getting to my feet. "But he's right. *I gotta get my shit together.*"

Time is running out.

TWO
LARISSA

"I'm done." I finish drying my hands and then toss the brown paper in the trash. "I mean it this time. Don't try to talk me out of it."

Bellamy bites the corner of her lip as she finishes rinsing her hands. While her voice may not betray her, her eyes certainly do.

"Don't laugh at me," I warn her.

"I'm not."

But she is. Suppressed humor at my expense splashes across her pretty face. I can't blame her for being amused by my slightly random and altogether unrealistic statement because I've said this before.

More than once, actually.

And even though I've always meant it, I *really* mean it this time.

"May I ask with what, exactly, you're done with?" Bellamy asks, flipping a long, blond lock of hair over her shoulder. "Because there are a couple of different options here, and I just want to clarify."

"Men."

"That's a very, *very* broad term, Riss."

I stand beside the settee in the ladies' room of Paddy's, my favorite restaurant in Savannah, and watch my best friend apply another coat of fabulous red lipstick. It screams confidence and badassery—two things that Bellamy Davenport certainly is. I'd like to think I am those things too, except, unlike Bells, I keep getting played.

This has been an unfortunate consistency throughout the past few years. I think a relationship has long-standing potential, and my lover thinks I'm nothing more than a glorified booty call. I'm all for a good one-night stand if the conditions are right. I'm not even totally opposed to a friends-with-benefits package.

What I am against, *vehemently*, are men who lure me in, sweep me off my feet, and then turn out to be egotistical, narcissistic, and completely selfish maniacs.

"Maybe I wanted it to be a broad term," I tell her. "Maybe I'm done with men altogether."

"But are you? Are you *really*?" She slips her lipstick back into her purse. "Because I know you and the men you so sadly choose to date—"

"Hey!"

"And I don't think men as a gender are your problem. And I think you know that."

I gasp in mock horror. "What are you saying? Are you saying *I'm* the problem?"

"I'd never even consider such a thing," she teases.

"Liar."

She spins on her heel and faces me. When our eyes meet, we start to laugh.

Bellamy has been my best friend my entire life. I can't remember a time when I didn't know her. She's always lived next door to my aunt Siggy—the best aunt in the entire world—and she's always been the wild to my calm.

More or less.

"You know what your problem is," she says pointedly when her laughter subsides. "It's not fair to yourself to pretend it's every man in the universe when, in reality, it's—"

"Athletes," we say in unison.

I sigh as dramatically as I can.

My weakness for the fit and delicious specimen who runs, jumps, and throws balls or hits pucks started in junior high school. It's not a revelation.

I had the biggest, most annoying crush on a boy who played centerfield on my cousin's all-star baseball team. I was twelve. He was older than me and had a swagger about him that appealed to me on a level I didn't know existed. He was a little headstrong and a whole lot cocky—just enough to seem forbidden. My thing with athletes—and probably bad boys, if I'm honest—started that summer.

My brain shuffles through the memories of my last few boyfriends.

There was Charlie—the hockey goalie with sweet eyes and it's-not-cheating-if-it's-not-penetration code of conduct.

Benny was next. He was a minor league baseball player who firmly believed my place was in the kitchen. But not barefoot. He liked me in expensive heels.

There was Christopher—a sports manager who was career-driven and egotistical and couldn't shut up about his day long enough to ask me about mine.

And, as if I had to prove to myself that I could do worse, I chose Sebastian Townsend. The golfer-turned-sports agent from Atlanta decided my take on monogamy—that cheaters should have their reproductive organs removed—was harsh, and I should *cushion my expectations*. Apparently, men are bees, and it's their job to pollinate the flowers of the world.

It's safe to say he didn't support the idea of one bee plus one flower equals happiness. He also didn't love—i.e., became enraged—at his theory working in reverse. Was one flower supposed to hope the one bee pollinating her had decent skills? Maybe she should be as free as the bee?

He took offense.

I'm not sure who ended it with who that night, but it went down rather spitefully … about as petty as Sebastian is tonight.

When I look back up at Bellamy, she's shaking her head. "Don't."

"Don't what?"

"Don't let *him* get in your head." She gets to her feet and towers over me in her nude-colored heels that are entirely unnecessary for a friend's birthday party. "Sebastian is a twerp. I know all of his little smug grins and bullshit waves, with his new girl shrink-wrapped to his side, are getting to you tonight."

"They are not."

"So, you're swearing off all men out of the blue? Riss, you like dick. You're not going to go all cold turkey like that. It's because he got to you tonight."

I get to my feet in a rush. "He did *not* get to me tonight. He pissed me off. That little line about how … *shameful*, or whatever word he used, it must be to show up to our friend's birthday party alone pissed me off."

"Yeah. Of course, it did. It was by design."

Anger pulses through me. "He used the word dreadful. *It must have been dreadful to have to bring Bellamy as your date*. I didn't even get a chance to tell him I wasn't here alone or with you as my date. Even though you are. But you know what I mean."

"Either way, fuck him! I'm a great date."

I smile through my annoyance. "He also told me not to worry. He told people our break-up was mutual and not that he had to let me down easy."

Bellamy balks. "It *was* mutual."

"Oh, trust me. I know. I was there."

"That little twerp."

I turn away from her and look in the mirror.

My reflection stares back at me. In my eyes, I see the truth. Sebastian didn't get to me tonight. *I did.*

I've known for a while now that I needed a break. Ever since Christopher ghosted me because work always came first, I've learned that something had to change. I've just refused to give it too much thought—probably because I didn't want to be here, standing in front of my reflection and knowing I have no one to blame for this mess of a love life other than me.

They say doing the same things while expecting a different result is ridiculous. That's what I've been doing. Dating different packages of the same contents over and over again. And somehow, I expect it to work.

I know better. I'm not a stupid person.

Theoretically, at least. The past doesn't speak well for me in this case.

Seeing Sebastian here tonight was fine. But having him try to rattle me on purpose and not have a moment to say anything back makes me disappointed in myself—almost as disappointed as I am that I dated him to start with.

No more. No more Sebastians for me. Period.

"You're a raccoon," Bellamy says out of nowhere. "A beautiful, thoughtful, slightly naïve but generally intuitive little raccoon."

"What?" My fingers go to the area beneath my eyes. "I paid a lot for this mascara. If it's getting all over my face, I'm taking it back for a refund. I'm sick of overpriced cosmetics that don't work."

I swipe roughly and pull my fingertips back. They're clean.

"I didn't mean that literally," she says, still chuckling. "What I meant was that there are millions of men out there—scuba divers and astronauts and bankers. And you're this sweet little raccoon digging around the dugout dumpster for its next meal."

She holds her hands out like claws and paws at me.

I swat them away. "I am not."

She raises a brow and takes a seat on the ivy-colored couch. I sit next to her.

"Yes, you are," she insists. "And you know what else? You deserve to pick out of *all* the dumpsters. Not just the one full of jockstraps and helmets."

"*Yeah.*"

"Yeah," she teases, bumping me in the shoulder. "So you tell your mama the next time she tries to hook you up with some overbearing jersey that you are not interested."

"What you're saying is that this is my mom's fault, right? I can blame everything on her."

"You can, and you should. She puts so much pressure on you to be attached to a guy—any guy—that she's definitely to blame for at least a part of this." She rolls her eyes. "The next time she starts in with her shit, tell her no. Stand your ground. No more setting you up on dates with guys she meets around your step-dad's baseball team or—surprise! So-and-so's prodigy is visiting from Chicago, so could you possibly show him around? Wink, wink. Oh!" She waggles her finger in my face. "Remember the time she volunteered you to tutor that newly single basketball player's kid?"

My jaw hangs open. "I forgot about that. I'm not even good at math. That poor kid sat with me for an hour a day for a month and still failed sixth-grade pre-algebra."

"See? No more. We've identified your problem—athletes. Specifically, ones your mother likes."

I can't argue with Bellamy. And she knows it.

"Noted," I say, shrugging helplessly. "I stand corrected. I'm not swearing off *all* men, just my type of men."

"If that's how you want to look at it. Just don't get pushed into the … cock pen?"

"Bullpen," I correct her, laughing. "It's a good thing you're pretty, Bells."

She grins. "I'm not nearly as pretty as my friend."

"If Sebastian looks at me with pity again tonight, I'm about to be petty."

"And that's why I love you."

She hooks her arm through mine and leads me to the door.

The patrons who came to Paddy's for a burger or bratwurst have all but disappeared. In their place is a younger and livelier night crowd. The restaurant's instrumental tunes switched to a slightly louder, punchier beat. I find my body moving to the bass as we make our way to the room hosting our friend's party.

I consider the ramifications of my self-imposed no-athletes rule when I nearly slam into the back of Bellamy.

"Check out that man in the suit to the north," she says, stopping dead in her tracks.

Instead of looking toward the door, which would be north, I look at the area where her gaze is situated. A tall, dark, and handsome man in a tailored suit stands by a plant still covered in clear Christmas lights.

I sigh. "Bells, that's south."

"Whatever. The point isn't the direction but the man."

"And what about him?"

She turns and faces me. "Imagine having to turn that guy down because you're on a sabbatical from men in general. That's why you don't do things like that. You keep your options open. Always."

"I …"

My attention is redirected when Sebastian steps into my line of sight. His smirk is deep and wide. He waves at me, and all I can do is wave back.

"Don't wave at him," Bellamy says through gritted teeth.

I wait for Sebastian to turn around before I speak. "What am I supposed to do? Not wave and look like I care?"

"Good point." She fires a glare to his backside. "I hate how smug he is."

"I hate a lot of things about him."

She rips her eyes out of his back and flips them to me. "He's gonna try to screw with you."

"I know."

I feel it in my bones. I also know how Sebastian operates, so it's a total no-brainer.

Unlucky for him, I know his Achilles' heel. Lucky for me, I have no feelings for him other than disdain, and if he tries to put me in a precarious position tonight, I'll have to repay him.

Somehow.

"You good?" Bellamy asks, her attention redirected to the man in the suit. "Because, if so …"

"I'm good. I'm great. *Super*. Waiting on my scuba diver," I joke.

She looks at me like I'm crazy, like she doesn't remember her scuba diver suggestion.

"Okay," she says slowly. "You do you, boo, and I'm going to go do me—or the suit, rather, if things work out like they're playing out in my head," she says with a wicked grin on her face.

The man looks up over a glass of amber-colored liquid and gives Bellamy a sweet smile. His eyes scream kindness and a naivete that will get him in big trouble.

"You're going to eat him up and spit him out," I tell her.

"I always spit them out." She tosses me a wink. "Swallowing is gross and reserved for the men who deserve it. That has yet to be proven."

I shake my head as she sashays across the restaurant like she owns the damn place.

Suddenly, the fact I'm alone in the middle of the restaurant becomes readily apparent. And knowing that Sebastian is probably just waiting to pounce on that little bit of information makes me want to scream.

"I need a drink," I groan, fluttering my lashes open and letting them fall on the opposite side of the restaurant.

Large, dark beams crisscross the ceiling and play a distinct contrast to the pale lavender walls. Bronze lighting fixtures and hazy yellow lights create a warm ambiance that speaks to my soul.

The entire front of the building is composed of windows that showcase the beautiful hotel across the cobblestone street. A bar tucked away to the right of the door.

I weave my way through the tables with much less grace than Bellamy. I'm about halfway across when the hair on the back of my neck stands up. If I were in an alley, I might think it was a predator ready to kill me. Here, I know it's just Sebastian.

And I, being the lady I am, cannot punch him in the throat.

"Why can't he just leave me alone?" I mutter.

My steps speed up, and I make it to the bar just as I feel his energy behind me. I glance over my shoulder and spot him, with his arm around the gorgeous redhead, heading my way.

I reach for the chair in front of me. Instead of finding leather, my fingers brush against something else. Something warmer. Something smoother and rougher all at the same time.

My heart jumps in my chest at the same moment my head snaps to the side.

Oh. Shit.

The most beautiful set of hazel eyes I've ever seen traps my gaze. The warmth of the chocolate brown is cooled by the spring green embedded in the orbs. Gold flecks twinkle as the man slowly withdraws his palm away from mine.

I open my mouth, but I've somehow forgotten how to speak.

"Hey," he says, his Southern drawl rippling across my ears. "You can have it."

I shake my head to try to jolt myself out of the haze I'm in. "I … I can have what?"

His full, pouty lips split into a sexy smirk. "I meant the chair, but if something else is on your mind, just let me know."

My heart flutters in my chest as a wave of heat courses through my body from head to toe.

A couple of days' scruff peppers a sharp, chiseled jaw. His skin is sun-kissed and imperfect, and there's the slightest mole beneath his left eye that gives a bit of softness to his appearance. His body is long, well over six feet, with broad shoulders and a thick chest.

It's one heck of a picture.

Slowly, *oh, so slowly,* the fog in my brain lifts.

"Can I buy you a drink?" he asks.

Sebastian's gaze pummels me from the side. It's as if it's intentional—his ego cannot stand the fact another man is paying me attention.

If that's the case …

A crazy idea pops into my brain. The longer I watch this man peer at me from under his thick lashes, the more it seems possible.

Crazy? Yes. But definitely possible.

"Want to do me a favor instead?" I ask before I can talk myself out of it.

My chest rises and falls in quick succession as he *and I* ponder my question. He narrows his eyes as he undoubtedly considers why a woman he just met might need his help.

His thick brows tug together. "That depends on what it is."

Blood pours through my ears as I realize I'm potentially playing with fire.

But what's the alternative? Sebastian gets to come over here and play poor Larissa?

Not an option.

"Are you going to ask or not?" he asks.

I look up and down his long, muscled body.

Too bad he's not an option.

Before I can overthink it, the hottie in front of me slays me with a playful quirk of his brow.

Screw it.

I take in a quick lungful of air. "I'm going to need an answer to two questions."

"Shoot."

"Quickly."

He grins. "I can't answer them if you don't ask them, beautiful."

I steady myself against the term of endearment and stay focused.

"Do you have a girlfriend?" I ask.

His eyes sparkle with mischief. "I like where this is going."

"That's not an answer, and we're running out of time."

"No," he says hurriedly. "Hard no. Definitely not. No girlfriend."

"Second question …" I take another deep breath and go in for the kill. "Will you be my fake boyfriend for five minutes?"

His grin knocks the breath I'm holding right out of me. "When do we start?"

THREE
HOLLIS

The blond-haired beauty who appeared out of thin air bends subtly toward me. And then, as if she's as surprised as I am by her proposal, she grins.

"We start now," she says.

There's an inherent playfulness to her tone, a definite levity in her words that appeals to me. But it's the slight edge hidden beneath the sweet lilt of her voice that has me curious.

And curiosity killed the cat.

I nibble on my lip as I study her.

She has straight hair the color of corn silk in the summer in Indiana. Her eyes are the greenest green, just like the turf on a football field before a game. A constellation of freckles are sprinkled across her nose that turns up slightly at the end, completing a compelling and sexy as hell picture in front of me.

This girl is no vixen. There's too much innocence about her for that. But she's not naïve either. She assesses me too carefully for that to be true.

"How exactly do we play this?" I ask, rolling my tongue around the inside of my mouth. "Any rules I should know?"

She glances over her shoulder but quickly turns back to me. "Could you just … I don't know, pretend you're really into me?"

"Absolutely."

"Great." She licks her lips as her gaze drops to my lips. "That's it. Just act like you like me, I guess."

Is she for fucking real?

As the question slips through my mind, she looks over her shoulder again. My eyes follow hers and land on a complete douchebag coming our way.

Suddenly, this is a route I understand.

Douchebag's hand wraps around another woman's waist. Her eyes dart between my new girlfriend and Douchebag.

My insides twist.

I have no idea who this guy is, but I don't like him. Not just because he's dressed like a tool or from the way he blatantly ignores me. Rude, sure, but I don't care. What's he to me? Not shit on my shoe.

You can always tell a guy's true nature by the women around him. By all accounts, this one is a dick.

I walk around the chair separating me from my new girlfriend.

"Want me to knock him out?" I ask.

Her eyes widen. "What? No! Why would you do that?"

"I haven't been in a fight for a long time, and he looks like he could use a good ass-whippin'."

Her jaw drops. "I don't … No. We're not …" Her face flushes, and she does everything in her power to remain unaffected by me. "No punching. Okay?"

"The thought of that turned you on a little, didn't it?"

The color in her cheeks deepen. She squirms, her whole body moving like it can't handle the energy contained in her tight little body.

"It did," I tease. "Huh. Good to know."

Her gorgeous lips part. Before she can say anything,

Douchebag, his girl, and about five-hundred bottles of men's cologne join us.

He looks at my new girlfriend as though I don't exist.

"I wanted to check on you before I left," he says. "It felt like the right thing to do, considering *your* situation."

Sure, it did, asshole.

My girl's eyes narrow so subtly that I'm not sure if anyone notices it but me. "Hello, Sebastian."

"We were just talking about you," I say, moving to stand directly behind my co-conspirator. I place both hands around her, lacing my fingers at her stomach and tugging her into me.

My blood heats as I invade her personal space. She smells like flowers and the ocean—a sweet, airy scent that feels like a cold drink of water on a hot day. The gray fabric wrapped around the deep curves of her body is soft against my skin.

She looks up at me and smiles. It's not the smile she used with Sebastian and not the one she flashed at me earlier. This one is simultaneously more shy and more mischievous. It's a juxtaposition that lights my libido on fire.

Game on.

"I can't wait to take this dress off you later," I whisper loud enough for Sebastian to hear.

Her jaw hangs open as a giggle of disbelief escapes from it.

"Don't act all innocent," I tease her. "I have the texts you sent me earlier, you dirty girl."

She twists in my arms and slaps at my chest. I clasp her wrist and hold it to my body. Her breath stalls in her chest as I lean down. I smile as my lips near her skin. Her body relaxes into mine as I grin.

A soft breath whispers into the air as I grow closer … and kiss her on the forehead.

She blows out the rest in a gush. Her eyes narrow as she looks up at me—partially amused and partially annoyed.

I grin. "Later, beautiful."

She exhales every drop of oxygen in her body as she tries to keep the irritation out of her chuckle.

"I'd like you to meet Catherine," Sebastian says in a voice a couple of octaves louder than necessary. "Catherine, this is Larissa."

Larissa. Noted.

Sebastian clenches his fingertips into the poor girl's side, closing the two millimeters between them. He then turns so he's almost standing sideways to me.

I didn't have Sebastian painted to have a lot of street sense. The little black sweater vest over an argyle sweater and a complexion that screams fancy skin creams gave that away. Still, I'm surprised a guy like this doesn't even have the sense not to turn his back on a guy like me—a guy who could break his jaw with the flick of my wrist. Not to mention, he's clearly trying to piss all over my girl.

Have I known her for longer than three minutes? No. But that's not the point.

Catherine grins sheepishly. "It's nice to meet you, Larissa. Your dress is so cute."

Larissa smiles at Catherine, relief sprinkled over her features. "Thank you. I like yours too. Did you get it at Halcyon?"

"I did. I love that store."

"Me too," Larissa says. "I almost bought that exact outfit a few weeks ago but wasn't sure I could pull it off."

Catherine laughs. "I thought the same thing about myself."

The girls exchange a friendly smile as Sebastian stews beside Catherine.

His jaw clenches as he looks at me. I lift a brow in a silent challenge.

I usually try to give people the benefit of the doubt and not judge a book by its cover or however that saying goes. But Sebastian seems to have gone out of his fucking way to print asshole on his forehead. There's another adage about trusting people when they tell you who they are.

I believe him.

Sebastian tries to hold my glare but gives up in a matter of seconds, just as I knew he would.

He clears his throat. "Catherine, would you gather our coats, please? I'll meet you by the door in a moment."

"Sure," she nearly whispers. "It was nice to meet you both." After a timid nod, she dashes away.

I instantly feel sorry for the girl. But there's no time to think about that. I have a job to do.

"Sebastian, this is …" A streak of panic flutters through my girlfriend's eyes as she realizes she doesn't know my name.

"I'm Hollis Hudson," I interject, more for Larissa's benefit than anything.

"I'm an old, *close* friend of Larissa's," Sebastian says, eyeing me carefully. "It's always nice to see her around."

"Well, I'm a *new, closer* friend of Larissa's, so I bet we'll all be seeing each other around." I run my tongue around my cheek and let my stare finish the thought.

He hems and haws around, looking back and forth between us as his displeasure grows by the minute. "How is your father, Riss?"

Larissa bristles at the nickname. "My dad is great."

Sebastian nods. He expected more from her—more freely given information that felt intimate to him. A wrinkled brow tells me he didn't get what he wanted. A set jaw tells me he's going to press until he does.

"Tell him hello for me," he says.

Larissa tenses in my arms. I rub my hands up and down her shoulders, giving them a gentle squeeze at the end. I want to tell this fucker precisely what I think, but I'm in a bit of a pickle here. I'm not really her boyfriend, or I'd jump right in and put Sebastian in his place.

And she already told me no punching.

I bite my tongue and wait for her to give me an indication about what she wants me to do. I'm not going to be in her life in the morning. I don't want to ruin shit she doesn't want imploding.

She takes a deep breath, her body heaving from the energy I think she's about to spew. I know one thing—if she loses her cool in front of this guy, it'll only encourage him and his antics.

I've seen this a hundred times before. There are people—men and women—who get off on riling people up. Sebastian is clearly one of those guys, and I'll be damned if I let that happen.

Not to my fake girlfriend.

"We have somewhere we need to be," I tell Larissa.

Larissa looks up at me in surprise. "We do?"

The expression on her pretty face changes from surprise to concern—surprise I said we had plans and concern she broke character.

I wink to assuage her worry.

"We do," I tell her, dropping my voice. "And you're gonna love them. Trust me."

She flushes the sexiest shade of pink. An impish smile displays little dimples in her cheeks. Whether she's playing along in her role as my girlfriend or if she really is reacting to the idea of us being together, I don't know. What I do know is that it's a hell of a turn-on.

"And what do those plans consist of, *Hollis*?" she asks, making my name sound a whole hell of a lot sexier than it ever has before.

The intimacy in her eyes and that fucking blush make my cock hard as hell. I move around as smoothly as I can to try to distract it.

"Do you want me to tell you right here in front of God and everyone?" I ask.

Her eyes sparkle.

Sebastian clears his throat, but neither of us looks his way.

"I took your advice from this morning and put together a little something. It'll be fun. I promise," I say, letting the last word fall on a hushed whisper.

Our bodies are only inches apart. From this angle, I can see straight down the top of her dress to the ample cleavage hoisted up like it was done just for me.

She throws her head back just far enough that her hair swishes against my arm. The ends tickle as they dust my hand, almost goading me to make more contact. And with Sebastian still standing there, she must want that.

So I give her what she wants.

I wrap my arms around her and let my hands come together at the small of her back. She's pushed against me, the curve of her breasts pressed snugly against the firm wall of my chest.

As I listen to her melodic giggle, I forget all about Sebastian and the show we're supposed to be putting on. Instead, I'm searching her eyes for a sign of what she really wants to do from this point forward.

Because I know what I want to do. And I have a room across the street in which to do it.

"Did you know," she says, sticking her fingers in my belt loop, "that just before I met you, I'd sworn off men? Like literally the moment before I met you."

"Well, I do always love a challenge."

She laughs. "You sort of fell into my life right when I needed you."

"Are you saying I'm an angel? Because I've been called that before."

Songs are written about smiles like the one on her face. It's a picture of a split second in time without worry—clear of any reservations or stress. And after all the hell I've been through in the past few months with letting my team down during every game, it's nice to be helpful for once.

And it's really nice having her in my arms.

"I need to get back to Catherine," Sebastian says from beside us. "It was nice seeing you."

"Goodbye, Sebastian," Larissa says without looking at him.

Instead, she looks at *me*.

We stand next to the bar with our arms around one another as though we've known each other for longer than five minutes. With each passing second, the look on our faces grows lighter and lighter until we eventually burst out into laughter.

"What the heck do we have here?" A woman slides up beside us as she tosses a strand of hair over her shoulder. Her face is painted into pure amusement.

Larissa's arms drop from my waist, and she takes a step back. She turns toward her friend. "I thought you were busy with Suit?"

The other girl shakes her head side to side. "I was, but then I look over, and here you are, taking my advice." Her bottom lip sticks out. "I'm so proud."

Both women look at me, but neither says a word. Feeling put on the spot, I shrug.

"I'm Hollis," I tell her. "Larissa's fake boyfriend."

"Well, I'm Bellamy, her best friend, and I feel like I just missed something huge."

Larissa looks at me, and her eyes shine. I'm drawn to her energy. It's clean. Happy. It's strangely comforting and exciting at the same time.

"Sebastian was walking up," Larissa says, turning to Bellamy. "And I just … Hollis was standing here, and I thought …" She makes a face. "I don't even know what I thought, to be honest."

"You thought I was hot," I say with a grin.

Bellamy bursts out laughing as Larissa hides her face.

A stunning, red-lipped siren by all accounts, Larissa's friend looks similar to many of the women I've hooked up with in the past. Yet tonight, the curvy little pistol has captured my attention.

"It's okay," I tease Larissa. "I'm used to it. It's hard to be me."

"I bet it is," Bellamy says with a grin.

I shrug like I might be kidding, but I'm not.

From the outside, it looks like my life must be sunshine and roses. Guys on campus want to *be* me. Girls want to be *with* me—mostly. This season kind of put a damper on all that. Social media pundits profess my prowess, and half of my professors call me out in class just to say my damn name.

No one thinks about the impossibility of figuring out who, if anyone, is real in my life. Who likes me for me and who likes me because of what they see on television? It's a difficult question to answer and one that'll get you all screwed up if you get it wrong.

Which I've done.

And hope to never do again.

Bellamy smacks her lips together and looks at her friend. "I'm going to go swap numbers with Suit. You going home with Hollis or me?"

"You," Larissa answers immediately.

It's such a quick response that I almost object. *Almost.* While it burns my ego a smidgen, I have to respect her decision. It's the logical one. Not the fun one but the one that makes sense.

"Cool. Find me when you're done." Bellamy turns and looks at me. "Nice job, Hollis. Thanks for bailing out my girl."

I glance at my watch. "She's still *my* girl, thank you very much."

I wink at Larissa. She pulls her eyes away from me and tries to hide her smile.

Bellamy shakes her head. "Stay out of trouble," she tells Larissa before tossing me a little wave and heading back to their table.

Larissa watches her friend disappear into the restaurant. I

shove a hand in my pocket and try to decide where to go from here.

Before I have it figured out, she flips her gaze to mine.

The air between us thickens. Larissa pulls the collar of her dress away from her body. My attention snaps to the movement, and she raises a brow when she catches me eyeing her. I grin.

"Thank you," she says, letting the fabric rest against her skin.

"For what?"

"For helping me with Sebastian. I'm standing here trying to decide if I should've done that. It feels kind of awkward now."

"Why? Wasn't I a good fake boyfriend?"

She laughs. "You were the best fake boyfriend I've ever had."

"I'm glad to hear it." I blow out a breath, hoping that the extra oxygen cools my blood a bit. "Who was Sebastian, anyway? An old boyfriend?"

She nods. "He doesn't even like me, really. He's just a dick."

"I have to agree with that opinion. At least the part about him being a dick."

Our gazes linger together, searching each other for the next step.

Do we just part ways?

Do I buy her a drink?

Do I even get her last name?

"Thanks again, Hollis. I appreciate it." She tucks a strand of hair behind her ear. "I guess I'll see you around."

"So, what? That's it?"

The questions come too quickly to be able to play it off smoothly. Even if she's not going home with me, that doesn't mean we have to end things now.

She looks at me out of the corner of her eye. "Yeah. That's it."

"You don't want a drink or something?"

"It's been five minutes. Your job here is done."

I balk. "But isn't that what women *don't* want from men? Every time it's only five minutes, all you hear are complaints."

She swats at me again, her laughter washing over me. The slight contact is enough to make my blood run hot again.

"You are a handful," she tells me.

"You could find out …"

She bites her lip and laughs. She's even prettier now than she was just a few minutes ago.

I clear my throat. "All joking aside, I'll be in town for a week or so. If you want my number, I could give it to you in case you run into any more scenarios where you need a fake boyfriend. Or … whatever …"

She wrinkles her nose. "It couldn't hurt, right?"

"I don't see how."

She tilts her head to the side as she mulls something over. Finally, she shrugs. "Pass me your phone."

I unlock it and hand it to her.

She looks at me suspiciously but takes it anyway.

Her fingers fly over the screen in a flurry. Soon, she's handing it back to me with a relieved smile.

"I put my name in and texted myself, so I have your number too," she says. "Just in case."

"Of course."

"Of course." She laughs softly. "I'll, um, I'll see you around. Maybe."

"Sounds good."

And with that, I watch her walk across the room and disappear through a set of French doors.

Before I can think twice, I pivot on my heel and exit onto the street. My phone still in my hand, I open my texting app.

Me: Blonde. Crew wins.

FOUR
LARISSA

"You don't have to scream at me," I say, wincing.

"I'm not screaming," my mother insists.

Her voice screeches through my car's speakers. I wince as my ears threaten to bleed.

"It might help if you held the phone to your ear and didn't put it on speakerphone while you do … whatever it is you're doing," I tell her.

She groans. The sound mixes with crumpled cellophane.

"You have me on speakerphone," she says. "What's the difference?"

"I'm driving. I'm being responsible. You're supposed to use the speakerphone in this situation."

The loudest static sounds through the car again as my mother makes a show of picking up the phone. I can't make out a series of muted protests and mumbles—which is probably a good thing for both of us.

"There," she says, her voice clearer and, thankfully, quieter. "Better?"

"Yes. Thank you."

"You're welcome."

I imagine the smile I hear in her voice and the way it touches both of her ears when she's happy. It's a look I don't often see on her. Sure, she grins, and with her chipper voice, she can sell the idea she's having a great time in life.

Mom is a gifted actress.

She's exchanged the exuberance of life for an overbooked calendar. The sparkle in her eyes that I saw when I was a little girl has been replaced with … something else.

Jack, my stepfather, provides well for her. He's a co-owner of the Savannah Seahawks, a minor league baseball team, and treats my mother to a lifestyle that most women only dream about. It's not like she's stressing about making ends meet. But she can't slow down long enough to enjoy the life she has, and that bothers me. I truly believe she adds more to her plate when I suggest she ease up.

"What are you doing, anyway?" I ask.

"Hang on a second."

I blow out a breath.

My head still hurts a little from the wine I drank last night in a futile attempt to sleep. My mind, and body, raced until the sun came up, thanks to my fake boyfriend.

The mixture of greens and golds in Hollis's eyes is unforgettable. I can't stop thinking about his smile either and how it sent a zap of electricity up my spine. The way his voice wrapped itself around my name and the way his hands did the same to my waist—it was too much to forget that quickly.

I know it's all because it was something new and exciting. That and Hollis is downright gorgeous. But even with that in mind, it was impossible to set him aside mentally and get things back in regular working order.

"I just had cosmetics delivered, and they pack the tiny boxes in boatloads of paper. You could fill a full-sized boat with this stuff. It's such a waste."

"So, stop shopping at those stores. Or may I suggest that you drive to the mall, walk inside, and buy your stuff yourself instead of shopping online?"

She gasps.

"I know. My bad. Forget I ever went there," I tease.

"You better hope I do if you want to stay in my will," she says, distracted. Finally, the crumpling stops. "There. Done. Now, what are you doing today?"

"Driving to Aunt Siggy's."

"What are you going to do over there?" she asks.

"She wanted me to come by and help her choose a few things for the New Year's Party. They're behind schedule, and you know how much she hates that."

I make a right-hand turn onto a tree-lined street. It's one of my favorite streets in Savannah. Large southern oaks stand guard at equidistant intervals, their branches heavy with spectacular doses of moss. The late morning sunlight streams through like the effect of a filter, creating the most beautiful and soothing environment.

My dad's brother, my uncle Rodney, and his wife, Aunt Siggy, have lived here my entire life. I used to beg my mom to let me come to play on the weekends and every day in the summer. Not only was their youngest son, Boone, my buddy, but their next-door neighbor was Bellamy.

It was the perfect situation. Lucky for me, Mom and Siggy maintained their friendship after Mom and Dad divorced when I was eight.

"I bet she's not behind for long," Mom laughs, knowing exactly how her former sister-in-law operates.

"I bet not either."

"When does her new line launch?"

"I'm not sure. Maybe around Valentine's Day, I think?"

I glance down at the delicate gold rope ring wrapped around my pointer finger. It has chips of sapphires and rubies, my two favorite gemstones. Aunt Siggy had it made especially for me on my twenty-first birthday.

It doesn't suck to have an aunt that's a jewelry designer. It definitely doesn't suck to have one that has five sons and one niece. Me.

"It's going to be great though," I say. "I've seen a few pieces and they're incredible. She went super feminine with this collection. Rose gold. Lots of sparkle."

"She'll kill it. She always does."

"Yeah."

"So, I'll see you tomorrow night then?" All of a sudden, her voice gets louder again, and I know I'm back on speakerphone. "The fundraiser starts at eight, but Jack wants to be there at seven. You could show up around seven-thirty, if you want."

My stomach twists into a tight knot.

Most people look forward to the week between Christmas and the New Year. It's filled with family, food, and free time to vacation or just hang out at home and read.

But me? Nope. It's one of the busiest weeks of my life.

The week between the holidays is always crammed with end-of-the-year engagements that I'm somehow obligated to attend. I don't mind them, usually. Jack's sports events are always fun and full of a ton of eye candy. My father's side of the family has get-togethers and dinners and is way more intimate and familial. But this year? This year, I'm not feeling it. This year, something feels off and I'd rather stay at home with hot cocoa and Hallmark.

"Do I have a choice?" I ask my mom.

"Is that a serious question?"

"I don't know. Was yours?"

I can almost hear her eyes roll. "Larissa," she says with an exhaustion that is more dramatic than necessary. "You act like it's not a terrific opportunity for you to come and rub shoulders with these people."

"Did you hear that?"

"What?"

"The sound of my eyes rolling into the back of my head," I say.

It's a joke that the audience didn't appreciate.

"What's that supposed to mean?" she huffs.

I sigh. "That means that you are obligated to attend these things. You're Jack's wife. It's his schtick. I'm his stepdaughter—"

"There are no steps in our family, Larissa."

I regrip the wheel and say a silent prayer for guidance.

"Has it ever occurred to you that being invited to these things is an opportunity that many people your age would kill to have? These are your future clients, Larissa. These are the people with giant checkbooks that will want their summer homes and expansive landscapes refreshed and beautified. They'll be looking for a landscape architect and having your name on the tip of their tongue once you graduate in May is how you network. Use this to your advantage, darling."

"I'm going to have years to build a business. I might not even want to have my business in Savannah," I say, although that's not true. I can't imagine living anywhere else. "I might not want to work on residences and estates."

"You're being difficult."

Learned from the best.

"I do expect you to be there tomorrow night," she says, matter-of-factly. "You didn't mention that you were not going to attend, and you come every year. So, show up with your date, please."

I pilot the car around a roundabout while trying to determine how to handle my mother. Usually, I would change the subject and never actually address it to avoid an argument. But Bellamy's voice keeps rolling around inside my head.

Stand your ground.

"If I do attend," I say, "I will be coming alone."

Her displeasure is evident. "You cannot come alone."

"And why not?"

"For one, Jack bought you two tickets. Those are not cheap."

"No one asked if I wanted them."

She groans. "Larissa, cooperate with me, please."

"I'll tell people my date got sick. They'd probably be grateful I came alone rather than bringing an ill guest."

"Can you just bring somebody so you aren't sitting by an empty plate?"

I squint into the sunlight. "Why does the idea of sitting alone bother you so much? It doesn't bother me. I'm great company. You should hear the conversations I have with myself."

She takes a long, deep breath. I can imagine her looking at the ceiling with a hand on her neck, mumbling something quietly about God giving her strength.

"Can we not do this right now?" she asks. "I have a ton of things to do and arguing with my baby girl is not on the agenda today."

"I'm not arguing with you. I'm just telling you I'll come despite not agreeing beforehand like an adult should have the right to do. But I'm coming alone."

"I don't understand you," she says, her voice clipped.

"That is obvious."

"All I do is try to help you. I try to give you every advantage in the world. I get you tickets to events, invitations to banquets—I surround you with men who could take care of you someday and—"

My eyes about bulge out of their sockets. "Whoa. Hold up. I don't know why you think I need taken care of."

"Because you do. It's not a personal fault. It's the way life works."

There aren't words in the English language I can string together to accurately display my outrage and shock.

"I want you to have a great life," she says, quieter this time. "I don't want you to make the same mistakes I have."

"I'm twenty-four. My job is to live my life and make mistakes so I can learn from them. I think maybe you didn't realize that when you were young."

She goes back to rumpling paper and I know she's mentally checked out of this line of questioning. It's what happens when a topic even remotely comes close to touching her past.

"I worry that you're going to end up alone someday if you don't start being serious about dating," she says.

"Would being alone truly be the end of the world?"

"Yes. It would. You need someone to love you and support you and to be there to help fight the world alongside you."

I can't argue with her. She's right. I want the relationship she's describing … if it's a real thing. And I'm not sure it is.

Mom grows quiet on the other end of the line. I can't tell if she's considering my stance or if I've hurt her feelings somehow. All I know is that I hate it when things between us get like this.

"I'll be there tomorrow," I tell her. Even as I say the words, I want to take them back.

"Thank you. Who will be your plus-one?"

"Nobody."

"Larissa …"

I slow down for a puppy crossing the street. It takes its sweet time, its little ears flopping around as it chases a butterfly. I use the vision to take a long, deep breath and try to recenter myself.

"Men have evolved with the understanding built into their seedy, hedonistic little genes that they don't need to be decent human beings to earn the affections of a woman," I say. "And I. Am. Sick. Of. It. I'll date again when I find someone who isn't a dickhead."

Or an athlete.

Once the puppy is safely across the street and into the arms of its human, I pull into Aunt Siggy's driveway. I sit in my car, engine running, and stare mindlessly at Siggy's bright red front door.

"Should I just arrange for a date for you?" Mom asks. "Because you are not coming alone. We paid for a plus-one, and it'll look ridiculous for you to be sitting next to an empty plate."

"God forbid," I mutter.

"Okay. I have a solution. There's a new third baseman on the Seahawks—"

"Mom. No."

"He's cute. He's from an excellent family. He's single. I ran into him in the offices last week, and he was sweet as pie. I've already planted a little seed about you—"

"I have to go," I cut in, my limit hit for arguing with her.

"And he seemed to be interested. Of course, it didn't hurt that there's a picture of you in Jack's office and—"

"I'm at Siggy's. Can we resume this later? Or not, but I bet you'll make me."

She groans. "I suppose. But by later, I mean tonight. If you don't call me, I'll assume you want me to make arrangements."

"I'm sure you will."

"I love you, Larissa."

"Love you, too. Bye, Mom."

I hang up and turn off the engine.

By this age, you wouldn't think I would still be having these conversations with my mother. I haven't lived at home since I was nineteen. But has that stopped her from trying to wield her influence in my life? *Hardly*.

Still, I'm thankful for her. Does she drive me crazy? Most every day. But what would I do without her?

Once I gather my things, I head to the front door. After a

knock that's unnecessary but makes me feel courteous, I enter the house.

A grand staircase greets me. The light from a heavy crystal chandelier makes it appear even more stunning. The dark and regal wood could tell a million stories if it could talk.

"Is that you, Riss?" Siggy calls.

"Yup."

"I'm in the kitchen."

I make my way down a long hallway with family pictures hanging on both sides and enter a bright kitchen. The cabinets are cream, and the floors a dark wood like the stairs. Windows flood the kitchen in sunlight, and it's my happiest place on earth.

My aunt turns around to face me. She's dressed in a black pair of pants and a white blouse. A large turquoise pendant hangs between her breasts. She's gorgeous with her long, dark hair and bright golden eyes.

"Bad morning?" she asks, her smile faltering.

I nod.

"Sit down and let me pour you a drink. Then we can talk about it while you help me decide between snowflakes or an icicles beverage bar."

I take a seat at her kitchen table.

"You are an aesthetic guru. I know you don't need my help," I tell her.

She leans into the refrigerator and pops out with two bottles in her hands. "Mimosas or tea?"

I raise a brow. It's returned with a grin as Siggy slips the tea back inside the appliance and replaces it with a bottle of orange juice.

"I respect your opinion. You have an excellent eye," she says as she pours our drinks. "I'm also surrounded by testosterone all day, and I need a little estrogen to balance it all out."

My heart warms with the compliment—especially coming from her.

"So what's happening?" she asks, handing me one of the drinks.

"Mom."

"Oh." She makes a face as she sits across from me. "That explains the look on your face."

"She's on my butt about not having a date for the Seahawks thing tomorrow night. And she's irritated I don't even want to go, but I think she should have the sense to ask me in the first place."

Siggy takes a long sip of her mimosa. "She just wants you to be happy, Riss. Everything she does is motivated by that. She can't comprehend how you don't see that."

"I know. That's why I can't get mad at her. But none of the world she lives in makes me happy—especially the having a date thing. I'm not into dating anymore, Aunt Siggy." I reconsider. "Well, maybe if he's super cute and not my type. My type of men don't work for me. Such a shame."

She laughs. "I can't imagine doing it now. It's terrible out there. I hear stories from my sons, and it makes me …" She shakes her head. "It makes me sick and nervous and, quite frankly, terrified."

I laugh too. "Well, I can see that, depending on which of your boys is telling the stories. I mean, if it's Boone ..."

"True," she says, pointing a finger my way. "Very, very true. I learned the hard way not to press him about his dates," she says, using her fingers to add air quotes.

I take a long drink of my mimosa and feel myself settle into the comfort of being here. It always has the calmest, most peaceful vibe about it that I gravitate toward. When my parents fought when I was little, I'd call my uncle, and he'd pick me up. During the rocky years after Mom and Jack got married, I'd come here and hang out. When I got my heart broken as a teenager, I'd be here digging through their refrigerator in the middle of the night.

"I swear my mom thinks I'm going to be old and alone," I say. "Do you think I'll be alone forever? Is there a chance of that? Should I be worried?"

Instead of sharing in my irritation, Siggy smiles gently.

I know what's coming. It's my aunt's smooth way of siding with me and siding with my mother in the same breath. She always makes me feel great about my decisions, but when I look back, I realize she got what she thought was best, and everyone walked away feeling good about it.

How she does it—I'll never know.

Siggy sets her glass down. "You know why she pressures you."

She's right. I do—at least kind of.

I distinctly remember my parents separating and the pure devastation it caused everyone in our family. I was too young to know what caused it. Even after all of these years, it's a topic that's yet to be explained. I just know that my mother isn't the same person I remember her being when I was a little girl and my dad lived with us. She was honestly happy then, I think.

I have theories about what happened to my parents—everything from an affair to financial problems—but the one thing I know for sure is that my mother never got over my father. Not really.

A part of me thinks she presses me so much because she doesn't want me to live without true, mind-blowing love—something I believe she's gone without since her divorce. And I think she married Jack because it was as close to that kind of love as she thought she was going to get.

Jack does love her. He's a saint for how much he indulges her. But Jack loves baseball as much as he loves my mother, and that's a platform she doesn't want to share.

I don't blame her for that.

"Why can't I just show up alone?" I ask my aunt, pulling my head back to the present. "Would it be that bad?"

"To her? Yes. It would."

I scoff. "Well, she's wrong. Society has drilled into our heads—into her head—that women need a man. We don't. I mean, maybe for procreation, but there are sperm banks for that. Procreation is even a moot point now that I think about it."

Siggy smiles. "You know you're right. And, honey, you could walk into that room tomorrow night and own it. It would kind of make me proud to see you that confident." Her grin grows wider. "But this means a lot to your mother. It gives her comfort to see you there beside her, and if you have a date, she feels like someone is taking care of you. That's what she really wants."

I sigh.

"You aren't going to solve this situation with your mother overnight, so you need to pick your battles with her."

"I pick this."

She sits back in her chair. "Then go hard, little girl. If it means that much to you, fight with her. Stand your ground. Refuse to go and dig in your heels."

It's a guilt-trip without even being one.

My resistance starts to fade, and I sit back in my chair too.

"Your mother, God love her, isn't you," Siggy says with a deep, thoughtful frown. "She was devastated when your dad left, and I truly think she thought she'd be alone forever. There she was in her early thirties with a young child. She thought she was damaged goods."

"That's crazy."

She nods. "She was raised with this mindset, I think. I know she took a lot of flack from her mother about raising a child alone. It was a different world back then."

I consider this. I never knew my grandmother or this about my mom. It does make sense.

She reaches across the table and pats the top of my hand, giving it a gentle squeeze before going back to her mimosa.

I sit across from her and sip my drink too. Her words fester inside me. I know she's right, but it doesn't mean that caving into Mom's irritating demands is right. Or easy. Especially when they're ridiculous.

"Don't you have someone who you wouldn't mind spending a few hours with?" she asks after a few minutes. "Instead of thinking of it as a prison sentence, couldn't you look at it as taking a friend out for the night?"

Instantly, Hollis materializes up in my head.

"What are you grinning about?" Siggy asks.

I didn't realize I was.

I try to tame the bolt of energy firing through my veins, but it's impossible. A chuckle sneaks by my lips. I shake my head—both at the thought of Hollis teasing me about sending him fictional dirty texts and my inability to stop being amused by him.

"The funniest thing happened last night," I tell her.

"And …"

I squirm in my seat. "I was at Paddy's downtown for a birthday party, and Sebastian was there. He made these comments to me early in the evening that basically inferred I was pathetic because I was alone. He's such an ass."

"I've met him. He is."

I laugh. "I knew he was going to come up and say hi. I could feel it. And I didn't want to be standing there alone because that would just stroke his ego."

Her face wrinkles in disgust.

"So I took matters into my own hands." I laugh as I remember Hollis's face when I propositioned him. "I found a boyfriend for a few minutes."

Siggy plays with the charm on her necklace and watches me closely, her eyes sparkling. "He was cute, I take it?"

My stomach flip-flops over itself.

"Yeah. He was cute," I say with a wide smile. "Ridiculously good-looking, actually. Built like a god. He had the sweetest smile but also the orneriest smirk that just … went right through me."

"Ooh, the smirk. I'm such a sucker for a good smirk."

"Me too." I laugh. "So, Hollis, the guy I knew for two seconds, was my fake boyfriend last night. In retrospect, I can't believe I asked him, and I can't believe he went through with it, but he did. He jumped right in and hugged me and sweet-talked me and put Sebastian in his place. He was just …"

My cheeks heat. My embarrassment at blushing only makes it worse.

Siggy leans against the table. Mischief fills her eyes. "So get him to be your date tomorrow."

I hold her gaze and feel her words sink into my brain. With each inch they settle, the more my stomach squirms inside my body.

He was fun. He did smell amazing. And the way those giant arms felt around me kept me from sleeping all night—mostly because I wasn't in them anymore.

But what would be the point? He's only in town for a few days.

I sit back in my chair.

In fact, isn't that the actual point?

I only need him for tomorrow night, and he did say to call him if I … *needed him for anything*. Maybe I'd enjoy more than one moment with his arms around me.

Or more …

No. Don't go there, Riss. He's too gorgeous not to want for more than one night.

I nibble on my lip. He *is* leaving town. And he's not on my stay-away-from list. But I don't even know anything about him.

Which is why you should stay away from him.

"I don't think it's a good idea," I say, refusing to look Siggy in the eye.

Siggy shrugs, a knowing grin on her face. "Then don't ask him. Go alone. But in the meantime, let's discuss snowflakes or icicles …"

FIVE
HOLLIS

Forty-eight. Forty-nine. Fifty.

I hop to my feet and stretch my arms out to the sides. The short burst of adrenaline from the quick workout provides me with both a distraction and a blast of endorphins—two things that I crave.

My body is rested. The wounds from the season are starting to heal. I can bend without groaning, and my shoulder only needs popped back into place every other morning now.

Despite the physical benefits of the season being over, I already hate it. The fact that I'll never have another season to look forward to is something I try not to think about.

Grabbing a water bottle off the dresser, I walk to the window and yank the curtains apart. The room floods with early afternoon sunlight, and I gaze down the street. Remnants of Christmas hang oddly in the trees and on the lampposts lining the sidewalks. They look as out of place as I feel.

"I'm out of place everywhere. So what does it matter?"

Taking a long drink of water and letting my heartbeat settle, I let my gaze slide up the street until it lands on Paddy's. A grin tickles my lips.

Larissa.

I've never known a Larissa before, but the name somehow fits her. It matches her sweet, kind smile and the vibe she put off that made me want to tease and joke around with her. But it also coincides perfectly with the sexy curve of her hips and the sparkle in her eye that made me want to do nasty, delicious things to her.

I glance over my shoulder. Tapping the beat to the song I was listening to on the side of my leg, I eye the device that holds Larissa's number.

It took every bit of self-restraint that I had last night not to shoot her a text. I constructed no less than fifteen possible ice-breakers—everything from *Hey, it's Hollis* (which felt like a vintage sitcom) to *Just checking that you made it home all right* (which screamed that, while I might be considerate, I might also be lame because no one leads with that) to *Wanna fuck?*

That one is self-explanatory.

They all felt legit. They all also felt wrong.

River told me to combine all three texts and hit send. Crew told me to sleep on it. And if there's one thing I know from lots of past experiences, it's to go with Crew's advice. He's never led me astray. River, though? Found myself naked and covered in strawberry-flavored lube once, thanks to him.

I stretch again and head for the shower. Before I can make it far, my phone rings.

I don't recognize the number. My body tingles, hoping it's Larissa on the other end—even though I have her number saved under her name, and this isn't it.

"Hello," I say, trying my best to sound cool.

It's a good thing I didn't lead with a line from last night—any of them—because the voice on the other end is not Larissa.

"Is this Hollis Hudson?" The tone is deep and gritty—decidedly not female.

"Yeah. It is. Who is this?"

"Hey, this is Lincoln Landry. How are you doing?"

Holy shit.

I run a hand over my head and try to ignore how the little boy who watched this guy play in the Majors is freaking out inside me.

Stay calm.

"I'm good," I say, trying to seem nonchalant about being on the phone with a Hall of Famer. "How are you?"

"Not bad. Thanks for asking. I just wanted to touch base with you and thank you for accepting the Catching-A-Care award."

I laugh. "What do you mean? Thank *you*."

"Apparently, you had my team over here worried you were going to be the first nominee who refused to accept." He laughs too.

"I …" I stammer as I try to figure out how to explain it and not seem disrespectful or unappreciative. Because I'm neither. "The stuff I do with the kids got exploited my freshman year of college. The school newspaper did a piece on it thanks to a girl I was …"

I gulp. *Choose a word, Hollis—one that doesn't make you sound like a dick.*

"Involved with," I say, finishing the sentence.

"So you were sleeping with her?" he jokes.

"Basically, even though there wasn't much actual sleeping."

"Ah, the best kind." Lincoln chuckles. "I get it. Been there, done dumb shit too. Lots of it. It's too easy to get in trouble when you're great looking and full of talent."

"You feel me then."

"Hell, yeah."

I grin. "Well, in that case, I was worried that your offer wasn't real. That the call was a scam. Besides the campus paper, I've managed to keep most of my shit on the down low, so I wasn't sure. There's a girl who threatened to ruin my life a while back, and … you can't trust anyone, you know?"

"You're damn right I do. I trust my family. That's it. Well, maybe my brother's bodyguard. It would be shitty of me not to trust him when he's taken a hit for me a time or two. Or ten."

"I get it. I have two guys on my team who I trust implicitly. That's about as far as I go."

"Sounds like you have one key of life figured out already."

"You mean I have to figure out more?" I joke. "I was hoping that was it."

He laughs. "You're still young. When I was your age …" He whistles through his teeth. "We'll just leave that there. There's not enough time, and if my wife walks in here, I'd be a dead man."

"Second lesson—no wife."

His laugh grows louder. "Nah, man. You have that one wrong. Get you one. Just make damn sure it's the right one. The wrong one will screw you up faster than that hit you took during that interception on the last play of the year."

I grimace. I'd hoped he'd missed that.

"Are you headed to the pros?" he asks. "I don't see any notes in your file."

I sink back onto the bed.

His question cuts through all the distractions I've managed to busy myself with over the past couple of weeks. It's a topic I need to address, and I know that, but I just don't want to. I don't know how.

There are reasons to go into the pros—lots of them. But there are a few that make me think I shouldn't, too, and I don't know how to separate it all out.

"I have an invitation to the Combine," I tell him. "I'm not sure what I'm going to do yet. I'm not sure I even have a shot now that I basically sucked this year."

"It's a big decision to go pro. It totally changes the trajectory of your life and puts everything in someone else's hands—where you live, what you can afford, how much money you make, how long you're in debt to an organization. On the other hand, it's full of opportunities. It's what a lot of people dream about. You can make a ton of money. Seeing your name on people's backs and having them buy tickets to see *you* play is something … it's incredible. There's nothing like it. But it's not as easy of a decision as most people think it is."

"That's kind of how I feel about it. Especially coming off this shit season …"

He sighs. "Confidence shaken a little?"

"I guess. I mean, I know I could go out there and perform, but it's … Do I want to do that? It's a lot."

"It *is* a lot. What do you think happened to you this year?"

"My head, I guess. Wasn't focused."

I was worrying about this shit already. Crew's grandfather died, and River's mom was sick. Everything else going on felt heavier than football.

I bite my lip as the weight of my life settles over my chest.

So many things to decide, so many choices to make, and not a fucking person in the world to talk to about it. Holidays always suck when you don't have a family. But it's times like this when you need a sounding board—or just somebody that actually gives a damn—that makes it the worst.

Sure, I can talk to River or even Crew, but they're dealing with their own stuff. Coach Herbert would talk to me, too, but it makes me feel even worse to have to get advice from a coach about personal life shit. That's not his job. He took me under his wing to coach, not to raise.

I'll be fine, and I know that. I'm always fine. I refuse to be anything other than that.

I just wasn't prepared to be so off-balance at the start of the season.

"You'll be alright," Lincoln says. "I know it doesn't feel like it all the time, but you will. Just follow your gut. That's the best advice I can give you. That's your second key to life right there."

My grin is shaky. "Thanks."

"Figure out why you love to play ball to start with and work from there."

"Football has always been a distraction for me. Therapy, I guess. I'm not sure it would function the same way at the professional level, you know?"

"Yeah, you're right, and you're smart for considering that." Papers shuffle in the background. "You seem to make good choices. Your coach said in the nomination letter that you're a leader on and off the field."

My brain stops at the words your coach.

Coach nominated me?

He told me he didn't know how the organization got my name.

Why did he do that?

"I know this is a very personal thing for you, so I appreciate you coming down here and accepting a few minutes of publicity. Other guys need to see the good that some of you do. There's a lot to be said for leading as an example," he says.

Flashbacks of drunk singing Adele's "Hello" at parties, eating my weight in brownies that I didn't realize had pot in them, and sleeping my way through half of Braxton's female body come barreling at me.

"You know, I'm not the best leader—on the field or otherwise," I admit. "I've had my share of … unfortunate circumstances."

Immediately, I remember calling Crew to come and pick River and me up at the police station after we took a dare to trick-or-treat a sorority house naked one Halloween. It would've been fine if we'd made it there. Getting pulled over while only wearing banana hammocks—also on a dare—isn't a good time.

"Haven't we all?" Lincoln says with an amused tone.

I laugh.

"When are you coming into town?" he asks.

"I'm here. I'm early, I know, but I figured why not come down and relax a little before my last semester starts? And your people hooked me up with this hotel, by the way. Thank you for that."

"Those people aren't my people. My people are always less organized and not as professional. My people are oversized children like their boss. You've been talking to my wife's people. She's much more professional about shit than me."

I laugh again. "Well, thank her for me then."

"Hey," he says, his voice rising. "If you're in town, why don't you come by for dinner one night? Thank her yourself."

My eyes grow wide as I watch myself in the mirror above the dresser.

"Really? That's … very cool of you, Mr. Landry—"

"Lincoln. Please. Mr. Landry is my dad. Trust me when I tell you that the differences between us are massive."

"Well, that's a very nice offer, *Lincoln*, but it's totally unnecessary. Covering the hotel was way more than enough."

"I agree. But you don't know my wife. She *won't* agree. As a matter of fact, when I tell her I talked to you and that you're in town, she's going to insist you come to dinner. It's just how she rolls. And, like it or not, you'll end up at dinner because she doesn't take no for an answer. If I didn't love her so much, it would be very fucking annoying."

I try to process the fact that I'm being invited somewhere with Lincoln fucking Landry.

What the heck is happening here?

What do I do? Do I just say yes because this is the coolest thing to ever happen to me? Or do I say no because why would a guy like this invite me to dinner?

"How about our house tonight at seven?" he asks.

"I …"

He laughs. "Just say yes. Unless you have other plans and really just can't, you don't have a choice. Trust me. I only golf once a week now. Before you know it, Danielle has you doing what she wants, and you're happy about it. It's fucked up."

"I mean, I don't have plans, so if you're sure …"

"I am. I'll text you the address in a little while. It's totally casual, so don't feel like you have to dress up or anything. Hell, I might even order pizza. You like pizza?"

I grin. "Who doesn't?"

He just laughs. "Okay. Great. And bring whoever you're traveling with—bring them all. We're cutting into your holiday the way it is, so we'll just make this a family affair."

Fucking great.

Forcing a smile, I nod even though he can't see me. "Okay. Sounds good."

"Cool. Well, I'll see you and your guest or guests tonight."

"Thank you, Lincoln. I appreciate the call and the dinner offer."

"Not a problem. See you soon."

"Goodbye," I say.

I sit on the edge of the bed. My brain tries to process the conversation but fires too quickly from one talking point to another. Ultimately, though, it lands on the boiled-down fact that I'm going to dinner tonight at Lincoln Landry's house.

Bring whoever you're traveling with—bring them all.

I scrub a hand down my face.

"Can I show up alone?" I ask out loud, hoping a voice will sound out of nowhere and answer me.

The idea of arriving at Lincoln's house by myself makes me want to puke. I'm used to either having an entire football team or at least River and Crew with me for all important events. If it's not a football thing, I usually just don't go. It's a survival skill I learned early on in life—opt out of everything you can. If you're not available, people can't invade your shit. It's preventative protection at its best. A life condom, if you will.

This was one of the biggest reasons I wanted to turn down

the Catching-A-Care thing to start with. I only agreed after a spirited argument to accept from Coach Herbert.

But now I'm not even sure if I *can* show up by myself. Will I seem like some kind of weirdo who comes by himself when he was instructed to bring his whole damn family?

Fuck.

My head hangs, the muscle pulling at the base of my skull. I have no idea what to do. All I know is that I wouldn't be here if Coach hadn't nominated me to start with.

I pick up my phone again and find Coach's number.

Me: Why didn't you tell me you nominated me?

It takes a few minutes of me staring at the screen before he responds.

Coach: I didn't want to hear you complain or argue with me. How are you doing, kid?

Me: Okay, I guess.

Coach: Need anything?

My chest sinks a little.

I need a lot of things, but nothing I can ask him for. He can't help me with it anyway.

Me: Nah, I'm good. Thanks.

Coach: Hit me up if you need anything, Hudson. I mean it.

I set the phone beside me and stare at the wall.

Over the past four years, Coach has been the guy to help me figure shit out. If he didn't have an answer, he made sure he found someone who did. Coach always did things in a way that didn't strip my confidence or self-respect, and I appreciated that more than I could ever tell him.

Not that I have told him that. But I think he knows.

He took pity on the kid in foster care from Indiana and offered him a football scholarship. He had hope in me when no one else did.

Now I don't even have that. I'm not his charge anymore. The end of the season axed that.

Standing, I lift my chin. I fill my lungs with air and then shove it all out of my body just as quickly.

Focus on what you can control.

Right now, that's dinner tonight.

The issue of showing up alone rears its head again, and I nibble on my bottom lip as I work through it.

I could show up alone or …

An idea percolates in the back of my mind as I take in the roof of Paddy's through the window.

I could ask Larissa to go.

My lips twitch back and forth as I try to work the idea all the way through. I don't really know her. Hell, I don't know her at all. But asking her to accompany me isn't any crazier than *her* asking *me* to be her fake date. She didn't want to be alone when what's-his-fuck came by the bar. I don't really want to show up at Mr. Hall of Famer's house by myself either.

If I go alone, all of their attention is on me. They'll start asking questions—poking and prodding into shit I don't want to discuss. Topics generally on the table for most people aren't items I want to break down over bread.

I got none of that.

But wouldn't it be just as awkward to sit next to a woman in that situation who I don't know anything about? And who doesn't know anything about me?

This isn't some sorority chick I'm taking to a Kappa party or a football banquet—a girl who doesn't care to know anything about me besides the size of my dick. I feel the conversations in the Landry house might be different from what I'm used to ... so I might need a different kind of date.

"Shit," I say out loud, unsure what to do.

I pick up my phone.

Me: Need help.

Crew's text comes immediately.

Crew: What kind of help?

Me: I'm not in jail or anything. Settle down, Hollywood.

Crew: When you ask for help, shit's usually fucked up.

River: He's not lying, Hollis.

Me: Well, you're usually with me, River. So fuck off.

River: Eh, good point. Continue.

I exhale an aggravated breath and type out my next message.

Me: I was invited to Lincoln Landry's for dinner.

Crew: That's awesome.

River: Hell, yeah!

Me: Either of you fools want to come and go with me?

I tap my foot against the floor while I wait for their messages. It doesn't take long.

River: What I wouldn't give.

Crew: I'd be there if I wasn't on the other side of the world.

River: You could just FaceTime me, and I'll be your phone date.

Crew: What about the blonde?

River: Back off, Hollywood. I'm the date. I already accepted.

Crew: <eye roll emoji>

Laughing, I get to my feet and pace across the room. The more time that passes after Lincoln's invitation, the more the anxiousness turns into excitement.

Me: About the blonde …

Crew: Yeah?

Me: Would it be weird to ask her?

River: It'd be weird to ask her lots of things, but not this.

Crew: Do you have her number?

River: Well, I take that back. It depends on how you ask her. You could make it super weird. You've made easier things weirder. Come to think of it, this might be a risk.

Me: Thanks, River. Fucker.

Crew: Can we focus here?

I stop moving and watch my friends banter back and forth while an ocean apart. It makes me feel good. Normal. Grounded.

Me: So yes or no to the blonde, Crew? Yes, I have her number.

River: I'll just sit here and pout that you're excluding me from this conversation.

Crew: Ask her. What do you have to lose?

River: HIS DIGNITY.

Crew: River—so help me God.

Me: LOL

Crew: I say go for it, Hollis. Just shoot her a text. If she says no, she says no. No harm, no foul. But if things went well, why not just toss it out there? You need to check in today with her anyway. It's the gentlemanly thing to do.

River: Reality check—Hollis is not a gentleman.

Me: Ok. I'll think about it. Thanks, guys.

Crew: You're welcome.

River: You're welcome.

Chuckling, I close the screen and take another look out the window.

I know exactly what I need—a run. Something to calm down my nerves and clear my head before I do something that's probably idiotic.

I slip my room key into my pocket and head for the door.

SIX
LARISSA

I pick up the plate I left sitting on the table after breakfast and shove it into the dishwasher. The piece of paper I was fiddling with as my bacon fried lays by the sink. I snatch it up.

The drawing is incomplete. It's a solid start to a garden design I've been dreaming about. Nice straight lines. Lots of open space. Tiered planters that I'm obsessed with. It's a beautiful, clean vision I can imagine filling with flowers of all shapes and colors.

Carrying the design with me into my bedroom, I flop on a chaise lounge to study the plan more closely.

I've been sketching gardens and flower beds since I was a little girl. Bellamy and I spent a summer one year with her maternal grandparents in Rhode Island. They had the most beautiful backyard that seemed to go on forever—just like their love of all things that bloomed. I watched her grandmother move gracefully around the plants each morning. She was so gentle, so careful with the flowers and vegetables that she seemed like some kind of goddess. Her grandfather worked alongside her doing the heavy lifting and pulling … and watching his wife adoringly in secret.

I came home, obtained a notepad and pencils, and went to town trying to capture that summer on paper.

I still am.

The sun coming through the window warms my skin. I set the paper down and sit quietly in the warmth of the rays. The light makes the wallpaper I hung last winter almost shine. Sebastian hated the idea and refused to help me. He also hated the navy background with the cerulean damask design.

My heart sinks as I realize Sebastian not only hated the wallpaper but he also disliked most of the things that I love. At the root of it, he might have even disliked *me*.

In retrospect, I'm not sure he had the capacity for the kind of relationship that I'm after. I want something wild yet stable. I'm after a connection to someone who extends beyond attraction or social circles. I want a love like Bellamy's grandparents, and a marriage like Aunt Siggy's and Uncle Rodney's.

I want something that's going to last forever.

And that terrifies me.

A little ball lays in the bottom of my stomach, reminding me from time to time that the kind of love I'm after in life might not exist for everyone. It hasn't come close for me—and not for lack of trying. Next to that ball lies another, slightly bigger one that houses the fear that I might find it someday, just as my mom found my dad. And that it might fall apart, just as it did between them.

"I need to take a few months and breathe," I mumble to an empty room. "Get back into classes and finish my degree. Bellamy is right. There's no need to add all kinds of pressure on myself about this. What is meant to be will be."

I hope.

My phone buzzes on the little table next to the chaise, and a text from my mom lights up the screen.

Mom: I have you a date lined up for tomorrow night.

I don't acknowledge her message with a response. Instead, I ignore it completely.

I stand and head to the window, wrapping a hand around the back of my neck. Stress builds at the bottom of my skull as I try to figure out how to deal with this stupid fundraiser. I know Siggy is right, and this does matter a lot to Mom. I know, too, that the holidays are even more problematic for her because it's the time of year that she and my father separated so many years ago. I believe she stays so busy these last few weeks of the year so she doesn't have to remember.

You need to pick your battles with her.

I nibble my bottom lip as I ponder choosing this battle. Fighting with her isn't what I want; it never is. But it *definitely* isn't the way I want to end the year.

Maybe if I just humor her now and then set firm boundaries in January ...

The strain in the back of my neck eases just a bit.

But what do I do about my plus-one?

My body fills up with a warmth that overtakes me from head to toe as I think about Hollis.

"His name is even hot," I say with a grin.

I turn from the window and mosey around my room.

So get him to be your date tomorrow.

A bubble of anxiety builds in my stomach as I contemplate Aunt Siggy's suggestion.

Taking Hollis isn't a good idea. I know it.

"If you want my number, I could give it to you in case you run into any more scenarios where you need a fake boyfriend. Or ... whatever ..."

Did he really mean that? Or was he just suggesting a hookup?

Given how he suggested that women complain when he only gave them five minutes, I'm going with a yes on the hookup.

But asking him to go with me tomorrow would have a definite starting and ending point. It would be a simple extenuation of the five minutes from the other night. *And* we would be in the presence of loads of other people, including my mom and Jack, which will dampen all things fun.

"And he's not an athlete, I don't think. I mean, he wasn't wearing some stupid hoodie with a team logo on it, so he's not even on my banned list," I point out to myself. "What would it hurt to take him as a friend to an event?"

My brain turns into mush when he grins. My knees give out when he smirks.

Dear lord, that smirk.

I moan helplessly.

My phone rings, ending my daydream before it even gets started. I look down.

"Hi," I say as I answer.

"Heya, Riss," my cousin Boone says. "What are you up to?"

"Pondering life and the choices we have to make," I say, sitting on the chair again.

He laughs. "That's deep for two in the afternoon."

I laugh along with him. "I'm guessing you're doing something less … intense?"

"You could say that."

The way he says it makes me wonder what exactly he's referring to. But it also scares me too much to ask.

Boone Mason is Aunt Siggy's youngest son. With four brothers, it was probably a given that he would be a handful. When you couple that with the fact his brother Coy was only eighteen months older than him and a complete and utter hellion, Boone didn't stand a chance.

The three of us grew up together—four, if you count Bellamy

—building forts in the woods and damming up the creek behind their house. We'd ride bikes, play home run derby, and hold fake *Star Search* contests that Coy would always win.

We were the Four Musketeers until Bellamy and Coy decided they hated each other.

"I spent the morning with your mom," I tell Boone.

He groans. "I'm so sick of hearing about her damn party. Did she poll you on snowflakes or icicles?"

I laugh again. "Yes. How did you know?"

"Because when I went by there last night to see if I could smuggle any food out, she was asking me."

"Your mom isn't giving you food anymore?"

"Yeah. But sometimes, I feel guilty. I'm a grown-ass man. I shouldn't be going to my mom's to get food, you know?"

"Exactly how does it make it better if you smuggle it out?"

He pauses. "I'm not sure. I think it just lets me keep some of my self-respect."

"You're an idiot," I say with a giggle. "We picked icicles, by the way. In case you care."

"I don't. I assure you, I don't."

I lean my head back on the chair and relax. Boone muffles the phone with what sounds like his hand and has a brief conversation with someone else. When he comes back, my mind is on Hollis again … and the fact he didn't call last night.

"Sorry," he says. "I'm back."

"No problem." I sigh, unsure whether I should bring up Hollis. I'm going to keep ruminating on him, so I might as well see what Boone thinks. "Can I ask you a question?"

"Sure."

"What do guys think of girls who make the first move, even if she didn't really mean it?"

"Depends."

I wait for more.

Still, nothing.

I roll my eyes. "Fine. That wasn't what I meant anyway." I shift around in the chair. "Let me rephrase this for you. What would a guy think about accompanying a girl somewhere if that girl had no desire to make something more out of it?"

"Why doesn't she want to do that?"

"Because maybe she just wants a man to be a gentleman for once and look out for a friend for a night."

I do want that, but if I'm candid, I want a man to be genuine and kind and above blaming me for *my* inadequacies—the reason they all seem to leave in some way or another. *God, I'm over that.*

"Because maybe she's tired of being burned. Maybe she's sick of finding herself in the same situations over and over with men who seem good at the start and then end up … tolerating her instead of loving her. Maybe she just wants to be alone for a while and break her bad habits so she can pick a guy with mental clarity, for once."

"Wow. Alright. Settle down."

"Sorry. That got a little aggressive there, didn't it?"

"A little," he teases. "And by she, I'm assuming we're talking about you?"

"Obviously." I sigh. "How would a guy react if I asked him to go somewhere with me as friends? Even if we aren't friends. And the sizzle between us isn't exactly *friendly*. Do you feel me?"

He taps his tongue on the roof of his mouth. "Well, I'm pretending we aren't talking about you because that makes things … weird and potentially skews my response. However, if it were me and a chick who had the hots for me invited me somewhere, my answer, I suppose, would depend on how well we got along. And if it's really a ploy to get us in a situation where we're gonna fuck, but she feels good about it. Like oops, we just happened to end up at this place where there's a bed, and the two of us, and we've had a couple of drinks." He laughs. "That's happened more times than you'd believe."

"Oh, great."

"You asked."

I sigh. "I expected you to be more … sweet about it, which I guess is my fault because when are you ever sweet?"

"I can be," he protests. "But only when it's necessary. I don't waste sweet behavior on just anyone, you know."

"God forbid."

"Not every situation calls for sweet behavior. Some women don't even want that, I'll have you know." He laughs. "So who is the guy, and where do you want to take him?"

Instantly, tension stretches across the back of my neck again. I place a hand at the base of my skull and squeeze.

"I was thinking about taking a guy I just met to Jack's Seahawks fundraiser tomorrow night. I don't want to go, but Jack bought me a ridiculously expensive ticket. Two, actually. So I have to go and take a plus-one, or else he's out like two grand."

"Want me to go?"

"Didn't you have some lewd love affair with Jack's partner's daughter or something a few years ago?"

He pauses. "I don't remember. Possibly. Sounds like it could be true."

"I think you did," I tease him. "And I think it ended rather poorly."

"Oh. In that case, who are you considering? Because it ain't gonna be me, pal."

A bolt of energy shoots through me, taking me by surprise. I get to my feet and pace around the room.

"I met a guy last night. You don't know him. He's just here for a little while. A few days, I think he said. Anyway, he pretended to be my boyfriend so Sebastian would leave me alone, and we hit it off in a way that … let's just say he's handsome and funny and had great shoulders—"

"This doesn't sound like it's going to end well."

I snort. "Right?"

He laughs. "Where did you meet Mr. Kryptonite?"

"Paddy's." I stop midstep as I remember the excitement at being in front of him. A shiver rips down my spine. "Anyway, we had fun, and he was super cute. I thought I could maybe ask him to go with me tomorrow, but …"

My voice fades. I'm not sure what to say.

"But what, Riss?"

"I don't know. I just … I really feel like I'm in a place in my life where I need a little perspective." I close my eyes and try to make myself clear. "I swore off men because I repeatedly choose the wrong ones—"

"Facts."

I open my eyes and glare as if Boone was standing in front of me.

"But Bellamy says it's not men but relationships that are my problem," I finish. "That I put too much pressure on myself or something. I don't know." I wince. "There was a raccoon analogy. It's all fuzzy after that."

"Leave it to Bells with the random analogy."

"This one was a doozy. Anyway," I say, trying to stay focused, "I feel like I'm screwing myself over after having just declared *last night* that I'm going to be single for a while. I made that decision sober and clearheaded, so I know it was a solid choice. Yet here I am, not twenty-four hours later, contemplating asking a guy to go with me to this event."

"He could say no, you know?"

"Yeah, but I don't think he would."

The idea of him saying yes doesn't help. It makes my insides all tingly.

"Riss, just … reality check here, okay? This guy, whoever he is, isn't even from Savannah, right? It's not like you're asking to date him or have his child. You can still be single for all intents and purposes if that's what you want and take this dude with you."

"Yes, I guess you're right."

The weight on my shoulders begins to lift, and I realize how much I'm pressuring myself.

I'm turning into my mom.

Finally, after what feels like forever, Boone laughs.

"Has it ever occurred to you, ever, that you can be just friends with a guy who you aren't related to?" he asks. "What I'm hearing—and correct me if I'm wrong—is that you just presume you'll end up fucking this guy because that's what always happens."

"You haven't seen him, Boone."

"For fuck's sake, Riss."

I laugh. "Okay. Yes. You're right. I presume things would escalate between us. And I just … I don't want to do that. I mean *I do*, but I shouldn't. I need to do what's right for me as a whole person. I need to lead myself to victory here and not just, well, you know. To the bedroom, I guess."

"I happen to find one-night stands quite victorious from time to time."

I roll my eyes. "Of course, you do."

Boone sighs into the phone. "Look, Jack will kill you if he paid that much for your tickets and you don't use them."

"I know. And Mom has already tried to hook me up with some random guy. Again."

"Ew, no. Your mom has awful taste."

"I know. Trust me. I'm half afraid to show up with Hollis as friends because she'd still be trying to parade me in front of her little picks like a dog in a dog show. Then she'll decide who I'm the best with and invite me to lunch that, *presto!* she can't make, but her man of choice will just happen to be there." I groan at the thought.

My cousin makes a sound that resembles blowing a raspberry. It makes me giggle. It's his *deep-thinking* sound, and it doesn't happen often.

"I got it," he says, his tone kissed with finality.

"What do you *got*?"

"Your solution. Hear me out," he says. "Call up the guy from Paddy's. You want to see him anyway. Tell him you need a plus-one to this fancy bullshit event but ask him to tell everyone you're dating. You've done that before anyway, so he won't think you're nuts … or not any more nuts than you were last night."

"Gee, thanks."

He laughs. "This solves your need for a date. It's a plus-one for the night only and a way to keep your mom from trying to set you up with every jerk in Savannah for a while. It also keeps Jack happy with his ticket purchase, and you can probably end up at the guy's hotel if you really want to, but that's a hard limit for me. I'm not about to talk to you about fucking guys, Riss. This is Bellamy's department."

"Noted."

I consider his proposal. It would work. It could be fun. And it might be the only way to solve all of my problems.

Sure, I could ask someone else. But I would have to see those people again around town. It would be easy to call them up in a moment of weakness too. But Hollis doesn't live here. I'll probably never see him again.

Come to think of it—this might be the only way to stay true to myself while keeping the peace with everyone around me for the time being.

"You have to admit it's a pretty great idea," Boone says.

It is, but I'm not about to tell him that. Not yet, anyway.

I sigh. "I need to figure out what I'm going to do. Thanks for helping me."

"Anytime."

"Talk to you later."

"Later, Riss."

I end the call. But before I even remove my finger from the phone screen, a text pops up.

Hollis: It's my turn to ask for a favor.

SEVEN
HOLLIS

"What the hell am I doing?"

I glance down at my phone and re-read the text I sent Larissa.

It's my turn to ask for a favor.

Could I have been any more pathetic?

Maybe she didn't notice. After all, she didn't ask questions. She simply volunteered to meet me here.

Groaning, I sit back in my seat and watch the door.

Paddy's is fairly quiet, which is not a surprise since it's two thirty. I worked at a restaurant on campus my sophomore year and learned that the hours between two and four thirty are pretty dead. That's precisely why I tried to work every shift I could that included those two hours. You basically got paid for sitting on your ass.

I spin my phone around and around. The sound the device makes as it slides across the wooden tabletop is smooth and almost melodic. I find myself humming a tune that starts slow. But as the minutes tick by and my eyes stay trained on the door, waiting for Larissa to walk in, the spins get faster, and the beat gets harder.

Fuck, Hollis. You're calmer than this before game day.

Finally, the phone jets from between my fingers and winds up leaned against a menu display.

My body pulses with the need to move—to run or do push-ups or lift some weights. Something. *Anything.* For a split second, I wish that I was back on campus and in my daily routine.

As much as I thought I'd hate everything about college except football, I was wrong. It was the first time in my life I had structure. Routine. Predictability. I could go to sleep at night in my bed and know that I'd be crawling back into the same bed the night after.

Unless I ended up at a girl's house, but the point remains the same.

I find it strange that the one thing I thought I'd hate most about Braxton College—the regime of it all—will be the one thing I look back on and wish I had the most. Because after graduation, who the fuck knows what's going to happen?

I squirm in my seat and shift my eyes to the door again.

I'm not sure if all this pent-up energy is from knowing that Larissa will be walking through the doors or if it's because I have a commitment to be at Landry's house in a few hours. Both are exciting in their own way. They're also equally nerve-wracking.

"She's just a chick," I whisper to myself. "A chick who owes you a favor."

But even as I say the words, I know they aren't true. She doesn't owe me jack shit.

She's about to be my fake date.

I imagine her next to me at some fancy table in Landry's dining room. The conversation in my mind is about football and the future—things that are inherently private and personal to me. If I imagine Larissa with me, it doesn't feel like a *fake* date anymore.

And that's enough to make my insides seize.

The fun of just screwing around diminishes when you start adding in real-life talk. I don't share those conversations with anyone, really. River knows the most because he has shit he needs to get off his chest too. We sort of talk about things and then blast abrasive rap music or go for a run and pretend it never happened.

I should've considered having to discuss things in front of Larissa before I got all impulsive and sent her that text.

Shit.

Do I really want to do this?

As alarm bells start ringing in my head, the door to Paddy's opens.

Larissa walks in.

Jeans kissing her thighs, a jacket skimming the curve of her waist, and a smile on her lips that feels like it's challenging me not to groan.

I'm not sure if she walks really fast or if my brain slows way down, but she's at my table before I have time to get settled.

"I just realized something on the way over here," she says as she sits across from me.

"And what might that be?"

She grins. She's even cuter this afternoon than she was yesterday—and that's quite a feat. Most women are much better looking in the evening hours than they are during the day. It's some kind of law of the universe that's never been fully explained.

"I realized that your little ploy of pretending to be my knight in shining armor was just that: a ploy," she teases.

I lean forward and rest my elbows on the table. Her eyes dance as I peer into them. They're clear and fresh with little lines coming from the corners that give her a playful energy.

"And how do you figure that?" I ask.

"Well, you told me that you were giving me your number in

case I needed you for anything." She sets her purse on the empty chair to her right. "But I bet you already knew you'd need me."

"Untrue. Although I appreciate your confidence that I would choose you automatically."

The corner of her lip turns upward. She mirrors my position by resting her elbows on the table.

"Was I your first choice?" she asks, her tone teasing.

"Absolutely."

"Okay. I just wanted to make sure a list of women didn't turn you down."

"Sweetheart, no one *ever* turns me down."

Her lips twist into an amused smirk. "I'm not sure if that means I should be the first or if I really have it in me to break your streak."

I point at her, my finger bouncing up and down. "You are a funny one."

She tosses me a wink.

Before I can say anything else, the waitress who brought me a drink earlier appears out of thin air. She asks Larissa if she wants anything. Larissa orders a tea just to be polite, I think.

Once we're alone, she looks at me again. "What do you need from me?"

"Well, I have a little situation that's not totally unlike yours from last night."

She raises a perfectly arched brow. "You have an ex-girlfriend you want me to help you with?"

"No. When you put it like that, it's totally different."

"Well, when you put it like that, it makes me more likely to help you."

She pauses and takes her drink from the waitress. After declining to order anything else, Larissa's attention is all mine again.

"You were saying …?" She takes a sip.

"I got invited to dinner tonight, and it was implied that I should bring whoever is traveling with me. Only I don't have anyone traveling with me. Hell, I don't even know anyone in Savannah."

"So I get the invitation because I'm the only person you know?"

"Yes."

She sighs dramatically. "That makes a girl feel good."

"Would you rather me lie to you?"

Larissa takes a second—a longer one than I expect—before answering. She makes a face like she's disgusted, and the gesture makes my stomach tight.

"I just realized something else," she says. "My first reaction was to say yes, I would rather you lie to me. But what does that say about me? Don't answer that."

I grin. "Although you asked me not to answer, I'd say it means you want someone to make you feel important. And I don't think that's a terrible thing to want."

She balks. "What are you? A philosopher?"

"Nope. I'll be getting a good ole bachelor's degree in business administration with a minor in music appreciation."

"I didn't know music appreciation was a thing."

"Yeah, well, I love music. All kinds of it. But I don't play an instrument and don't want to learn. This let me take all the music classes I wanted to without taking saxophone lessons or some shit."

She laughs, the ends of her straight hair hitting the small of her back.

The anxiety I felt earlier is long gone and, in its place, is a feeling of manageability.

"So you need me to accompany you to a dinner tonight. Is that right?" she asks.

"Yeah."

"And we're going as friends?"

I suck in a long, deep breath.

Going as friends will probably work fine. But would it feel *pitiful* if I tell Landry that I picked up a random girl I just met and asked her to go with me? Because it seems like it would. And if there's one thing I don't want, it's Landry's pity.

"Friends is okay. But maybe we could pretend we've known each other for a while? You don't have to want to fuck me, but maybe you didn't meet me last night either. Make sense?"

Her cheeks flush. "You want me to lie?"

I shift in my seat as my eyes lock onto hers. "About which part?"

A smile slips across my lips as a fire begins to burn inside my body. The flames lick at my veins, and all I can feel is my body heating.

Her tongue darts out, and she licks her lips. I think she's doing it to fuck with me. If she is, *it's working*.

"Before I agree," she says, "I have something to ask you."

"What's that?"

"Another favor."

"What do I look like? A favor boy?"

She sits back in her chair and exhales. "You look convenient."

"I've heard that before."

She tries not to look amused but fails. Miserably.

"Okay. In all seriousness, what do you need from me?" I ask.

"My stepfather, Jack, has this charity fundraiser thing he does every year. I wasn't going to go, but he's bought two tickets for me. If I don't go, it'll be the start of a war in my family, and I'd just like to get through the holiday season without anyone melting down."

I cross my arms over my chest. "I'm not from here. I can't ask anyone else—hence, you by default." *Which I'm not mad about.* "But you, on the other hand, are from here. Or I suppose you are. So why not ask someone else?"

"To be honest, my mother will have someone there as my date if I don't bring one. And while that seems fairly innocuous, it's not. It's a long and convoluted story that ends with my mother trying to marry me off to some random athlete that she thinks will simultaneously make me happy and save me from a life of eating TV dinners alone." She sighs. "So I need a date, a fake one I won't actually fall in love with, to save me from an arranged marriage."

She smiles triumphantly.

I tilt my head to the side. "There's one problem I don't think you've accounted for."

She makes a face.

"You don't think you'll fall in love with me?" I grin. "That's very bold of you, Larissa."

She levels her gaze on me. The sparkle is still there but also a heavy dose of confidence I wasn't expecting.

"On the contrary, I think it's very bold of you to think I will, Hollis."

"Your naivete is adorable."

"And your confidence is admirable."

We watch each other like two gamblers in Vegas—both of us waiting for the other to fold.

This is a side of her that I didn't expect. It's a whole lot sexy, and a little badass, and I could really, really get into it.

But I won't.

"I think the logical thing for us to do is to establish some boundaries for this relationship pact," she says. "I mean, if you're still considering this whole thing."

I rub a hand down the side of my face. "What kind of boundaries?"

"Well, our interaction and relationship—both in reality and

the one we are putting on for everyone else—is rooted in friendship. We might be acting like a couple but not a couple-couple. Not all over each other," she says. "More like friends that might be trying something new."

I get what she's saying. It makes a lot of sense.

"Can we fuck and still be friends, though?" I ask.

She's not sure if I'm teasing or not.

Her eyes shoot to the ceiling, her little rosebud of a pout parting and gasping for a quick breath of air.

I'm not kidding. I'd love to break her down and have her reeling from it for days. But that's not what we're doing here, and it's probably for the best. I'm not sure she's used to that sort of thing, and I'm definitely not a guy like she's used to.

Case in point: Sebastian.

"I'm just kidding," I tell her. "I don't think you can handle me."

She sighs, knocking a strand of hair out of her face. "You're an asshole."

I shrug.

She sits up and takes a drink of her tea. When she looks at me again, she's composed.

"If I do start to fall in love with that wicked charm of yours, all I'll have to do is remember this conversation, and I'm sure I'll be able to deal," she says.

"Yeah, well, women usually take it as a challenge."

"Not me. I'm challenged out. Just looking for the easy road from here on out." She pulls her purse onto her lap and sorts through it. "What will your dinner thing require? A dress? Casual? A bottle of wine?"

"Casual. I think. He said pizza."

She looks up. "Pizza is good."

"Pizza is great."

She nods and takes her hand out of her purse. "Okay. For my thing, you'd need a suit and tie. Would that be a problem?"

"Nope. I have one with me for the event I'm here for to start with."

"Can you make small talk?" she asks.

"I'm making small talk now, aren't I?"

"Good point."

She puts her purse back on the chair and focuses solely on me once again.

The need to move, to burn off excess energy comes rushing back again. My leg bounces up and down as I wait for her to figure out what she wants to do.

Because I know what I want to do.

I want to make this deal.

It'll help me out of a bind. Fortunately, it'll help her too.

And the fact I'll get to hang out with her and watch her laugh and banter back and forth isn't that bad either.

She wrinkles her nose. "So do we have a deal?"

"I'm in if you are."

She shoves her hand across the table. I take it in mine.

Her skin is as soft as I remember, and her perfume brings me right back to the sea. Feeling the warmth in her palm and the sturdiness in the weight of her hand causes my leg to stop hopping around under the table.

We shake gently, easily, our eyes glued together.

She slips her hand from mine entirely before I'm ready, which is weird because I don't do the hand-holding thing. I mean, I've done it. Sometimes you have to in order to keep the peace. But it's never once been something I wanted or enjoyed. It feels intimate—like parents and their kids or girlfriends and boyfriends—and when have I ever had that?

Never. And despite what Lincoln said earlier, it's not something I'll probably ever have. That shit makes me uncomfortable.

Still, I miss the stillness from Larissa's touch, and that throws me a bit.

"Guess we have a deal then," she says softly, her eyes finding mine.

She has beautiful eyes.

"I can pick you up tonight around six thirty. I drove here from school, so I have my car."

"Great. I'll text you my address."

A smile ghosts her lips as she gets to her feet. I stand, too.

My heartbeat thumps away as I watch her. She takes her purse in her hand and smooths her shirt down with the other.

I want to follow the movement and take in the beauty of her body, but I can't look away from her face.

I wish I could ask her to stand still, to never leave that spot just so I could stay right here and feel this … balance. This calm before what I'm afraid might be a storm because there's always a storm brewing. It's a fact of life.

"I'll see you tonight," she says.

"Six thirty."

She grins. "I'll grab a bottle of wine. Don't worry about that."

"I wasn't." I hadn't even thought about bringing something to dinner.

"I saw the panic in your eyes when I mentioned it before. But don't worry—I have many, many extra bottles at home that will work."

"Well, if you insist …"

She laughs as she turns on her heel and walks away.

I stand beside the table and watch her, wondering what just happened here. She's a chance encounter. Temporary. The perfect solution to an imperfect situation.

Yet … there was a vibe between us. Our energies fell in-sync so easily that being around her feels like being around one of my guy friends. It's easy. It's fun.

Except that I wouldn't mind fucking her.

I shake my head. *You're here for a few days, Hudson. Then*

Savannah is in your rearview, like so many people and places before Larissa.

So many people.

I heave a breath and find a smile spreading across my cheeks.

Maybe so, but I'll get this girl for two nights. And that's better than what I usually get—nothing.

EIGHT
LARISSA

I turn side-to-side and check out my reflection.

The jeans from Halcyon fit me pretty well despite being a new-to-me brand, and the powder-blue top makes me look like I have more cleavage than I do. It looks decent and definitely casual, and Hollis said the dinner tonight was casual.

Then why does casual feel so wrong?

"And why am I trusting a guy's take on the dress code?" I groan, scrunching my face up in frustration.

I turn around and take in the mess on my bed. Nearly every top I own that could remotely be labeled as *casual* lays in a heap.

I go back into my closet and thumb through the few remaining items. My eyes end up falling on a turquoise wrap dress that I borrowed from Bellamy a few months ago. I take the hanger off the rod and carry the dress into my bedroom.

With the late afternoon sunlight creating a spotlight on me, I hold the dress up to my body. I turn from one side to the other.

"I mean, it's kind of casual," I say, still unsure. "But is it too much for … I don't even know where we're going."

I blow out a breath and feel my spirits sink.

"Just pick something, Larissa," I mutter as I hang the dress on the back of my closet door.

I wander around my room and try to remind myself of who I am. I am not a girl who gets worked up about what she wears or puts this much effort into getting ready. Ever.

I wonder vaguely if this is what other girls feel like. Does Bellamy get this obsessed about getting dressed every morning?

Probably. And it's probably why she looks phenomenal in everything she wears.

Ugh.

I just don't have it in me to care this much.

I walk over to my desk and take a seat. I open my laptop and check my email. Coupons for ice cream, newsletters from romance authors, and shipping updates fill my inbox. But there's one message buried in the middle of the list that stands out. I click on it.

The email from my academic advisor at school is short and sweet. The last few classes I need to take to finalize my bachelor's degree are written in black and white. I needed an urban design course but had failed to take the prerequisite math class. My new advisor promised me he would work it out, and after some shifting around and an online course, I'm thrilled to see it finally confirmed on my schedule.

A rush of relief mixed with excitement flows freely through me. I sit back in my leather office chair and revel in the feeling of things going according to plan.

Landscape architecture was a no-brainer for me. It's creative and artistic and gives me access to sunshine and fresh air—two things I need to feel alive. It was the only career option that would allow me to create something beautiful or something practical—or something practically beautiful—*and* feed my soul.

I let myself imagine what life might be like in just a few months. While everyone seems to think I'll go into residential landscape design and work with my family's friends and acquaintances, that's not at all what I want to do.

My dreams are much bigger than designing golf courses and sculpted lawns. I want to create actual spaces and transform specific areas that make people feel at home.

I want to do something more than inspire one family. I want to do something bigger, something bigger than *me.*

Designing gardens for convalescent centers so people who can't go home can still sit outside and feel safe and relaxed is on my bucket list. I hope to create green areas in the middle of the city for commuters to find a bit of calm in their day. I would die over the ability to tuck in a little garden somewhere with a flow of energy that others can flock to when they need a shot of happiness or hope. My goal is to use my skills and passions to make other people's lives better—to extend the gifts given to me.

The summer that Bellamy and I spent at her grandma's house changed me in a deep, molecular-level way. I needed to be surrounded by life and colors and calm to survive the disruptions in my life during those months. My heart *craved* that peace. It was desperate for it. And now that I know what can deliver that kind of respite from life's stresses, I want to be able to bring that to others.

It's a secret I stumbled onto and one that I can share with the world.

I rock back and forth in my chair, relishing in the idea of the future, and make the mistake of looking over my shoulder. Instantly, I'm reminded of my very real *first world problem* of not knowing what to wear.

Better to overdress and impress than underdress and obsess, my mom says.

"This time, you just might be right," I say out loud.

I get to my feet and grab my phone. I press Bellamy's number.

"Hey," she chirps after barely the first ring.

"Hey, Bells."

"What's up?"

"Well … I was wondering if it would be okay if I wear that turquoise dress that I borrowed from you a while back. Do you know the one?" I glance at the fabric draped on the hanger across the room. "It's a wrap dress that has a very faint cream-colored checkered design on it."

"I forgot you had that."

I laugh. "It must be really hard to have so many clothes that you don't know what you're missing."

"*Oh*, like you have any room to talk."

I roll my eyes. "So can I wear it? I mean, I could've just put it on, and you wouldn't have known, but I thought I'd ask first."

"I don't care. I didn't even know I didn't have it, so it's not like I'm attached." She smacks her lips together as she eats something. "Where are you going?"

The thought of saying Hollis's name makes me smile. The idea of being with him again makes me shiver. The realization that I'm going to have to tell my best friend what's going on has me bracing myself because she's not going to just gloss over it.

There's no way.

"I'm just helping out a friend and going to dinner with them," I say as breezily as I can manage.

Bellamy reads right through my attempt at evasion.

"And who might your friend be? Because it's not me. And not that I'm your only friend or anything, but I do feel like I would know if you had plans to go to dinner with someone."

Her tone is teasing but pointed enough for me to know she's going to press until she has an answer. There's also enough of a smugness to tell me that she already knows the answer.

I hold back a laugh. "You'll be pleased to know that I took your advice."

"This is starting off strong."

"Your girl over here talked to her mother about Jack's event and put her foot down. I told Mom that she wouldn't be picking out my date. Period."

She pauses. "So, you're going alone?"

"I didn't say that."

She sighs before smacking her lips together again.

"What are you eating?" I ask.

"Cheetos. The hot ones. My mouth is on fire."

I laugh.

"Don't try to distract me," she says. "I know where this is going, but I'm going to make you tell me."

"Why?" I whine, hoping I'd managed to get away with not telling her. It's not a big deal. But just in case things don't work out the way I imagine, it would be easier not to have to explain it to Bellamy later.

"Because it's more fun that way," she says. "Also, I knew this whole thing between the two of you wasn't over last night."

"What are you talking about? There's no *whole thing* between me and anyone."

"You might be able to trick yourself or him or your mother or whoever, but you aren't going to trick me."

"I'm not trying to trick anyone," I tell her, slipping out of my jeans.

"Good. Because I saw you with the hottie last night. I saw the way he looked at you like he wanted to eat every part of you and—"

"Ew!"

"Don't *ew* that. You write way too much off too early."

"Anyway …" I say, trying to distract her.

"Anyway, I saw the way he looked at you and the way you looked at him—which was not a whole lot different than he looked at you, but I'll keep my descriptions vanilla to protect your innocent little ears."

I laugh, bobbling the phone between my hands long enough to slip out of my shirt.

"I almost called Boone and bet on how long it would take you to see him again," she says. "But I got distracted by Suit."

"How'd that go?"

"It went. He *accidentally* called me late last night, and I purposely picked up. We talked for a bit, and then he came by and stayed for a while. I'll let you fill in those blanks," she says, sighing. "But he left before dawn. I probably won't see him again."

I make a face. "And why not? Was he weird?"

"No. He was fine," she says, brushing him off like a crumb off her shoulder. "Just not for me."

"You do realize that you're going to end up murdered in your sleep one of these days." I take the dress off the hanger. "You need a hotel room that you can use to meet up with guys in or something."

"I have a security system. If I get murdered, find the footage in the cloud and nail that sucker to the wall."

I laugh. "I'm glad you've planned ahead."

"You know me. I'm always planning." She laughs too. "So back to … what's his name again?"

"Hollis."

The name ripples off my tongue.

"That really is a great name," Bellamy says. "And it matches him. You know, it's really weird when people don't match their names. Like when you meet a beast of a man, and his name is Clyde. But then you might walk into the library and spot a geek sitting by the history section, and his name is something like *Mauricio*. So sexy."

I put Bellamy on speakerphone long enough to tug the dress over me. I smooth the lines out around my hips and then adjust the wrap to cinch my waist and enhance my boobs.

"Not bad," I mutter, checking myself out again.

"Where are you going with Hollis?"

I pick up the phone and take her off speakerphone. "I actually don't know. It's a dinner he was invited to, and they asked him to bring his family. He's in town alone and doesn't know anyone but me. So I'm going with him."

"That's convenient. Lucky you. And you might get luckier if you don't get all weird about it and start ruling things out before they can become options."

"That's already been taken care of," I say, running my fingers through my hair. "We're going to the dinner and Jack's thing from a baseline of friends. It doesn't matter as much tonight for his thing, but Mom has to think I'm taken so she stops trying to match me with random men. We just need to sell it so that Mom thinks I'm forming a friendship with Hollis to see if more is there post-graduation since he doesn't live here." I shrug and drop my hand. "So we're friends. It's completely platonic."

She snorts. "Yeah. That's gonna work."

"What?"

"You really believe that you're going to spend two evenings with *Hollis* and manage not to touch him. Or be begging for him to touch you? Come on, Riss."

I swipe my lip gloss off the dresser with a little more force than necessary. "Yes, Bellamy. I do."

"Okay."

"Don't okay me like that," I say, coating my lips with another layer of gloss. "Just because this mutually-beneficial situation makes it seem like I'm getting all willy-nilly with my take on dating last night, I'm not. Two platonic nights with Hollis will keep my eyes focused on him. There will be no looking at all the delicious athletic man specimens tomorrow night. I'm still anti-athlete. I will be for eternity."

"I love how you always just go all-in. It's eternity or bust!"

I laugh. "It's called commitment, and I'm not the one who has a problem with that."

"Ouch," Bellamy says, knowing I'm talking about her and her refusal to even date a man seriously. "So what does Hollis do? What's his deal?"

"I don't know. I don't know much about him, really. He was a good-looking single man standing by a bar when I needed him. I don't know much else."

"And *I'm* the one who's going to end up murdered?"

"He's not a murderer."

"All you know is that he's hot. There have been hot serial killers."

I gasp. "What are you trying to do here? Get me to cancel?"

"Hardly," she scoffs. "I was just pointing out a touch of hypocrisy on your part. I'd totally go with him."

I set the gloss back on the dresser and try to ignore the hint of jealousy that settles in my stomach. I really don't know what to do with it.

There's no reason she couldn't go with him—not that she was saying that. She wasn't. She wouldn't do that. But the idea of Bellamy going with Hollis tonight makes me feel a certain way that I don't love.

"Okay, Bells. I gotta go. Hollis should be here soon," I say, shaking my head and hoping the crazy thoughts leave.

"Have fun. Make sure your tracking is on so I can find you if you end up in a ditch."

"You are a terrible friend," I joke.

All she does is laugh.

"Talk to you later," I say.

"Call me as soon as you get home. I want all the details."

I grab my purse. "There will be no details that you're interested in hearing." I head into the hallway with a final look at myself and deposit my purse near the door.

"You'll have no good details because you're lame."

"I'm not lame. I'm just trying to figure out my life over here and not just roll in the breeze."

"When did you get all judgy?" she teases me. "You get a hot boyfriend, and all of a sudden, you're a little judgy friend."

I laugh. "I'm not judging you, and he's not my boyfriend."

"Let's reconvene this conversation in a week."

"Let's not."

"You go rock my dress and look hot and call me later. Love you. Bye."

"Bye, Bells."

Before I even hit the button, the doorbell rings.

My head whips toward the door as I end the call. I drop my phone in my purse and check the mirror one last time.

"You got this," I whisper.

I take a deep breath and tug open the door.

It's a damn good thing I hold onto the frame with the other hand.

Hollis is downright edible—a word I can never tell Bellamy after our conversation today. It's safe to say I won't even remember thinking it because I'm reasonably sure my brain just went dead.

He's dressed in a pair of dark denim jeans that fit a set of muscled thighs like gloves. A black collared shirt is stretched across his broad shoulders.

His forearms are thick and heavily roped. On one wrist is a series of leather bracelets in a variety of styles.

He runs his hand through his hair, making the strands fall to one side. I know many guys will stand in front of the mirror forever to make their hair appear as though they don't give a crap about it. But I really don't think Hollis spent any time on it.

And that makes it *so* much hotter.

He stands on my doorstep, smelling like rich leather and chewing a large wad of pink bubble gum. He makes no secret of looking me up and down, letting his gaze sizzle my skin with each sweep.

I shiver as I force a swallow and try to remember how to speak English.

"Hey," he says, the words kissed with a sweet, slow drawl that's not quite Southern.

I clench the doorway even tighter. "Hi."

"The gentleman in me wants to say that you look beautiful." He smirks. "But the man in me wants to tell you that you look fucking hot."

My cheeks flush. "Well, thank them both for me, okay?"

His smirk deepens.

"Let me get my purse, and we can go."

I turn away from him and grab my stuff. I use the opportunity to get some fresh, un-Hollis-scented air and to let myself settle just a bit.

You're friends. He's a super-hot Boone. Go into it thinking that.

I turn as he blows a bubble. As it snaps, he winks.

Shit.

"What's your last name?" I ask him as I step outside.

"Hudson. Why?"

I shut the door and lock it before dropping my keys into my purse.

"Just in case you kill me. That way, Bellamy knows who to look for," I say.

He chuckles. "Hopefully, she'd call the cops."

"You'd be lucky if she did that and didn't come after you on her own. She's a savage."

A black Mustang sits at the end of the sidewalk. It has dark window tint and blacked-out rims.

It's exactly what I would imagine Hollis driving.

"Is this your car?" I ask.

"No. I stole it."

I look up at him to see him grinning.

"Yes, it's my car. It was a graduation present of sorts."

"It's nice. It fits you."

He seems to take this as it was intended—as a compliment. He smiles and opens the passenger's side door.

"What's your last name?" he asks.

"Mason."

"Good last name," he says.

What's that even mean?

I climb into the car and halfway fall into the low-sitting seat. When I look up, he's grabbing the window frame and looking down at me. The look in his eyes is full of mischief and innuendo, and I feel it fire through my veins.

"We're just friends, right?" he asks.

I nod because I don't trust my voice.

He nods too and closes the door.

"This is going to be a long night," I whisper. "And much harder than I thought."

NINE
HOLLIS

"I think this is where we're going," I say as I pull into a driveway.

A large brick mansion towers in front of us.

I don't know what I expected Lincoln Landry's house to look like, but this exceeds any expectations I might've had.

The house is grand, the biggest fucking house I've ever seen, with clean black shutters and window boxes full of some sort of green plant that drapes over the sides of the boxes. Lawns extend along both sides of the structure that would be perfect for football games. To cap off the vision is a Tennessee Arrows team flag flying proudly from a flagpole near the front porch.

"Quite a place, huh?" I ask, shifting the car into park.

"Yeah. It is. Who lives here?"

"This guy used to play baseball for the Arrows," I tell her. "That's a professional baseball team. His name is—"

"Lincoln Landry."

I raise a brow.

If this girl turns out to be a sports fan on top of being hot and funny and willing to spontaneously do shit like pretend to date a guy, then I'm done. I'm taking her home and calling it a night.

I'll be sure that the universe is pulling a trick on me, and that she's really a dude. Or the host of some reality show. Or working for an ex-hookup and going to poison me.

"I know him," she says simply.

"You like baseball?"

She sighs. "No. I know him. Personally. Well, sort of. My cousin Coy used to play baseball with Lincoln a long time ago. They were on the same high school team together and played ball all summer. I used to go watch with my aunt Siggy."

"You *know* this guy? I mean, I know it's a small world and all, but … really?"

She laughs. "It's a small world, but it's even smaller down here." She studies me for a moment. "Where are you from, anyway? Your accent doesn't scream Georgia."

"I'm from Indiana. Land of corn and coal."

"Sounds delightful," she jokes.

I shift in my seat to face her. "So back to this you knowing Lincoln thing. You're telling me that a girl I randomly met in a bar knows the professional baseball player I'm here to see. And that's completely random?"

"Stranger things have happened."

"I beg to differ," I say, still unable to process this new information. "Anyway, are you ready to go in?"

She holds up a finger. "Before we do that, I have a question for you."

"Shoot, Shooter."

She makes a face but continues. "Why are *you* coming here? Not that it's crazy or anything, just … random, as you say. I'm just curious. Humor me."

There's a right or wrong answer here. I can see it in the curiosity in her eyes and the way she nibbles on the end of her fingernail.

"Well," I begin. "He has a Catching-A-Care program that … I don't know what all it does, honestly. But there's a banquet I have to go to next week here in Savannah, and he invited me for dinner tonight to get to know me or something."

She closes her eyes and shakes her head. "Not what I mean. Who are *you*, Hollis? In adjectives."

I glance quickly at the front of the house before looking at her again. She sits next to me with her eyes squeezed shut, and if I was a betting man, I'd swear she was whispering a prayer.

"Adjectives?" I sigh. "Okay. I'm a man. Handsome. Charming. Studly. Humble," I add for good measure.

She opens her eyes long enough to give me a look of disapproval. The way her nose wrinkles up is adorable.

"I'm a student," I tell her, pausing to see when she'll have had enough. I'm also not sure if that's an adjective, but whatever. She doesn't stop me, so I continue. "Ferocious. A football player—"

"Ugh," she groans immediately.

"What?"

"I knew it," she moans, hitting the headrest with her ponytail.

I have no idea what's happening here. I only know she's slightly freaking me out.

"Larissa?"

"I should've known." She looks at me, resolution in her eyes. "You're an athlete."

It's more of an accusation than a statement, and I'm not sure what to do with that. I've been accused of many things in my life but never of being an athlete. It's usually more of a positive connotation, a conversation starter.

"Yeah. That's what I said," I deadpan.

She smacks her lips together. "Everything is starting to make sense."

"I'm glad it is for one of us."

She glances toward the door and then back at me.

"It's too late. We're already here," Larissa says.

"It's too late for what?" I run a hand through my hair. "What are you even talking about?"

"It's too late to have you take me back home."

I flinch. "What? Why do you want to go home?"

"Because you play football."

She scrunches up her face in a way that I think is supposed to express her dislike of my sporting habits but instead makes me laugh. This further annoys her.

"Let's get this over with, shall we?" she asks as she grabs the door handle and steps outside.

I scramble to get out. Before I can get around the car, she's already standing at the front.

I grin at her. "I need to know why me playing football is such a problem for you?"

"Just because."

We start up the walkway to the house. Her arms are crossed over her chest, but I don't get the feeling she's mad at me. Just … at the football player in me.

I don't know what to do, so I laugh.

She stops at the top of the stairs and sighs.

"Look, do you remember last night when I told you I had sworn off men right before I met you?" she asks.

I nod even though I don't actually remember. I'm not about to fight Larissa on this. Not with her already riled up about something I don't understand.

"Well, I didn't swear off all men, Hollis. Just one specific little category of them." She takes a deep breath. "*Athletes.* I promised myself I was not even entertaining the idea of being with an athlete in any way, shape, or form."

She turns away from me and rings the doorbell.

I take a step forward and nudge her with my elbow. When she looks at me, I smirk.

"Does this mean you were entertaining the idea of *entertaining me* tonight?" I ask.

"Ugh," she groans, looking at the giant chandelier hanging over our heads.

"Because, if you were, I'm technically not an athlete anymore. My season is over. So if you wanna ..."

Before I can get the thought out, the door swings open. Lincoln greets us with a broad, genuine smile.

"Hey, Hollis," he says, extending a hand. "It's good to see you. Thanks for coming, man."

We shake hands. Lincoln steps to the side to allow us to enter his home. I look at Larissa and wait for her to enter first.

"Don't I know you?" Lincoln asks as she walks by.

She smiles up at him adoringly. "Yes. I'm Larissa Mason. Coy Mason's cousin."

He tilts his head back and laughs. "That's right. Coy Mason. How the hell is he, anyway?"

"He's okay. He's Coy, so you know how that goes."

"That I do. Just saw him on the television a couple of days ago on one of those entertainment news reports, actually. And I hear him on the radio all the damn time. Danielle loves his music." Lincoln shuts the door behind me. "How do the two of you know each other?"

"We met in a bar," I say, figuring it's best to leave it simple and as vague as possible.

Lincoln looks at Larissa and winks. "I won't tell your cousins that you're picking up men in bars."

She grins. "I'd appreciate that."

He turns and heads down a long hallway, motioning for us to follow. "Come on. Let's get some food."

The house smells warm, like apples and cinnamon, and it's precisely what I imagine the homes smelling like in the old fifties sitcoms I watch late at night.

The hallway is decorated with pictures and random art pieces that make no sense to me. Music, I understand. Abstract art? Not even a little bit.

A living room sits to our left. It's painted light yellow and has oversized green couches facing a fireplace. On the right is a long dining room that looks like something out of a magazine that I would flip through at the doctor's office. It's immaculate, yet you can tell by the little touches of personal effects that people live here.

I look down at Larissa to see her watching me. She smiles.

"Hollis, Larissa, meet my wife, Danielle," Lincoln says as we enter the kitchen.

A woman much shorter than Lincoln is standing in front of a counter. Pizza boxes are lined up behind her as she watches us walk in.

"It's so nice to meet you, Hollis," she says. After wiping her hands on a white towel, she tosses it over her shoulder. "I'm so glad you could make it tonight."

Her energy is a bit shocking as she heads my way, and I'm not sure what I'm supposed to do. I half-ass stick my hand out in case she wants to shake it—in case that's what I'm supposed to do. But she bypasses it all together and pulls me into a hug.

My body goes stiff as I look over her head at her husband. I keep my arms at my sides.

She pulls back and smiles before turning to Larissa.

"And you," Danielle says, "have to be Sigourney Mason's daughter? Niece, maybe? I know I've seen you around."

"Siggy is my aunt," Larissa says easily. "Although we're both blond with green eyes, so you're not the first person to ask if we're related." She takes a bottle of wine out of her purse like some kind of fucking magician. "We brought you this."

"Thank you, sweetheart," Danielle coos, taking the wine from Larissa. She sets it on the counter. "I just love Siggy and her shop. I go in there all the time—"

"She's not lying," Lincoln chimes in.

Danielle rolls her eyes. "Ignore him. He's just upset I put him on a budget."

I can't help but laugh at the look on Lincoln's face. He glares playfully at the back of his wife.

It reminds me of Kim and Philip, the last foster family I stayed with. She definitely called the shots in that dynamic. It was hilarious because Philip was loud and slightly obnoxious, and Kim was this tiny little thing. But she could bend Philip to her will without saying a word.

There was something extraordinary about their relationship. There was something special about their family as a whole.

And the whole memory of them feels like a stake being shoved right through my heart.

I shake away all of that and focus on what Lincoln is saying.

"Hollis, come on over here and fill your plate," he says. "We aren't fancy around here. Just make yourself at home."

I glance over my shoulder. Larissa and Danielle are in an animated conversation about jewelry, and I don't really know what to do. *Do I just grab a plate and put pizza on it? Do I need to wait for someone to give me a plate?* I don't know how to make myself at home in a place like this.

Larissa catches my eye. With the skill of a master, she scoots away from Danielle and toward me without missing a beat.

"I prefer rose gold," she tells Danielle. "But I really don't love expensive jewelry. I'm always afraid I'll lose it, and the stress isn't worth it to me." She stops next to me. "Are you hungry?"

I nod.

She pats me on the shoulder. "I heard your stomach rumbling in the car."

She's lying because I'm not even hungry. But I appreciate how she seems to know that I'm a bit out of my element here.

I watch as she finds the plates stacked next to the pizza boxes, something I clearly missed. She hands me one. We fill our plates while Danielle grabs us drinks, and then we all find our way into the dining room.

"How are you enjoying Savannah, Hollis?" Danielle asks as we sit down at the table.

"I haven't had a lot of time to sightsee yet, but it's really nice so far. I love all the moss hanging from the trees."

"That's what Savannah is known for," Danielle says.

"Who came down with you?" Lincoln asks. "It's always so interesting to see who guys your age bring with them. You can tell a lot about a person by their entourage. Sometimes they come with parents and grandparents and aunts and uncles. Sometimes it looks like a whole damn gang. Other times, they bring their wives and sometimes even their own kids already."

Lincoln takes a big bite of pizza.

I take a deep breath and blow it out quietly. "I came by myself. It's just me."

"Oh," Danielle says but tries to cover her surprise up as quickly as she displayed it. "Sometimes people come alone too. I quite like a little trip by myself sometimes. This guy I'm married to can get overwhelming."

"Bullshit," Lincoln says.

I sit with my pizza untouched on my plate. The Landrys are so friendly and welcoming, but it feels a bit like some kind of interview. And I don't love where it seems to be heading.

My foot taps against the floor, matching the beat of a Post Malone song. Larissa's hand falls to my thigh, and I stop moving.

I look at her. My leg feels like it's on fire, the heat extending out from the weight of her palm on me.

I've only actually touched her when we were screwing around in front of her ex. It was silly and fun and in front of the world. But to have her hand on me under the table in a way that feels resoundingly more personal—it feels different.

And good. *How the hell does she do that?*

"Tell us about yourself, Hollis," Danielle chirps. "What are you going to school for?"

"Business administration," I say. "Just like every other athlete in the world."

Lincoln laughs. "Let me guess, minor in communication?"

"Music appreciation, actually. I try not to communicate with anyone I don't have to."

Lincoln's laughter grows louder, and I chime in even though I'm not kidding.

"What about you?" Danielle asks Larissa. "Are you going into the jewelry business like your aunt?"

I turn to face my date. Larissa's cheeks flush. A strand of hair has fallen out of the high ponytail she had it in, and I'm jealous of the way it flirts against her lips.

She removes her hand from my leg and clasps it against the other one in front of her.

"No," she says. "I'm actually graduating in May with a degree in landscape architecture. I was afraid I'd end up hating it by now, but I think I love it more every day."

"That's how I felt about working in the Children's Hospital," Danielle says. "And I think that's how you felt playing baseball, right, Lincoln?"

Lincoln swallows a bite of pizza. "Yeah. Absolutely. I wanted nothing more than to live and breathe it. Until I met you, of course."

Danielle swats at him again, making him chuckle.

"Are you wanting to live and breathe football?" Lincoln looks at me. "I think it really comes down to that."

"I'm just not sure."

"What's your family telling you?" he asks. "My dad was all for me going pro. My older brother Graham was all against it. It was quite the contentious conversation for a while."

My face gets hot as I lick my lips. My gaze falls to my plate because I don't really want to look at either of them.

I force a swallow down my throat. My spit feels like it's on fire.

This is a question I'm not good at spinning. It's too direct, too intense.

Deflect. Deflect. Deflect.

"Yeah," I say, "I think my parents would be pretty happy if I went to the league. I mean, it's a pretty big deal."

"I'm sure they'll be proud of you either way," Danielle says.

She keeps talking, but all I see is her lips move. I don't hear a word. My brain is too busy replying to her silently because there's no way I can, or will, verbalize how wrong she really is.

I'm not going to tell her that going Pro would be the only way I figure my parents might bother to remember they had me. And then, even if they did, they'd only try to find me to see if they could benefit from it somehow. I can't sit here and share that the last time I saw my father was a rainy morning when I was six years old, and the last time I saw the woman who gave birth to me involved a couple of ounces of dope.

Danielle sits across from me, her hands flying through the air as she tells my dining partners a story. I watch her, the sound muted by my errant thoughts, and wonder for the briefest moment what life would've been like with someone like her as a mother.

I can imagine her hugging her kids with the warmth she hugged me with tonight. I bet Danielle has cookies for them after school and does their laundry. She probably even tells them a story at bedtime. I'm sure she remembers their birthdays and even lets her kids believe in Santa Claus and the Easter bunny instead of telling them the truth to prevent any expectations of presents or baskets.

I don't tell her either that there's a hole inside me—a cave so dark and deep that sometimes it threatens to suck me in. The abyss gets wider during the holidays. It gets darker around my birthday in April because no one sits at the proverbial table to celebrate with me.

Hell, there's not even a table for anyone to sit at.

"Hollis?" Larissa whispers. She lays her hand on my arm.

I snap out of my daze and look at her pretty face. Only then do I realize I've missed something, and everyone is looking at me.

"Huh?" I ask.

"Lincoln just asked you if you have any siblings," she says softly. The tenderness in her gaze makes my chest feel like it's caving in.

"Oh, sorry," I say, clearing my throat. "I do. I have a little sister named Harlee."

Who I haven't seen since I was six.

Larissa's hand drops to my thigh again, and she gives it a gentle squeeze. The contact grounds me and gives me something to focus on—her.

"Anyone want dessert?" Lincoln asks as he gets up from the table. "You like cake, Hollis?"

"I love cake," I say without taking my eyes off Larissa.

She smiles at me—a genuine gesture that's void of pity. And I cling to that for dear life.

TEN
LARISSA

The evening sky is inky with bright silver stars sparkling overhead. Hollis and I roll quietly through the outskirts of Savannah on our way back to my house.

I settle into my seat and try to relax.

Hollis turned on the radio as soon as we got into the car. Besides an occasional glance my way—a movement coupled with a smile that's unmistakably softer than what I'm used to from him—he's been focused on the road ahead.

In turn, I stare at his profile and try to figure out the man sitting beside me.

He's a conundrum, a complexity that I can't entirely unravel. I equivocate him with confidence and fun, but watching him tonight with the Landrys exposed another side of him different from his quick-witted levity.

His jaw is tense. The corners of his eyes crinkle as if the thoughts going through his head aren't exactly welcome. His wild hair makes a show of just how many times he's run his hands through it since we climbed in the car just a few minutes ago.

My thoughts are interrupted when he reaches up and turns down the music.

"Are you okay?" he asks.

A gentleness touches the severity of his features as he searches my eyes. I fight the urge to reach out and touch the side of his face.

I can't do that. I'm not sure if it's appropriate, but I'm positive it's unwanted.

"I'm good," I tell him. "Are *you* okay?"

He lets his gaze linger on me for a moment. Long enough to tell me he's not totally okay.

"Yeah. I'm fine." His tone is clipped. It's not angry or frustrated, but the words are coated with a finality that doesn't sit well with me.

It's a lie—a white one, maybe. But he knows I suspect something is amiss with him.

What do I do? Pretend I don't see it and just let it go? *Wouldn't that make me a jerk?*

"I don't mean to be rude or anything," I say carefully, "but you don't seem fine."

He regrips the steering wheel. "And I don't mean to be rude or anything, but you don't seem to know how to stop asking questions." He looks at me over his shoulder, a small grin playing against his lips. "Stop pressing me, and I *will* be fine."

I grin back at him. "You obviously don't know me well enough to know that pressing is my forte."

He drags his eyes away from mine and settles them ahead once again. "I guess that's a good thing about our situation then, huh?"

"What do you mean?"

"I mean that we don't have to know each other well enough for anything."

He's doing to me what he did to the Landrys. He's giving me

enough of an answer to feel like he was a participant in this conversation when, in reality, he's just changing the subject.

I reach up and turn the radio completely off. "No, I suppose we don't have to know each other at all. But that doesn't mean I don't want to know things about you."

He half-laughs, half-snorts. "Why?"

"Why what?" I ask, my feathers getting ruffled.

"Why do you want to know things about me? Like, I get why you wanna know my name and that I'm not a serial killer. And if you are curious about my bill of health—I'm clean."

The cocky little grin he casts me is supposed to make me think about something other than interrogating him.

It works.

Lucky for me, I'm strong enough to stay *somewhat* focused on the task at hand. Only a small part of my brain watches Hollis's fingers tap the steering wheel and wonders what they would feel like on my bare skin.

"Wow. If you'd given me your birthday, you would've shared almost as much as a prisoner of war."

He looks at me out of the corner of his eye. He's amused, though he's trying desperately not to show it. "Why do you need to know anything else about me?"

"I don't know," I say, trying to ignore the way his lips look fuller, more kissable, in the shadowiness of the car. "Isn't that what friends do?"

"We're friends now?"

"Oh, for heaven's sake, Hollis."

He turns to me with a megawatt smile.

I roll my eyes. "Are we not friends? Did we not agree to help each other out of our current predicaments *as friends*? Because I'd like to think I'm taking a friend around my family tomorrow night and not some random dude who doesn't care if I live or die."

"Wow. Okay. You just took this to the next level." He laughs. "Live or die? Larissa, really?"

"Again, I wouldn't know. It wasn't included in the three things you shared with me."

"I don't want you to die," he says, humoring me. "And my birthday is April fifth."

I grin smugly. "That's a start."

His shoulders relax, and his grip eases on the steering wheel. I bet it's because he thinks I'm distracted from the original topic. But as he silently revels in his assumed victory, I plot my pivot.

"But we still aren't friends?" I ask, easing my way back in.

"All right. *Fine,*" he says as though it pains him. "We're friends. Does that make you happy?"

I shrug. "I was happy before. Our friendship status has no bearing on my happiness."

"Then why are you so dramatic about all this?" he asks with a laugh.

"I'm not."

"*Oh, my god.*" His mouth falls open, and his head hangs forward in exasperation.

It's my turn to laugh. "I was just trying to get to know my new friend like a normal person."

"People know too much about each other. There's no mystery anymore."

"I disagree. I think knowing things about other people helps you connect."

He glances at me, eyeing me suspiciously. "Maybe some people don't want to connect."

Sitting up, I look at him like he's crazy. The sudden movement causes him to flinch.

"Why would someone not want to connect with other people?" I say, holding my hands out. "That's … lonely, cold, and a terrible way to live."

"Maybe for you."

He can't really think that. That can't be his actual truth.

I rest my head on the seat again and wait for him to continue, to finish off the thought that feels incredibly incomplete. Much to my surprise, he simply reaches over and turns the radio back on.

I reach up and snap it off.

"Dammit, Hollis," I say, frustration thick in my voice.

He looks at me in disbelief. "Did you just turn off my radio?"

"Yes. I did."

"Why?"

"Talk to me," I plead.

"*I don't want to talk to you*," he says, mocking the whine in my voice.

I narrow my eyes. "Maybe I don't want to talk to you now either, asshole."

He laughs, and his easy way about him has returned. "Yes, you do," he teases.

"*Oh*. You want me to want to talk to you. That's the problem, isn't it?" I say, only half-kidding.

I felt the way his body relaxed when I touched his leg at the Landry's. His entire body sort of stilled. It was remarkable. I realized at that moment that he might not want that sort of invasion of his privacy—because I'm pretty sure that's how he'll see it if prompted—but maybe he needs it. Perhaps it's good for him.

He shakes his head at my theory.

"Not everyone wants to be an open book, you know?" he asks as we swerve around a pothole.

"No. I don't know. I am an open book."

"I gathered," he mumbles.

The lights along the highway bounce inside the cab of the car. Hollis shifts in his seat and rests his left elbow next to the window, toying with his bottom lip.

The wrinkle is back around his eyes, but he's not frowning anymore. I take that as a good sign.

Finally, he looks at me again. His eyes are warm but still guarded.

"I think you're a nice person," he says.

"You think?"

"Yeah, I think," he says.

"Gee, thanks."

"What?" He laughs. "That's more credit than I give most people. I usually shut down women well before it even makes it to this stage of the game."

"Someone really burned you, didn't they?" I ask, narrowing my eyes.

He narrows his back at me. He pauses before pulling his attention back to the road. "Yes. They did."

"You know, last night, I'd basically lumped all men—all athletes, no less—into one group. And after spending time with Lincoln tonight, and you, I guess," I say, rushing over the last part, "I feel as though that lens prescription isn't totally accurate. Maybe you've lumped women into a similar kind of box." I force a swallow. "That's not fair—to them or you."

I flop back against my seat and stare through the windshield.

We drive along the highway until we get to my exit. When his GPS instructs him to, he takes the off-ramp. The sound of the automated voice is the only thing that breaks the silence.

The car rides smoothly onto the side street, the rumble of the muffler hypnotic. I think about what tomorrow's conversation might sound like after Hollis meets my mom and Jack.

Instead of Hollis being the commonality amongst the group like tonight, it will be me tomorrow. He will be the one hearing things and learning things; he will be the one with questions.

If he wants to know more about me but, right now, I'm not convinced he does.

Which is fine. It's fine, Riss. Cut him some slack.

"If it makes you feel any better," I tell him, "there will be less time for me to ask you questions tomorrow night. It's going to be so loud and so chaotic."

"I'm looking forward to it."

"Really?"

He nods. "Yeah. I'll get to give you the inquisition on the way home."

My cheeks split into a smile.

"That's the difference between us. I'll tell you whatever you want to know," I tell him. "I'm an open book. I want you to be sure you're on a fake date with a nice person."

"You don't think I'm nice?" he jokes.

"You'll do."

He chuckles as we pull onto my street. He pulls up in front of my house and kills the engine like he's done it a million times before.

"Wait," he says as I reach for the handle.

I stop and turn to see him watching me.

"You're right," he says. "It's not fair to lump you in with everyone else. Not all the way, anyway."

I smile. "Thank you. I shouldn't have to pay the price for some other woman's sins," I say politely. "Can I ask you a question now?"

"No."

I pout.

He laughs as he climbs out of the car.

I noticed at the Landry's that Hollis was irritated that I didn't let him open my door. I'm not used to that kind of thing from guys, so it didn't even cross my mind. But now I sit and wait for him to jog around the front of the Mustang and do me the honors.

"Thank you," I tell him as I get out.

"You're very welcome." He shuts the door. "Thank you for going with me tonight."

"You're very welcome. It almost feels like a real date with the door opening finale."

He shakes his head as we make our way up the sidewalk.

"I liked it. It was a good move," I tell him just to keep the mood light.

With every step we take, my heart starts to beat faster. The closer we get to the door, the more I begin to panic about what to do internally. Light mood or not, things are about to get tricky.

Do I invite him in? Do I want him to come in? What does it mean if I invite him in?

Can I just admit I want to have sex with him?

No, no, don't do that. It's just the first date.

It's not even a real date!

I sneak a peek at him.

But he's so freaking hot.

We make it to the doorstep before I can come to grips with my feelings.

Hollis stands next to me with his hands shoved in his pockets. His hair lays against his forehead as he watches me dig through my purse for my keys.

His cologne envelops me in my small porch as I push the key into the lock. It turns, and I push the door open.

"Do you want to come inside?" I ask, hoping he can't hear the slight quiver in my voice.

I'm still unsure what I want him to do. It's a split decision. My brain knows it's not a good idea, but my body is in strong disagreement.

He smiles. "No. I gotta get going."

Relief coupled with disappointment rolls through me. I don't know which is stronger.

"Big plans tonight?" I joke.

"Yeah. I gotta call River and check on his mom."

I furrow my brow. "What's wrong with River's mom, and who is River?"

"River's my best friend, and his mom has cancer. He's been pretty fucked up about it, as you can imagine."

My heart sinks in my chest. "I'm sorry to hear that. I'll say a prayer for her tonight."

"Thanks." Surprise riddles his voice. "And thank you again for going with me tonight."

"I was happy to do it."

We watch each other. The air between us changes. There's a current swishing back and forth—pushing me and pulling me toward him and away again.

I should just let him go and not say anything else. I shouldn't make this complicated or personal. But I can't help but want to ease the uncertainty present in his eyes.

"I know, or I expect, that you'll go back to your hotel and replay the conversations from tonight and wonder if you said the right things." I tuck a strand of hair behind my ear. "Or I assume you'll do that. Do guys do that? Girls totally do."

He nods. "Yeah. We do. Probably worse than you."

"I don't know. I'm great at it," I scoff. "Anyway, I just want to tell you that you did great. Lincoln and Danielle loved you, and I had a great time with you."

He runs a hand down his cheek and cups his chin. He watches me, one brow raised to the sky.

"And I was just teasing you tonight," I add since he seems to have taken the first part well. "I think you're a totally nice guy."

"Well, I was just teasing you too. I think you're a totally nice girl."

We exchange a grin.

He moves his weight from one foot to the other. I hold my breath, not sure what's coming but fairly certain *something* is.

There's a wariness in his eyes that makes me wonder if he's going to kiss me. He leans in, ever so slightly, and I'm a little breathless.

I feel so small next to him, and I shouldn't feel so comfortable. I should be darting inside and shutting the door and calling Bellamy with the details of tonight. Instead, I'm contemplating what his lips taste like and where his hands will fall when he kisses me.

His teeth graze over his bottom lip. *Slowly*. And as he releases it, I'm mesmerized by how red his lips are.

God, this man is sexy.

A host of butterflies take flight in my stomach while I wait for him to make up his mind or make the next move.

Please let it be the next move.

I force a swallow as my nerves start to get to me.

He reaches forward, his hand stalling midair before grazing the side of my cheek. The confidence I expect from him is mixed with a surprisingly sweet hesitation.

He's beautifully confusing. What you see isn't all you get.

"You're so damn beautiful," he whispers, stroking the side of my face. "Thank you for coming tonight."

I can't shake myself out of the almost-trance I'm in to find the words to respond, so I nod.

I hold my breath as he searches my eyes for something. Whether he finds it or not, I don't know, but his hand falls to his side.

"I better get going," he whispers, finally taking a step back.

A rush of breath escapes my lips as I look at him like he has to be kidding.

Resolution is seated in his face as he forces a smile for my benefit. "Good night, Larissa."

What?

He says it like an apology. As though he knows what I expected, and he is to blame for that.

I lift my chin.

"Uh, good night, Hollis," I say, hoping I don't stumble over the words too much. "Be safe."

Be safe? Oh, my gosh, Larissa.

"I'll text you tomorrow and make sure everything is still a go." He walks back down the steps.

I nod, watching him turn and jog down the sidewalk.

My heart sinks in my chest. It kills the butterflies.

Dammit.

I go inside and shut the door. My nerves are racing over the non-kiss, and I can't help but wonder if I was too pushy. *Or too obvious.*

I wanted that kiss so damn bad that I could almost taste it. I was sure Hollis wanted it too.

Maybe I just can't read men anymore.

Or maybe it's that Hollis isn't what I expected him to be.

I sigh.

Maybe I shouldn't be kissing him in the first place.

My purse hits the table with a thud. But before I can walk toward my room, a knock raps quietly behind me. I spin around and look through the peephole to see Hollis.

I swing the door open with a flourish.

"What the—"

Hollis steals the words from my lips. He presses his mouth to mine with a mixture of tenderness and aggression that takes my breath away.

His mouth is hot, his body is hard as he presses it against mine. His fingers are rough as they cup my cheeks.

My brain misfires, unable to process this quick turn of events. By the time I get myself together, he's pulling away.

A deep smirk offsets a broodiness in his eyes that has me reaching for the doorframe to keep from falling over.

"My mom," he says as he walks backward again.

"Huh?" I ask, my brain still clouded from the kiss. "What do you mean?"

"She's the one who burned me."

I stand on the porch, mouth hanging open from both the kiss and his admission, and watch him climb in his car. He starts it up, and, with a rev of his engine, he rips his way down the street.

I touch my fingers to my cheeks, mimicking his hold on me.

My brain replays the past few minutes just as I told him I always do. His touch was gentle yet strong. His kiss was sweet but still utterly suggestive. But as I sort through each touch, each sensation, my mind settles on one thing.

She's the one who burned me.

"What the hell does all of this mean?" I ask out loud.

With a final look at the empty street, I step back inside and close the door.

ELEVEN
HOLLIS

A man smiles my way as we pass each other on the sidewalk.

"Good morning," he says, giving me a friendly wave.

I nod. "Good morning."

I hunker down in my jacket, my hands stuck in the pockets, and make my way across the street.

The sun is brighter than I expected before lunchtime, and I squint as I look up into a cloudless sky. Air moves breezily around me, ruffling the storefront canopies along the sidewalk.

The shops are still dressed for Christmas. Wreaths still hang on doors. Tinsel is draped around windows despite the holiday having passed. It reminds me of the little towns in movies that some girls in the sorority houses watch after Thanksgiving. I've only seen a few minutes of them at a time, and that's enough for me.

I venture along the road and feel the fresh air on my face. It helps to wake me up out of the fog from last night.

Sleep never comes easy for me. Last night, though, it was pointless to even try.

I take out my phone and check to see if River texted me back.

As if I didn't have enough to worry about last night, River was more upset than I'd ever heard him, and I fucking hate I can't be there to help him. Not that I can cure cancer and fix his mom. But I know it helps him to see our faces in the morning, and he's up in Vermont without Crew or me.

The screen is blank. No missed calls or texts from River or anyone else.

I shove my phone back in my pocket and continue down the sidewalk.

My brain skips over all the things that have taken up space over the past twenty-four hours.

Like kissing Larissa.

Fuck, that girl is more than I bargained for.

She just worms her way inside my head and makes me do and say shit I don't do or say. I don't kiss—not like that. Not like I want it.

And I don't talk about my mom. Ever.

"What the fuck came over me?" I grumble.

A mix of emotions has flooded my psyche since I opened my damn mouth to Larissa. Frustration at opening that Pandora's box, irritation with myself for admitting that shit out loud, and a sadness that hit around three in the morning that only further pissed me off.

A part of me wants to say to hell with sticking around and just head back to campus now. It's the simple answer, and it's probably the right one, too. Anyone that has ever known anything about my life's history has done one of two things—pitied me or judged me. It just depends on how much they know.

And now Larissa knows the start of it.

If I thought she was nosy before, what's she going to do now?

What would she do if she knew the truth?

Why did I open my mouth?

I clamp a hand against the back of my neck and try to squeeze the stress out.

A little building with a bubblegum-pink door is ahead of me. A woman exits the shop, and a spicy, cinnamon-y aroma fills the sidewalk in front of a sign, also in pink, spelling *Judy's*. It redirects my attention from my fuckup with Larissa to my growling stomach.

A bell jingles as I open the door.

"Good morning," a woman says happily from behind a stack of boxes. "Welcome to Judy's."

I give her a nod and look at the various knickknacks and displays.

Clothes hang on hooks, and bags in bright floral prints are showcased on stands. Shelves are stocked with little jars, books, and pottery.

"Can I help you find anything?" The old woman comes out from around the boxes. She has silver hair puffed up on top of her head, and she's as wide as she is tall. "We have something for everyone in here."

"Nah. I'm not looking for anything, really. Just killing time."

I pick up a small jar of sunflower honey—something I didn't even know existed. It has a little yellow ribbon around it that starts to slip off as I handle it. I secure the ribbon and set the jar back down.

The woman takes off her glasses. "What are you killing time for?"

I'm taken aback a little bit by her forwardness, but her sweet little grandma vibe disarms me.

"I have a date," I tell her. Even though it's only partially true, it's the easiest answer.

"I bet you do. You're a cutie pie."

Laughing, I turn to face her. "Well, thank you."

"You're welcome. You remind me of one of my grandsons. I have seven—and three granddaughters. But," she says, whispering conspiratorially, "if I was your age, your girlfriend better watch out because *whoo-wee*."

She winks as she walks in front of me and heads toward the back of the store.

"You've left me speechless," I tell her with a laugh.

"Story of my life. I've been leaving men speechless for seventy-five years." She motions for me to join her by a large glass case. "Are you hungry?"

I walk toward her and look around. The back of the building is a sandwich shop decorated in flamingos, of all things. It's pink and white with a bright pink neon sign spelling out her name like you'd see in a bar.

It's so random and so … *eclectic*. It seems to fit her.

"See anything in there that looks good?" she asks, rapping on top of the glass with her knuckle.

I peer inside the display. Cookies, cakes, and the reddest cherry pie I've ever seen sit behind the glass. Perfectly squared brownies are arranged on a plate. Cupcakes with tie-dye swirled icing are piled on a stand.

It looks like heaven.

"Everything looks delicious," I tell her. "Did you make all of this?"

"Sure did. Been cooking all my life. My mom was the best cook and baker I've ever known. I'm not as good as her yet, but I still have some time."

I smile at her. "I didn't know your mom, obviously, but I can't imagine that she could have done much better than this."

She beams, wiping her hands on the hem of her purple apron. "I'm Judy. What's your name?"

"Hollis."

"Well, Hollis, get your butt in a seat and let me get you something to eat."

I sit in a booth along the paneled wall. "Do you have a menu?"

"Only for paying customers."

"Well, that's me." I get situated on the plastic seat. "What do you serve here?"

She busies herself behind the counter and doesn't bother to look up. "Do you like bacon?"

"Who doesn't?"

"Exactly. That's the right answer."

I sit back and watch her work. She whistles softly while she heats up bacon on a small grill. The sound is simple and melodic, and I strain to hear the words. It's a beat I've heard before, but I can't place it.

"Tell me about your girlfriend," she says.

"Ah, well, she's not really my girlfriend."

Judy looks at me over her shoulder. "I get it."

I read the look on her face.

"No. It's not like that." I laugh. "It's really not. We are more of a situational, convenience-based, and probably a little hormonal-based thing, if I'm not lying."

"It's okay, sweetheart." She looks back at what she's doing. "I'm not going to say a word."

"It's *really* not."

"Okay. It's not."

There's something about the way she just agrees with me that makes me want her to believe me. I *need* her to believe me.

"I'm helping a friend out," I tell her as if it matters. "We're going to an event of some sort together. So it's a date, but it's … not. We're playing pretend, I guess."

The words aren't all the way out of my mouth before I taste them. The idea Larissa is pretending when she's around me—that her kindness and caring are just an act—tastes bitter.

"Well, I played house with my husband for fifty years, and it always felt like we were playing pretend. He was always so much fun, my dear Ronnie. You just never knew what that man was going to say. I woke up every morning for fifty years, and every day felt like the first one." She glances at me over her shoulder. "That doesn't mean there weren't fights because, God love him, he got on my nerves some days. But being married to him never really felt like work."

"You are the first person I've ever heard say that."

She laughs. "Marriage is always work. Don't let me fool you. But aren't all relationships? I mean, look at you and me. I've had to work on getting you to talk and stick around for a little while. Had I not done that, you might've turned around and walked out of here."

She has a point.

"You're right," I admit. "But marriage seems like it's on another level. Like once you get married, you're thrust into this life with another person and connected to everything they do—good or bad. And then you have kids and not only have to feed and clothe yourself but them too ..."

I shrug as if that proves my point.

Judy walks toward me, holding a plate. "You're absolutely right, Hollis. It is another level, and *my, oh my*, is it hard." She sets a sandwich in front of me. "My Ronnie and I had five kids, and it was the hardest and longest years of my life. But I wouldn't trade it for the world."

I consider her words as I pull the plate across the table.

"This looks great," I tell her. "Thank you."

I smile at her.

"Of course. You're very welcome."

Relaxing back in the booth, I stretch my legs out in front of me. It's the first time since our last football game that my head didn't hurt at least a little bit in the back. This morning is also the first time that I haven't felt like my insides were sawed into a hundred little pieces, and I had to piece them back together like a jigsaw puzzle and hope they fit.

Judy starts to sit down across from me. She groans a little as she bends.

"Can I help you?" I ask, starting to get up.

She motions for me to sit down. "I'm fine. It just takes me a little longer than it used to. Oomph." She drops into the seat. "There we go. All is well now."

"I'm glad."

I take a bite of my sandwich. It's bacon with an egg and some kind of white cheese and practically melts in my mouth. It's much better than the Ding Dongs I had for a midnight snack and an early breakfast.

"Not sure I should believe you, Judy."

"About what?"

"That you say that you're seventy-five."

"Not a day older or younger," she says, pride ripe in her tone. "Still looking pretty good, don't you think?"

I swallow. "I was just wondering if you'd let me take you out to dinner."

She tips her head back and laughs. "Oh, child. Because that's what you are—a child. You couldn't handle this old woman."

"I don't know about that," I tease. "I'll have you know that I've handled my fair share of women."

She lifts her chin. "That's what my last boyfriend said. He couldn't keep up with me." She leans forward. "I think he thought I was old and done. Heck, there might be snow on the roof, but that doesn't mean there's not a fire in the furnace if you know what I mean."

Somehow, I swallow my spit, and it goes down the wrong pipe. My cheeks turn red as I sputter.

She watches me try not to die with amusement written all over her face.

"Sorry," I choke out. "You, uh, caught me a little off guard there."

Instead of responding, Judy takes a napkin out of the dispenser and wipes it across the table.

I go back to my sandwich.

"You don't sound like a Georgia boy," she says, wadding up the napkin. "You sound like a Midwestern."

"Good ear. I'm from Indiana. The good ole Hoosier State."

She nods. "What are you doing down here?"

"I have a football thing in a few days," I tell her. "I decided to come a little early and … kill some time."

"Sounds like you have a lot of time on your hands."

She says it like she's just making conversation. But she's not. She's curious.

I take the last bite of the sandwich and sit back in the booth while I chew. Judy pins me to my seat with a sharp yet kind eye.

"What's a college kid supposed to do on winter break?" I ask her. "Kill time."

"I think most kids are home with their families during winter break."

I narrow my eyes. She narrows hers. We have a battle of the wits that I'm not sure I can win.

Finally, I shrug.

"Well, if you haven't noticed, I'm not a normal guy," I say. "I do the whole path less traveled kind of thing. Keeps me mysterious."

She senses something is amiss, and I can see the wheels turning in her head. I stay calm and act as though I'm here to chat when, in reality, I'm trying to find a segue out of here.

"When is the last time you had a home-cooked meal?" she asks.

I laugh. "That's what you're worried about?"

"Well, heavens yes. Now answer the question."

"I'm fine. Don't worry about me," I tell her, already regretting saying anything. "Can I get a check?"

"No, but you can answer my question."

I lean forward. "What if I don't want to?"

"Then I'll swat your behind." She grins. "Go ahead and don't answer me. I might like it."

Our laughter blends together as we get to our feet. I hold out a hand and help her stand. She presses her free hand against the top of our joined grasps and pats it.

I look down into her face and feel the warmth she's radiating my way. I appreciate it.

"You just never know who this old world is going to throw in your path. Do you believe that, Hollis?" she asks.

"I don't know. Should I?"

"Yes. You should." She takes her hand off mine and releases my other one. "I have to think that seeing you today wasn't random."

"Wasn't it?"

She shakes her head.

"No," she says. "The world put you here so I could feed you."

Judy's eagle eyes watch every move I make. There's something about women—the older they get, the more refined they get. You can't get anything past a mother. I know this for a fact. But a woman with grandkids? A woman who's seventy-five? If she wants to read me, she will. And there's not a damn thing I can do about it.

I think back to just a few days ago, to the last day of the semester when I took off from campus. Crew was gone, and I knew River would be going too. I didn't want to be alone. I didn't even want to be the last guy there. It always feels worse if you're the one left behind. I know.

Sure, I could've gone with River. If he knew I really didn't have anywhere to be on Christmas, I'm sure he would've demanded it. I lied to him and told him I was meeting up with someone and would be fine.

"How long are you here?" she asks, looking up at me with the bluest eyes.

"Just a few days."

"If you need anything, you come by and see me. You hear?"

I smile at her. "Only if you let me pay for that sandwich."

She closes her eyes and shakes her head. "I won't hear of it. You're one of mine now. You may call me Grandma." She squeezes my hand before letting it go. "You wait right here."

It takes her a moment to get her feet under her and steady herself. Then she shuffles through a doorway behind the counter.

I watch the spot she just vacated and replay her words. *You're one of mine now.*

The sentence pokes its way through the shield I put up to keep people away … just as she did.

Even though I'm sure her words were a Southern slang or term of endearment kind of thing, they still feel good. And despite my natural reaction to shrug them off, I let what she said sit with me for a minute. Because no one has ever laid claim to me like that.

"Judy, you're something else," I mutter as I look around the shop.

Racks of shot glasses and bells with pictures of the beach painted on them are for sale near the cash register. I walk around the corner until I see a rack of little bracelets. They're obviously not actual gold or silver, but they're dainty and have little charms on them.

I finger through the line of dangling chains until I see the third one from the end. It's a pinkish-gold color and has a tiny little succulent charm hanging from it.

"I prefer rose gold. But I really don't love expensive jewelry. I'm always afraid I'll lose it, and the stress isn't worth it to me."

My jaw works back and forth as I replay Larissa's words to Danielle last night.

"I'm actually graduating in May with a degree in landscape architecture. I was afraid I'd end up hating it by now, but I think I love it more every day."

I lift the bracelet from the display and turn it over in my

hand. It's silly and costs a whopping fifteen dollars, but it reminds me of Larissa. It's delicate and pretty and makes me smile when I hold it.

"You're fucking stupid," I mumble to myself.

"Where did you go, Hollis?" Judy calls.

I walk around the corner and see her standing by the cash register. She's holding a box.

"I'm right here," I say.

"Here." She presses a box big enough to fit an entire cake into my hands. "I made you a snack for later."

"You didn't have to make me a snack."

"Yes, I do."

"Judy …" I look at her warily.

She shushes me with a wave of her hand. "You call me Judy again, and we're going to have a problem. I'm Grandma. I told you that. Don't make me get a switch."

I can't make sense of her or the craziness inside me—least of all rationalizing all of it at one time. So I laugh and ignore as much of it as I can.

"Well, at least let me pay you for it. And my sandwich and this bracelet." I hold the jewelry up in the air. "I'd like to get this, please."

She smiles. "For your girlfriend?"

I give her a playful warning glare. "No. For *my friend.*"

She winks at me. "But I need to make sure she's good enough for you. Bring her by so I can meet her."

The box starts to slip in my hands. Luckily, I catch it just in time.

This is the first fucking thing I've caught all year.

Her mouth opens to talk, but the phone rings instead. "I need to get that."

"What do I owe you?"

She swats my shoulder. "Go on. Enjoy your day. And come back and see me before you leave town."

I watch her walk to the back again and lift a phone to her ear. After a few minutes, it becomes apparent that she's not going to come back. I have to wonder if it's not an excuse to get me to leave without paying.

I sit the box on the counter with the bracelet on top. Then I take out my wallet. I fish out thirty dollars because I'm not sure the price of any of the food or what's in the box and lay it on the cash register.

"Hollis!" Judy chastises me from across the store.

I laugh. "Have a good day, *Grandma*!"

"You little rascal!"

I pick up the box and stick the bracelet in my pocket. The bells chime as I leave.

TWELVE
LARISSA

"What do I do now?" I ask an empty kitchen.

I've asked myself this question a hundred times since Hollis kissed me senseless and then left like some kind of libido assassin.

My head continues to spin from his abrupt switcheroo—going from a difficult yet playful pain in the ass to a straightforward yet confusing man who I'd like to kiss me again.

And that piece of the puzzle is why it's complicated.

And frustrating.

It's also why I was up all damn night.

My lips stung from the memory of his being pressed against them. I tasted the heat of his mouth until the sun came up. I can still, even all these hours later, recall exactly the way his palms were prickly but his fingertips were soft as they gripped my cheeks.

I liked it. *I like him.*

Even at the Landry's house when he was quiet, I was glad I was there with him. In the car when he was refusing to cooperate, he made me laugh. And even when he walked away and left me hanging, I wasn't upset.

And Lord knows I wasn't mad about him coming back to kiss me, nor was I anything but shocked that he shared the crux of his refusal to talk.

I tidy up the countertop and rinse my bowl. I'm too preoccupied to get it in the dishwasher, so I leave it in the sink next to the plate that housed my cheese and crackers at two this morning.

I check the clock on the oven before making my way to my bedroom.

"You just have to keep your head about you," I tell myself. "You can't really walk away now. But you can remember that this isn't a repeat of your past boyfriends where you should be worried. You know how it ends. *And you hate it*."

I groan. Flashes of Sebastian and his superiority complex come blitzing through my mind. I'm reminded of Charlie and the way his phone would be lit up like a Christmas tree after away games and of Benny's mercurial position on monogamy.

"Yes, I freaking do hate how it ends. And it always ends with those guys," I say with a groan. "At least the ending with Hollis is planned out. That makes this doable."

My stomach twists as I slip on the emerald-green dress I chose to wear tonight. It's a stretchy velvet that gathers on my left shoulder and leaves my right one bare. The waist is hugged with two braided pieces that cinch me in and deepen the curve of my waist without the strangulation of a corset.

Even though I bet Hollis is hot as hell in a suit, I'm not wearing a corset.

I glimpse down at my phone to check for missed calls. It's only the two-hundredth time I've looked since he texted me around midnight that he would be here to pick me up this evening. I was quick—maybe too quick, in retrospect—to return his message and then waited for a follow-up that didn't come.

Naturally.

Ignoring the lump of uncertainty in my stomach, I find a pair of diamond earrings and put them on. I slip on my nude heels and exaggerate my breathing in hopes it evens out.

"You should've just had him leave the Landry's and bring you home as soon as you found out he was a baller," I chastise myself. "All of this was too easy. You were attracted to him because he's your weakness all summarized into one frustratingly handsome package."

I stand straight and look at myself in the mirror.

I imagine Hollis standing next to me. With the heels, I'll probably come up to just under his nose. I envision his broad shoulders filling out a black suit jacket and his handsome face smiling down at me. I shiver.

A sound squeaks from the hallway, pulling me out of my daydream.

"Hey, Riss! Where are you?" Bellamy's voice shouts from the foyer.

"My room."

"Are you decent?" she asks. "Boone is with me."

"I'm dressed."

A few seconds later, my cousin walks into my bedroom. He stops in his tracks.

"Holy shit, Riss."

"What?" I look down to see if there's a hole in my dress somewhere, or maybe I have on two different shoes or something. "What, Boone? Does this look bad?"

When I look up, he's smiling.

"In a purely I'm-not-your-cousin-and-just-a-guy opinion, I really hope you're trying to drive this dude crazy tonight because you look gorgeous."

I scrunch up my shoulders and grin. "Thanks."

"Here." He thrusts a box my way. "Looks like I made it just in time. It's from Mom. She said this is a prototype, and she thought you might need a little good juju tonight."

I take the black box from him and open the lid. A delicate rose gold bracelet with a tiny heart lays inside.

"This is so pretty," I coo.

I slide it out of the box and onto my wrist as Bellamy comes bursting into my room like a hurricane. She holds a box of Cheez-Its in her hand.

"Did you bring those with you?" I ask.

"Nope. Got them from your pantry." She sits on my bed and reclines back. "I don't know why I never buy these. They're so good."

"Why would you when you just get them for free from me?" I ask.

"Good point, Riss. Good point."

Boone and I exchange a look. He shrugs.

"Did you guys come together?" I ask.

"Nope. We pulled up at the same time," Bellamy says. "What're the odds of that?"

"Wade left this geeky magazine at my house the other day," Boone says about one of his brothers. "I was flipping through it, and they suspect that people who spend a lot of time together can sense what the other person is doing and feeling."

Bellamy tosses a Cheez-It into the air and catches it in her mouth. "What am I feeling right now then?"

"Hungry, I'd guess," Boone says.

"Exacto." Another orange square goes up and comes down with precision. She crunches it loudly. "I think Riss is feeling like she's gonna get some of her football player boy toy. You look hot."

I avoid Boone's eyes and set the jewelry box on my dresser.

"Football player?" Boone asks, lifting a brow.

"I didn't know," I groan.

Bellamy chomps on another cracker. "She doesn't even have to know. She just walks to the athlete dumpster and starts digging like a brain-dead raccoon."

I glare at her.

"I don't even want to know what that means," Boone says, eyeing Bellamy.

"You're right. You don't," I agree.

Bellamy puts the snack box to the side and sits up.

I heave out a breath. Turning back to the mirror, I pretend to be engrossed in smoothing out a nonexistent wrinkle in my dress.

"I'm going to be okay this time," I say as much to myself as I do to them. "I have this one under control."

"That's probably a lie, but I'm all for you embracing your heart's desires," Bellamy jokes. "And I get why your heart is desiring that."

Boone rolls his eyes. "What kind of football does he play?"

"College. Somewhere …" I say, unable to come up with the name of a university. "He's getting some recognition from Lincoln Landry's nonprofit. I went with him to Lincoln's house last night."

Boone's eyes light up. "That's a good sign."

I turn to face my friends. "I think he's a good guy. He's nice. He's funny. He's—"

"Incredibly good-looking," Bellamy adds.

Ignoring her, I continue. "He's a little guarded, but that's normal for some guys, I think. Right?"

"Can be," Boone says.

I look back and forth between them. They're both watching me, waiting on me to continue my take on Hollis. I don't know what to say, though—mostly because I'm not sure myself.

I grab a roller of perfume and dab it on my wrists and behind my ears.

"You know what," I begin again, "he's only here for a few days. I didn't know he was a football player, or I would've abstained from all things *him*. But here we are, and I'm not mad about it."

"But you will be," Boone points out.

"I will not."

I look at Bellamy. She's sitting on the edge of my bed, pursing her bright red lips. She's sending me telepathic messages of encouragement. I feel it. When I grin at her, she laughs.

"You will be fine," she insists. "Trust your gut."

"I am. And it's telling me to just remember this isn't real. We're just going to be faking things tonight for Mom's benefit, and I'll never see him again." I look back at the mirror. "I can handle this."

My reflection looks back at me. I look self-assured and confident, and I try to absorb as much of that as I can.

Before I can add anything to my little pep talk, the doorbell rings.

My head whips to Bellamy's.

Boone heads toward the doorway. "I'll get this."

I start to object but stop because it's pointless.

Boone's steps fall down the hallway. The door opens. His voice mixes with Hollis's as they exchange hellos.

My blood pressure spikes as Hollis's presence infiltrates my house. A rush of excitement sparks through me as I stand tall and motion to myself.

Bellamy does a quick once-over and gives me a thumbs-up.

I grab my nude-colored clutch, take a deep breath, and head for the hallway.

My heart is beating so hard that I think I might pass out.

"I had a friend who went to Braxton," Boone is saying as I make my way toward the foyer. "He played lacrosse. There was some bar there that he was always talking about that had something to do with aliens."

I can't see Hollis, thanks to the way Boone is standing. But as soon as I hear Hollis's voice, a chill causes a flurry of goose bumps up my arms.

"The Truth Is Out There," Hollis says with a laugh. "That's

our favorite place. It's kinda crazy with all the alien bullshit, but it's fun."

Boone steps to the side to look out the window. As soon as Hollis is in my line of sight, I almost die.

"Holy shit," Bellamy whispers from behind me.

Holy shit is right.

"Look at him," I whisper back.

Hollis is in head-to-toe black—suit, pants, shirt, and long, skinny tie. His shoulders fill out the jacket and make him look wider and stronger than even before. His waist is wrapped in a black belt.

He looks polished and sophisticated with a side of rogue thanks to his hair. It's a sight that I wasn't ready to behold.

He looks absolutely divine.

His eyes grow wide as I grow closer. "Wow, Larissa. You're … fucking gorgeous."

Boone turns around. His brow is crinkled. "We can go with *beautiful*."

"Beautiful, then," Hollis says with a smile. "That works."

We stand like two teenagers going to prom, facing each other but scared to actually touch. Suddenly, this seems like a terrible, rotten idea because I have no idea how I'm going to keep my wits about me tonight.

I don't think I can.

My brain screams at me to stay in check while my body begs for a free pass. My mind can't deny that a free pass—especially under the circumstances I just carefully laid out to my friends—wouldn't be the end of the world.

If the opportunity presents itself.

What do I have to lose?

"Boone," Bellamy says, "this is our cue to go, good buddy."

He sticks a hand out to Hollis. "It was nice to meet you. Nice car, too. Is it fast?"

"Oh, hell yeah," Hollis says, giving his hand a shake. "I'll take you for a ride when we have more time. It's a twelve-second car."

"No shit?" Boone asks.

"Yeah. River and I did it on this abandoned stretch of the way just off the campus. It used to be an old mine road or something, and we ran it just to see what it'd do. Quarter-mile in twelve seconds. Not too bad." He smiles proudly.

"That's awesome," Boone tells him, side-eyeing me before turning back to Hollis. "Hey, are you coming to our New Year's Eve party?"

Hollis looks at me. I can see the hesitation in his eyes because we haven't discussed that. We haven't discussed anything after tonight because our relationship pact ends after Jack's party.

"I haven't brought it up," I say so that Hollis doesn't have to stumble his way through it. "He might have plans."

"You gotta come," Boone says. "We'll all be there."

"Not me," Bellamy says.

I look at her. "Really, Bells?"

She shakes her head adamantly back and forth. "Not if Coy is coming."

"He's my brother. What are we supposed to do? Not invite him?" Boone asks, rolling his eyes.

"Sounds like a plan to me," she says.

"Just avoid him," Boone tells her.

"Trust me. I try. I avoid him like the fucking plague, but he *is* the fucking plague. I'd rather just avoid him from my house."

I'm not entirely sure what happened between the two of them, but it's been going on for a long time. Coy seems less hateful about Bells than she does him, but it doesn't matter. She loathes Boone's brother.

Or so she says.

Boone sighs. "Anyway, I hope to see you there, Hollis. It's a great time. I promise."

"Yeah. Okay. Thanks." Hollis smiles at Boone. "We'll see how things go."

Boone looks at me and grins. "Call me tomorrow."

"I will. And tell your mom thanks for the bracelet."

Hollis looks at the gold circling my wrist and gulps. His hand goes into his pocket, and he frowns. I can't think about it too much because Bellamy is hugging me.

"If you get Cheez-Its on this dress …." I warn her.

"I hope that's not all that gets all over this dress tonight," she whispers in my ear.

I shove her away, making her laugh. "Get out of here."

She exchanges a quiet goodbye with Hollis, and I'm glad I can't hear it. The mischief in his eyes tells me it was something that would've embarrassed me.

As soon as the two of them are gone, the energy in the house changes. It gets hotter. Thicker. More alive.

"You look beautiful," he tells me. The grit of his tone scratches wonderfully over my ears. "I meant it when I said that earlier."

"And you clean up well. I love the suit and tie on you."

"Do you?" He looks down at himself. "I don't wear this shit often. I feel like a monkey."

I laugh. "Well, you look handsome."

He reaches for my hand. I hesitate before putting my palm inside his.

I hiccup a breath as our skin makes contact, and I feel the warmth of his hand as he closes his fingers around mine.

"Ready?" he asks, looking so deeply in my eyes that I think he can see my soul.

"Yup."

"Let's go then."

With a final exchanged grin, we head out the door. And even though I know where we're headed, the rest of the night is a mystery.

Like the man holding my hand.

THIRTEEN
HOLLIS

Holy shit.

I mumble the words under my breath as I take in the activities around me. I don't know what I expected when I agreed to accompany Larissa to her stepfather's event, but I think it was all along the lines of something like a football banquet. A table of food with caterers, even. I figured there would be a stage for people to get up and talk about a bunch of shit nobody really cares about.

This is not that.

A large ballroom in a ritzy hotel in Savannah sits in front of us. It's filled to capacity with men and women whose Audis and Mercedes surround my Mustang in the valet.

I look down at Larissa.

That fucking dress has given me a hard-on since the moment I saw her. It was difficult to hide in front of her cousin, and it made the car ride here uncomfortable. Every time I look at her, I have to battle not throwing her over my shoulder and carrying her out of here.

The fabric is soft and hugs her body in a way that makes me jealous. Her exposed shoulder showcases a swath of tanned skin, and the slit up her right leg is a tease if I've ever seen one.

I might not have had the nicest car in the parking lot, but I have the hottest date. Period.

Larissa looks up at me through thick, dark lashes and smiles nervously. "Hanging in there?"

"I feel like you didn't accurately describe what we were getting into," I tease her. "I heard some work event for your step-dad, and you brought me to a who's who of Georgia."

She giggles. "This is one of the more low-key affairs of the year. You should see the Fourth of July thing. They get a boat and caterers, and there are fireworks. Last year, someone brought a giant floating duck that attracted a shark, and things got a little hairy."

"You're kidding."

She shakes her head. "Nope."

"Can I get an invitation to that?"

She laughs.

A woman approaches Larissa. I'm briefly introduced, but her name slides right by me. They get involved in a conversation that I lose interest in immediately. Instead of trying to follow along, I gaze around the room and wonder what her stepfather does for a living.

The walls of the banquet room are covered in black bunting. Lights shine behind it that somehow make the room feel like a forest or some kind of magical cave. Trees and shrubs have been brought in to add to the effect.

It's definitely on a level I'm not used to. The five-piece band is playing smooth jazz, the commercially-oriented crossover jazz. From memory, I know it became dominant in the eighties. But it suits the opulence of the night and is doing exactly what it's intended to do by creating an easy-listening ambiance.

Maybe my music minor isn't a bust, after all.

Round tables are set up throughout the room, and I know

from a communications class I took that the arrangement encourages conversation. I wonder if all the conversations tonight will include the life-sized ice sculpture of a man with a baseball bat pointing at the sky in the middle of the room.

Larissa touches my arm and brings my attention back to her.

"Okay," she says. "Sorry about that. That woman is a talker."

"It's cool."

She exhales. "My mother knows we're here. Are you ready to start our mission?"

"I'm ready and willing."

"Good. Before we go over there, her name is Trista Cunningham. Her husband is Jack Cunningham."

I gasp. "They have the same last name?"

She smacks my arm. "Don't be a dick."

"Anything else *less obvious* that I need to know?"

Her gaze sweeps around the room before it comes back to me.

"Jack co-owns the Savannah Seahawks. They're a minor league baseball team. These people are management, players, former players, businesses that sponsor different ballpark events, or bankers. You get the idea."

I nod.

"But," she says, lowering her voice, "none of that specifically matters to us. Our mission is solely on my mom."

"Right," I whisper conspiratorially.

Something about her enjoys this little game of us teaming up to … do whatever it is we're doing. But I get it. I kind of like it too.

"Give me my marching orders again," I tell her. "I'm supposed to make your mom think I'm totally obsessed with you, right?"

"Well, I mean, if you have to be obsessed, then do." She pretends to be flattered, making me laugh. "But really, I just want her to think I'm seeing someone so she'll stop setting me up with random guys who I have no interest or business dating. Because if you weren't here, she would've set me up with someone, and she'd be naming our future children by now."

"Rude."

She shrugs. "It comes from a good place. I think."

"I'm going to warn you," I tell her. "If she's after cute grandkids, you're in trouble. One look at me, and she's going to think about how she hopes her daughter breeds some of these genes into your gene pool."

"Breeding your genes into my gene pool?" She lifts a brow. "When you say it like that, it's such a turn-on."

I laugh. "Would you like me to rephrase?"

"No."

She swats me again, but this time, I grab her wrist. Her eyes go wide as they meet mine, and her breathing stalls in her chest.

We haven't talked about the kiss from last night. And while we might not have talked about it, I know she's thought about it. She's replayed it ten times in her mind since I've picked her up. I'm not judging her because every time I catch her looking at my mouth, I'm thinking about it too.

Logic tells me that kiss was a mistake. Why bother kissing a girl who I know on a cellular level could get under my skin? I've made it a mission in my life—went completely out of my way—to avoid anyone I think might be able to get to me.

Honestly? It hasn't been that hard.

I'm down to fuck. One-night stands are fine. Great, actually. I'm game for a friends-with-benefits situation too. But none of those circumstances involve kissing.

Sex is different. It's an exchange. Kissing, though, is a connection. You can fuck someone and not have to face them. You do what you want to the other person's body, but it has nothing to do with them as a person. Intercourse is a pleasure transaction. Kissing is a communication, an intentional decision to face someone and form a personal connection.

Fuck. That.

Yet I kissed her last night. Even worse, I want to kiss her again against my better judgment.

She squirms her hand free and lays it flat on the lapel of my jacket. Her breathing gets quicker.

"Would you rather I demonstrate?" I ask.

She tries to hide her smile. "Does that mean you're thinking about kissing me again?"

"This isn't about me," I tell her, lowering my face toward hers. "This is about what suits you right now."

She forces a swallow. Notes of amber in her perfume float through the air as her body undoubtedly heats.

I'm playing with fire here. And I just can't stop myself.

"This is a public place, Hollis," she says as if that would stop me.

"Does that mean whatever you're thinking about is not PG-13?"

She flushes the prettiest shade of pink as she fingers the edge of my jacket. "I'm just thinking that I need to be the object of your affection while we're here. Can you do that?"

I nod. "I can do that."

She pats my chest, and I take a step back. She looks simultaneously relieved and disappointed at my movement. The thought that she liked me that close to her sends a surge of testosterone through me.

"Okay," she says, clearing her throat. "Let's go see Mom and Jack."

"Let's do it."

She turns to walk away, and I instinctively want to grab her hand. I stop myself, but then I realize that if I was her man, I'd sure as hell be holding onto hers right now.

Play the part, Hollis.

I reach out and take her palm in mine. Our fingers lace together.

She looks at me over her shoulder and then down at our interlocked hands.

"What?" I ask. "You wanted to be the object of my affection."

"Fair enough."

She looks away but not before I see her satisfied little smile.

We wind through the faux forest, pausing every now and then when someone says hello to Larissa. She introduces me to each person as her boyfriend. Much to my surprise, the sound of that doesn't make me cringe.

She chats easily with each person, asks questions about their business or child and even someone's cat. Her attention to detail is awe-inspiring. Judging by their contented expressions, each person walks away feeling like the most important person in the room.

How the hell does she do that?

I spot her mother before we even get close. She has Larissa's blond hair and curvy figure. She also wears a version of Larissa's smile. It's not as warm or quite as kind, and I can't really imagine her throwing her head back and laughing like her daughter either. But the resemblance is close enough to pick her out of a room.

"Hi, Mom," Larissa says as we approach them. "Hi, Jack."

They smile as they see us coming.

Jack holds a glass tumbler of dark liquid, and Trista clutches a glass of pink-colored wine. They both do a quick assessment of me. I'm not sure what Jack thinks, but I can tell I pass Trista's inspection.

Trista tears her eyes off me long enough to say hello to her daughter.

"Hi, Riss," she coos, pulling my date into a hug that requires me to let go of her.

"Hey, Mom."

As soon as she releases her mother, I take her hand again. I don't think she minds.

"Glad you could make it, Larissa," Jack says, smiling kindly. "And who is this strapping young fellow that you have with you?"

"Mom, Jack, this is Hollis," she says.

I extend my free hand to Jack. "I'm Hollis Hudson. It's nice to meet you, sir."

He seems to appreciate the respect. His handshake is firm. "We're glad you could join us."

Trista's wineglass sways in her hand as she takes a closer look at me. "Where did you meet Riss?"

"At Paddy's," Larissa says before I have a chance to answer. "We both reached for a chair at the same time."

Jack taps on the side of his glass, drawing our attention his way.

"Your name is familiar to me," he says, looking at me. "Are you from around here?"

"No, sir," I say. "I'm from Indiana, but I do go to college at Braxton. It's not that far from here."

His eyes narrow. "You play football, don't you?"

I grin. I love it when this happens. In the right audience and in the right year—which this is generally not—it's pretty cool to be me. I hope, for Larissa's sake, this is that audience.

"I do. Or, I did. I was the tight end," I say, talking over the snort from Larissa. "This was my senior year."

"I didn't get to follow college football much this year. You had a hell of a season last year, though, didn't you?"

Thank fuck he didn't follow this year. He may not be quite as warm if he had.

Not that it really matters.

"Yeah. We won the National Championship. We had a great team and great coaches. It all worked out really well."

He nods, still thinking. "Did you ever play any baseball?"

"No. No, I didn't." I laugh. "There are too many games a year and not enough opportunities to … express myself."

He laughs, reading between the lines and understanding that I like to hit and get hit.

"I played football and baseball back in my day," he says. "To be honest with you, I preferred football, but my body just wasn't cut out to take the abuse, so I ended up focusing on baseball."

"Well, by the looks of everything tonight, that choice has served you well."

He smiles broadly. "I like this guy. Good job." He tosses me a wink before excusing himself to get another drink.

Larissa gives my hand a gentle squeeze. I squeeze it back.

So far, so good.

Trista watches me over the rim of her wineglass. I wonder how many drinks she's had because her eyes are just a touch glassy.

"Getting Jack's endorsement is quite a feat," she tells me. "I'm not sure he's ever particularly liked someone who Larissa has been involved with."

The idea of Larissa being involved with anyone sends a ripple of jealousy through me, which is crazy. I've never felt jealous over a girl before. Women are easy come, easy go.

Maybe I just ate too many cookies from Judy's box this morning.

"Well," I say, forcing a swallow. "I guess he has good taste. He chose you, didn't he?"

She appreciates this. "That's very true."

"I'm sure he just wants what's best for Larissa," I say, upping the charm factor. "You have an amazing daughter, Mrs. Cunningham. I'm honored to be here with her tonight."

Larissa lays her head against my arm. This doesn't go unnoticed by her mother.

"Well, Hollis," Trista says, impressed. "I'm delighted to

know that you are here. Larissa looks positively smitten with you."

"And I am with her, as well. But how could you not be? Just look at her."

"That's what I think too. She's an incredible girl and I'm just …" She touches her chest. "Just thank you for coming tonight. I hope we can have dinner soon."

"I would love that," I lie. "But I'll be going back to school soon. I need to finish my education so I can be worthy of your daughter."

Larissa pinches my hip and I try not to laugh.

Trista beams. She looks over our head and waves at someone. "If you two will excuse me, I need to say hello to Petra. But we will have a dance later, Hollis. Mark my words."

"Absolutely," I tell her. "I can't wait."

"I'll find you soon," she tells me before disappearing into the throng of people.

Once she's gone, I spin Larissa around to face me. She's beaming as she gazes up at me, and I feel a hint of pride that maybe she's proud to have me here.

"I think that went well," I say, feeling her out.

She tilts her head back and laughs. "You think?"

"I think so. I just hope it went well enough that your mom bought it hook, line, and sinker and doesn't try to set you up with someone else. Because, unlike Jacky boy, I can take a hit, and I can deliver one even better."

She rests a hand on my chest again. "You did great with my mom. Nailed it."

I shrug. "Did you doubt me?"

She laughs. "No. Not really."

"I can charm anyone."

She raises her chin. "Do you think you've charmed me?"

"Maybe."

I hope so.

She looks around the room. I can tell she's considering her answer because lines appear between her eyes. I think they're adorable but know from experience never to mention shit like that. Women don't think it's as cute.

"What would I have to do to charm you more?" I ask.

She grins. "You've done just fine. Don't lose any sleep over it."

A man dressed in a gray suit with a lavender shirt stops at Larissa's side. They speak easily. By the time she introduces me, white noise screams in my ears, and I miss his name.

It's not like it matters. He was wholly unimpressive.

"Did your mom send him over here?" I ask.

"Hollis Hudson, are you jealous?"

I cross my arms over my chest. "Nope. Don't lose any sleep over it."

She laughs loudly and freely.

"Is it wrong that I don't like some pudfucker coming by and hitting on my girl?" I ask.

I use the term without thinking.

She doesn't miss it.

"Your girl?" she asks, raising a brow.

"For tonight, anyway."

We watch each other closely. Somehow, using that term shifts the energy between us.

She turns her body to face me. "You know what I told Bells before I came here?"

"No."

"I told her I'd trust my gut."

I nod. "Sounds like a solid plan."

She presses her lips together. "Well, my gut tells me we should put a stamp on our fake relationship, so everyone here knows I'm taken." She looks up at me through those damn lashes again. "Because I would hate for you to get in a fight over me."

Instantly, my cock strains against my pants.

I wrap an arm around her back and pull her into me. She doesn't fight it, doesn't resist at all. In fact, she leans against me and brings one arm lazily over my shoulder.

I'm fairly certain that it would always feel like a level of heaven to have her—a woman so beautiful and funny and smart and classy—up against me. But we aren't in a frat house or a bar or even at a place that I invited her to like last night. We are *here* —with her people. People with money and class. People I don't associate with much because I'm the poor college kid who barely scrapes by.

To have her in my arms is amazing. But to have her willingly in my arms in this situation? It's another fucking level.

I grin. "Sweetheart, you're going to need to define what *put a stamp on it* means to you because the definition going through my head might get the police called for public indecency."

She sways back and forth just enough so that her body rubs against my groin. I think it's by accident, but the twist of her lips tells me it wasn't.

"I'm warning you," I tell her.

"Warnings are for chumps."

I chuckle. "Is that so?"

"People only issue warnings if they don't want to have to follow through." She shrugs cockily. "I don't know what you're warning me about, Hollis, but I hope it doesn't mean that you're taking options off the table."

I can't believe what I'm hearing.

"Are you goading me?" I ask her, surprised. "Because you don't know who you're fucking with, and you just might be out of your league, little lady."

She runs her fingers against my lapel again. "You know what I think about you?"

"No, but I'd love to."

"I think you're all talk and no action."

I stare at her dumbfounded. “Aren't you the girl who was telling me how you have this problem with guys like me?”

She nods. “I do have a problem with guys like you. *I like you,*” she says, annunciating each syllable clearly. “But *you*, specifically, I have a *definite* problem with.”

I lock my other hand at the small of her back and pull her into me even closer. The half an inch that was between us a moment ago is gone.

“Please, tell me. What is your *definite* problem with me?” I tease.

“I always end up in terrible relationships with guys like you,” she says slowly. “I don't know if it's the athlete part of it that's the problem or if it's the way that I interact with them, but me getting involved with guys that play sports—or work in the sports field, for that matter—is a no-go. Flat-out. But you, Mr. Hudson, are a special kind of trouble.”

I'm not sure if we're still playing here. Is someone watching, and we're supposed to be making a show of being an item so they leave her alone? I don’t know, but I'm going to roll with this to see.

If she wants me to act like I’ll fuck her, I will.

And if she wants me to actually fuck her, I'll do that too.

She’s sexy as fuck, and I’m horny as hell. *And have been since the first time she looked up and into my eyes.*

“I've been called troubled before,” I admit, playing along. “By lots and lots of people.”

“I can see why,” she says, playing with the hair at the nape of my neck.

The contact makes me crazy. The weight of her hand on the sensitive skin of the back of my neck heats my blood and makes me shiver at the same time.

My pulse kicks into overdrive. My body almost trembles as I stare into her hooded eyes.

“You pose a different sort of problem for me,” she says.

I'm trying to stay calm and let her work out whatever this is. But with every brush of her fingertip and every sway of her hip, I find it harder and harder to be patient.

"What kind of problem?" I ask.

"Well, I had sworn off guys," she says, "but *really,* I swore off *relationships* with guys."

"So, a relationship with girls is okay?"

She silences me with a look.

"Sorry. Continue," I tell her, enjoying the feeling of having her in my arms.

"I can't really have a relationship with you, now can I?" she asks. "Because you're going home in a few days. Our relationship pact expires tonight. I'm not going to run into you or find myself in precarious situations with you all winter, now am I?"

"Nope."

"So …" She brushes against me again. This time, there is absolutely no possibility that it was anything but intentional. "What could it hurt if we... *indulged* in this little charade we have going on and ended it on a high note?"

She stills. Her bottom lip goes between her teeth as she gazes up at me like a little vixen that I thought she wasn't.

I can feel every beat of my heart pound against my rib cage. I'm aware of every shallow breath she takes as she awaits my reaction.

I'm also acutely aware of how bad I want to be inside her little body right fucking now.

I shift my weight from one foot to the other to get rid of some of the energy building inside me.

"You're playing a dangerous game," I tell her.

"And why is that?"

I run my nose down the side of her cheek. She holds her breath as I smile against her skin. It's pure torture for me, but she deserves a little payback since her touches have been driving me insane for a while now.

"Because if you don't stop," I say, lowering my voice, "I will find a place, and I will fuck you. *Hard.*"

She tries to stay composed, but her eyes give her away. Her pupils dilate as my words sink into her brain.

Finally, her head tilts to the side, and she grins.

"What are you waiting for?" she asks, the words coming out in a rasp.

Game on.

FOURTEEN
LARISSA

Oh, my God.

Hollis locks our hands together and, without hesitation, makes his way to the front of the restaurant. We weave in and out of bodies, around circles of people talking about the stock market, and dodge men in bow ties carrying plates of hors d'oeuvres.

None of the people we pass know what we're doing or why we're leaving the event like we're on a mission.

Something about the secret—that only Hollis and I know what we're up to—makes my blood pound even harder through my veins.

"Excuse us," I say as a waiter nearly blindsides us. There was no way he anticipated two people darting by him, and I feel sorry he had to rebalance the baked brie on his tray.

But my sympathy only lasts for a moment. Before I know it, we exit the restaurant perched at the top of the swanky Jamison Hotel that Jack's company rented out for the night.

I come to a halt behind Hollis, almost stumbling on my heels like a little girl wearing them for the first time.

A double-elevator bay sits to our right. Two large doors are closed to our left. Straight ahead is a balcony that overlooks the Savannah River.

Hollis looks around before tugging me behind him until we stop again—this time beneath a brightly colored painting of fruit.

A slight breath escapes my lips as he guides me in front of him. I land against his hard chest, and he locks his hands against the small of my back.

"Still feeling this?" he asks as he studies me intently.

"Yes."

No other words are needed.

The corner of his mouth upturns as he drags a finger down the side of my face. A flurry of goose bumps breaks out across my skin.

I reach up and rest my arms against his shoulders, letting my fingers play in the silky strands of his hair. He leans his head against the crook of my elbow.

"Do you want to be *fucked*, Miss Mason?"

Something about the way he poses the question—and lingers on the one particular word—strikes a match inside me.

I return his playful grin. "I thought that's where you were taking me."

"I was. *I am*. I just want to be sure."

The truth is, I *am* sure. I want him. I want him so freaking bad, and I'm positive he wants me too.

The beauty of it—the way that I tell myself that it's okay to give in and go for it—is that he's safe. We are on the same page about what *we* are, and that's a means to an end.

Unlike the men before him, this won't end badly. There's nothing *to* end. And that is beautiful.

I tear my gaze from his and look around the elevator landing. There's nowhere for us to go. We could go out onto the balcony, but the odds someone would interrupt us is near one-hundred-percent. A bathroom is just gross. A room is too expensive and completely overkill for a quickie.

"I'm sure," I say. "But I don't know where we could pull that off."

He looks at something behind me, and a twinkle lights up his eyes.

"Where there is a will, there is a way," he says.

I heave a breath. "That sounds worrisome."

"Do you trust me?"

"Hollis …"

He brings his hands—both of them—to my face. He cups my cheeks and looks me dead in the eye.

My breath hiccups as I lose all sense and sensibilities.

"Do you trust me, Larissa? Because if you don't, we'll go back to your stepdaddy's party and have a good time. I'm perfectly fine with that."

I wrap my hands around his wrists. I can feel the muscles in his forearm and the meatiness of his palms.

I'm suddenly aware of just how much I don't want to go back inside Picante yet. My body screams with the need to touch his. My breasts ache, my legs feel heavy. The panties I almost didn't wear are soaked.

"I trust you," I say matter-of-factly.

He bends down and presses a quick, chaste kiss against my lips. When he pulls back, the smirk that's settled where my mouth just was is enough to almost elicit a moan.

"Follow me," he says softly.

He takes my hand again and leads me to the elevator. Much to my surprise, he presses the button to go *up*.

I furrow my brow. "That sign says the terrace is closed for a remodel."

He grins and doesn't say a word.

"*Ooh*."

The bell rings, and the elevator opens. We step inside. Hollis pushes the *R* button.

The motor spins, and the elevator car begins to move.

I stand on one side of the box. Hollis stands on the other. He stands with his legs shoulder-width apart and rubs a hand down his cheek. He never takes his eyes off me.

Watching him watch me and knowing that he's thinking about what he's going to do to me in a short matter of time has every cell in my body short-circuiting.

My skin already feels like it's a hundred degrees. My stomach feels hollow except for a knot that grinds against the lower part of my abs.

Each second that goes by might as well be an hour and, by the time the doors slide open, I'm ready to just strip out of my dress if it will speed things up.

Cool December air slams into us. We step onto the rooftop and take in our surroundings.

A brick wall that's waist-high or more sits along the edge. A water tank and pieces of ductwork are partially hidden by a half-wall painted with what I think is intentional graffiti. On the other side of the landing are a bar and a few tables that typically serve as a hangout for Picante guests. The rest of the space is open and showcases the spectacular view beneath us.

It's almost as breathtaking as the man beside me.

"It's so pretty out here," I whisper, taking in the stars and the way they reflect off the water.

"You've never been up here?"

"Not at night."

I turn around to see him. His eyes are still hooded, but something else floats around those orbs. I try to make sense of it, but in what I'm beginning to understand as typical Hollis style, he puts up a shield to keep me away.

He grins. "Come over here."

I take my time as I close the distance between us.

A breeze swirls around me as I reach Hollis. I shiver, but I'm not sure if it's from the cool air or the heat of his stare.

I'm on the edge of losing control and falling into his arms. It's too easy. It feels too safe with him, so much so that it causes me to stutter-step at the last minute.

He quirks a brow.

You're allowed to trust yourself. You're capable of handling this with him. It's a completely different situation.

I take a deep lungful of air and stop inches in front of him.

"Is this close enough?" I ask.

"Honestly?" He grins. "No."

"How close do you want me then?"

Hollis reaches down and pulls me up and into him. He captures my mouth with his before I realize what's happening.

I melt against his chest.

Our mouths move together in perfect unison. His lips are soft yet commanding, and I'm more than willing to let him take the lead.

Sliding my hands beneath his jacket, I rip his shirt out of his pants. I plant my palms onto his back.

The muscles on his body are thick and developed. His back is chiseled and hard, and as I move my hands to his sides, I feel the bulge of the top of the V that makes every woman on earth crazy.

Every move he makes causes his muscles to ripple under my touch. It becomes obvious why I have a thing for athletes—their bodies are on fire.

My legs buckle, but he is one step ahead of me. He scoops me up like I'm a doll.

I moan into his mouth as he takes me by surprise and parts my lips with his tongue. He explores me, staking his claim in a delightful, delicious act of desire.

I run my hands through his hair, feeling the strands slip through my fingers.

His assault on my lips is unending. As though he can't bear to stop what we finally started.

Carrying me across the rooftop, he sets me down on a lounge chair. The plastic is cold and hard, but it only barely registers. He breaks his kiss long enough to sit next to me.

We take each other in as we pant to catch our breath. His eyes are wild as his hand grips my thigh beneath the slit of my dress.

"You make me crazy," he growls.

"I've heard that before."

He chuckles, his need thick in his tone.

His hand slips between my thighs, and he pushes them apart.

I shimmy up in my seat and spread my knees as far as my dress will allow. I can feel my heartbeat between my legs and my desire coating the inside of my thighs.

There's nothing I can do about it.

He's already there.

"Hollis," I say, my body arching toward him.

"You are wet," he teases. "Can you feel that?"

He swipes my panties to the side and parts my folds with his finger.

"Mm-hmm," I say, closing my eyes.

He toys with my opening, flicking my swollen bud back and forth. I yelp at the contact.

"Where did all that mouth of yours go?" he asks, grinning. "Where's the Larissa who was goading me earlier? Huh?"

"*She's* trying not to come all over your fingers."

He sucks in a breath. "*Fuck.*"

The lace of my panties scratches against the inside bend of my leg, creating a crazy sensation that makes me moan. He leans forward and captures the sound with his tongue.

He kisses me like I've never been kissed. It's controlled and wild and sweet and a promise of something more lascivious.

I grind against his hand, getting both the pump of his finger and the contact with my clit. He lets me have my way—lets me use him to bring myself to the precipice of an orgasm.

I wind my fingers in his hair as I hold his face near mine.

He pulls away, pressing kisses across my jaw and to my ear. I toss my head back to allow him as much access as he wants.

My hips swirl, needing more and more until Hollis buries his head in the crook of my shoulder.

Shots are fired in my belly, and an explosion of colors bursts through my vision. My knees fall to the side as I pulse around his fingers.

"*Do. Not. Stop*," I say, each word a separate syllable.

"So bossy." The words are whispered over the shell of my ear. "But I have no plans on stopping, baby."

The orgasm keeps coming, keeps building until it becomes so sharp, so intense that I shout in response.

"Shh," Hollis says with a chuckle. "We don't need to attract attention."

I peek open my eyes as he slows his pressure on my body.

"Sorry," I say, wincing.

He presses another kiss to my lips. His eyes are filled with amusement.

"Never apologize for that. Ever," he says, removing his hand from between my legs. When he draws it back, it's coated with my wetness. He holds it up in the air and grins. "Now, that's hot."

"It's not. But whatever."

He laughs.

I get to my feet, emboldened by the confidence he's given me, and pull my dress up to my waist. He watches me like he's fascinated. I hold his gaze as I step out of my shoes and remove my panties.

The air whips around my wet, bare skin. I keep my dress bunched with one hand, and with the other, I slip my shoulder out of the top.

Hollis reaches over and carefully tugs it down until my breasts are exposed.

"Oh, shit," he breathes as he takes a pebbled nipple between two fingers. "Riss."

I grin at his use of my nickname. "Are you just going to sit there, or are you going to fuck me?"

His eyes snap to mine. "There's my girl."

I laugh as he gets to his feet and takes off his jacket. He throws it at the foot of the chair. He tugs his shirt out of his pants altogether and unfastens his belt with ease.

Snap.

Zip.

Down goes his pants until they're pooled at his feet. A condom appears. He remains in front of me with his cock wrapped and standing at full attention.

"That's impressive," I say, grabbing it in my hand.

"That's better than the alternative."

I laugh. "Sit down. All the way back." I shove his chest until he's sitting in the spot I just vacated.

"Now what?" he asks me.

"Enjoy the ride."

He groans from the base of his throat as I climb up on the chair with him. He palms his cock, and I lower myself onto him.

I take him in inch by inch, my eyes rolling into the back of my head as he fills every bit of me. He pulls a nipple into his mouth and rolls it around with his tongue. The juxtaposition of the cold air and the heat of his mouth is enough to make me want to scream in pleasure.

He grips my hips, his fingertips biting into my skin, as I guide myself up and down his length.

His teeth graze my nipple before he switches to the other side. He guides me, helping set the tempo that works for him, as I slide him in and out.

His hips flex, pressing himself deeper—so deep that it can't go any more.

"That's all I can take," I whimper, the pinch of pain so delicious that it almost topples me over the edge again.

"Just keep doing that," he says through gritted teeth. "*Oh, my god.*"

The growl that follows comes from the base of his throat and is so gravelly, so raw that it flips a switch inside me.

I slam down on his cock and grind myself against him. His chin lifts to the star-studded sky when I work myself in a figure eight. I lift, I tilt, and I take him as deep as I can. And when he moans his release, his fingers dipping into the curve of my hip so tightly that I couldn't stop if I wanted to, I find my release again.

"Hollis!" I shout, unable to contain the rush of pleasure coursing through me.

"Don't stop." He moves my hips up and down as he continues to milk the end of his climax.

His handsome features are even sharper in the shadows of the night. And to know the look on his face is because of me? That's a high I've never imagined.

Finally, his grip eases, and his movement stops. He opens his eyes, and they snap automatically to mine.

The greens and golds are glossed over, and he looks as relaxed as I've ever seen him. It makes me wonder what he looks like when he wakes up in the morning.

"I did," he says, still inside me.

"You did what?"

"I enjoyed the ride."

I'm literally floating from how incredible this was. I more than enjoyed the ride.

"I'm glad," I say, aiming my best smug smile at him.

I'm actually finding it odd that I have no regrets. Keeping my dress bunched up in my hands, I climb off him.

He jumps off the chair with more energy than I have and takes in our situation.

"You need to clean up," he notices.

I nod.

He looks around and spots his jacket on the edge of the chair. He digs through his jacket, and something falls to the ground when he pulls out a tissue.

"This is all I have," he says, handing it to me. "It's new. I just shoved it in there this morning."

"Thanks." I use it to clean between my legs as best as I can. Then I drop my dress.

We get ourselves sorted in silence. But my attention keeps going back to the item that fell from his jacket.

Once I'm dressed properly and he's shrugging on his jacket again, I walk over to the end of the chair and scoop up a delicate rose gold bracelet. There's a tiny succulent on the band. It's adorable and reminds me of something I'd totally buy for myself.

I watch Hollis as he smooths out his jacket, oblivious to what I'm doing.

"Hollis?" I ask, holding it in the air. "This fell out of your pocket."

"What?" He spins around. His sight falls on the bracelet, and he stops moving. "*Oh.*"

I hold the piece in my hand. "What is this? It's so pretty."

His Adam's apple bobs in his throat. "Oh. Um …" He forces another swallow. "I picked that up this morning. I was in a store, and it was there. It wasn't twenty bucks, I don't think."

My heart tugs in my chest as I watch him fumble over his words.

I grin. "I didn't ask you how much it cost. I asked you why you had it."

He narrows his eyes. "You ask a lot of questions. Does that ever stop?"

"Nope."

"Good to know," he says, his cheeks just a touch pinker than I remember them.

"Did you get this for me?"

He grins too. "Maybe."

"Then why didn't you give it to me?"

He shifts his weight from one foot to the other.

Is he … *embarrassed?*

Oh, my heart.

"It was an impulse purchase. You took the wine to the Landry's, so I thought maybe I should bring something tonight for you."

"But you left it in your pocket?"

"Well, you were already wearing one, and this one felt … stupid. You know what? I'm done answering your silly questions."

He leans in to kiss me, but I turn my head and his lips land on my cheek.

"I want this," I say, letting it dangle from my fingers. "Can I have it?"

He sighs against my cheek. I think he smiles too, but I can't see him. "I bought it for you."

"Then help me put it on."

He leans back and takes the bracelet. With the care of a surgeon, he fastens it around my wrist.

"Look, it's perfect," I say. "How did you know?"

"You said you liked rose gold jewelry. And you're going to school for something in landscape. Right?"

I nod, shocked he remembered—especially since I didn't say those things to him.

"And you said you didn't like expensive jewelry." He smiles. "But I don't think you meant fifteen-buck pieces, huh?"

My heart is so full. It was such a sweet gesture that I almost can't stand how giddy I feel. I mean, I just had mind-blowing sex with the most divine man I have ever met. Ever. And *two* orgasms.

In my blissful haze, though, all I can think is *wow*. Out of all the men I've dated, none of them have ever shown such genuine thoughtfulness. This is the sweetest thing a guy has given me.

He's a good man. A sexy, good man.

I think my heart might burst.

I rise on my tiptoes and kiss him on the cheek. "This is exactly what I meant. Thank you, Hollis."

"Yeah, yeah, yeah," he says, blowing it off. "Let's not get too sentimental and shit."

I roll my eyes and chuckle as we walk toward the elevator. "You sure know how to ruin a sweet moment, don't you?"

"It's a gift."

It really might be.

FIFTEEN
HOLLIS

"Let me help you in," I say.

Larissa holds onto my arm and hums against my jacket. Her cheeks are pink from the three glasses of wine she drank with her mother after we returned from the rooftop. She dozed off in the car on the way back to her house, but I'm not mad about it. I kind of like her when she's not talking a mile a minute.

Although I missed her crazy questions.

We stumble up the sidewalk. I help her get her key in the door. She steps inside and pulls me right along with her.

"I guess I'm coming in," I crack as I shut the door behind us.

She turns on the light, squinting when the chandelier overhead shines brightly on us. She winces as she wakes back up.

"Who let me drink this much?" she asks, pressing a hand to her stomach.

"Your mother."

She laughs. "Figures. Are you hungry?"

I shrug noncommittally.

"Follow me," she says.

We walk down a hallway and into the kitchen. The floors are a dark hardwood, and the cabinets a deep navy blue. The handles are some kind of copper or brass. I know from working construction all summer for the past four years that this isn't cheap. Not in the least.

She rummages through a pantry tucked into the wall next to a Sub-Zero refrigerator.

Her dress is a bit rumpled but still beautiful despite everything. It managed to make it through a formal dinner of halibut and prime rib, as well as cigars on the balcony with a couple of baseball players from Jack's team who were cool as hell. I even got on FaceTime with Crew and River so they could say hello.

I miss those fuckers.

I spent almost an hour shooting the shit with Jack and his buddy Milo. They own a bunch of ground in Ohio, near where I grew up in Indiana, and invited me to go hunting with them next fall.

Then Larissa and I spent a couple of hours of dancing to everything from The Mamas and the Papas to Post Malone—something I thought I'd never do and probably will never do again. But somehow, this girl gets me to do whatever she wants.

It's a good thing I'm going home soon. This could be a problem.

"Bellamy ate all my Cheez-Its," she says. "Do you like cookies or beef jerky? Or …" She reaches into the back of the cabinet and pulls out a familiar white box. "I have three Ding Dongs."

"Ding Dongs are my favorite food."

"Seriously?" She peers at the box. "I don't even know why I have these. They might be expired."

"They never expire. That's the beauty of a Ding Dong."

She tosses me the container. "Here. All yours." She reaches back inside and grabs a package of chocolate chip cookies. "Let's eat in bed."

"Haven't you heard the saying about eating crackers in bed?"

"Yeah," she says as she walks by. "And the saying goes that hot guys can always eat crackers in your bed."

"Ahhh. Excellent point. You haven't even seen my abs yet."

"I didn't tell you what you had to do to get in my bed," she jokes. *I think.*

I follow her back down the hallway to her bedroom. I stop in the doorway.

The wallpaper is a dark blue with the coolest design in a different shade of blue. It gives so much dimension and texture to the walls that it's fascinating.

"Love the wallpaper," I say, stepping fully inside. "It almost looks like velvet."

"Right? I love it so much. Sebas… Never mind."

"Yeah. Never mind."

My jaw flexes at the idea of that bastard being here. Of course, he was. He was in this room, this house … in her.

I have to shove the thought out of my head.

I take off my jacket and lay it over a chair. She disappears into what I assume is a closet. I take my shoes and socks off, grab my Ding Dongs, and climb into her bed.

The bed is huge, a king, I think, and piled with pillows of all shapes and colors. The bedding is soft as fuck—all fluffy and cloud-like. I get situated on the pillows and feel the weight of the world float away.

When Larissa comes back out, her hair is down and brushed out, and she's wearing a long T-shirt.

I watch her move across the room like some kind of angel. I'm well aware that my mind is fucking with me, but I can't help it.

She's even more fucking gorgeous now than she was earlier. Who would've thought that was possible?

Larissa climbs into bed, and I hand her the cookies. She slips under the covers.

"So …" I say, taking a bite of a Ding Dong. "Now what?"

She shrugs. "I don't know." She takes a cookie from the container and nibbles along the edge. "Wanna talk?"

I lay my head back against the headboard. It hits with a thud, making her laugh.

I sort of knew this was coming. It's what she does. Larissa asks questions. But I've discovered that as much as it annoys me when she does it, it annoys me less when it's her and not someone else. And it annoys me even less when she doesn't do it.

Maybe this is because, down deep, I kind of like her dedication to figuring me out. It might also be that I like her resiliency. No matter how hard I try to deter her, she pushes.

Because she just might care a little.

I take another bite of my treat, letting my head fall over so I can look at her. She watches me out of the corner of her eye and tries not to grin.

The longer we sit in silence eating our junk food, the more I feel myself giving in to her iron-clad will.

I sigh. "Fine. Three questions."

She shimmies to sit upright. Her eyes glow. "Anything I want?"

"I reserve the right not to answer anything I don't want to," I say, ignoring the face she makes, "but, yes. You can ask me three things. But I get three back to you."

She squeals. I roll my eyes.

She pretends she doesn't already know what she's going to ask. It's adorable.

"Okay. First question," she says. "What is your hidden talent?"

I fill my mouth with my cake. "Singing."

"Singing?"

I nod.

"Okay. Sing."

I laugh, shaking my head as I swallow. "I can't just sing on demand."

"Yes, you can."

"No, I can't."

She sticks her bottom lip out. I reach over and flip it with my thumb.

She swats my hand. "Sing your karaoke song," she says.

"My karaoke song. What's that?"

"The song you sing when you karaoke. Duh."

Flashbacks of karaoke with the football team at The Truth Is Out There come rolling back through my memory. It always happens on the nights we drink—nights that don't happen very often. Not for Crew, River, and me, anyway.

"So?" Larissa prompts.

I stick out my bottom lip. "'Hello' by Adele."

"What?" She smiles broadly. "Go. Sing. Now."

"Again, I just can't sing when prompted. I'm not a fucking canary."

She laughs. "Come on, Hollis. Sing for me."

I can tell by the glimmer in her eyes that she's not going to let it go. She's going to hound me until I finally break down, so I might as well do it now.

I clear my throat and begin to sing the first few bars of Adele's hit song. The smile dims on Larissa's face as I get to the part about a million miles.

"Oh, my gosh," she whispers. "Hollis. *You're good.*"

I let the line vanish off the tip of my tongue and shrug. "I'm not good. It's fine. It's just my party trick."

"No. Don't sell yourself short. Your voice is amazing."

I blow her off. "Okay, my turn. What's your hidden talent?"

"You can't ask me what I ask you."

I grin. "Oh, I can. And I did."

"I don't have one." She pops a cookie in her mouth. "I'm talentless."

I doubt that. I turn over onto my side and watch her. "Answer it, or we'll be here all night."

She rolls over to face me too. "That's fine. I live here."

I brush a piece of cookie off her lip. "Answer. It."

"I really don't have any hidden talents, but I can speak English, French, and bits of Russian."

"No shit?"

She nods. "I had to take a foreign language in school and fell in love with it. I'm learning Russian on an app on my phone."

"Huh. That's cool. Not what I was expecting, but I love it."

"Great." She smiles at me. "Question number two is one I'm just using for scientific research, okay?"

"Okay."

"How do you feel about monogamy?"

"Interesting change of direction."

She waits patiently for me to answer.

"I feel like if you've committed to someone and you've agreed that's what you're doing, then you honor that. Your word is your word," I say.

"But do you think it's something that can be done?"

"Of course."

She studies me. "Is it something you do?"

I wish I had another Ding Dong at my disposal, so I didn't have to answer this.

"Not really," I say, watching her face fall. "I'm not against it. By all means, if you're going to be in a relationship, monogamy would be the way to go."

"So you don't really do relationships?"

I wrinkle my nose at her. "Only the ones with pacts for a limited number of days. What about you?"

"I think monogamy is the only way to have a true connection with someone. I think our society undervalues it."

"Probably true."

Her face darkens as she prepares her third and final question.

She shoves the cookies away from her and focuses squarely on my face. It makes me squirm because, while I have no idea what she's going to say, I already know I don't want to answer it.

"Third question—what did you mean when you told me that your mom is the one who burned you?"

I sit up. I'm acutely aware of how closely she's observing every move I make. I also know she's expecting an answer to this—to the one question I avoid from anyone.

My heart sinks as I think about my mom and the circumstances surrounding her leaving Harlee and me.

I don't want to answer this. I want to avoid it like I always do because it's not something I talk about to anyone—not even Crew and River. But, for the first time in my life, I can feel a small fissure in my heart that wants to allow some of the story to come out.

Maybe it'll help lighten my load. Maybe I won't feel so ... alone.

My heart pounds in my chest as I try to figure out where to start and how much to tell her.

The beauty of telling her is that it won't matter. I can walk out of here tonight and never see her again.

That's supposed to make me feel better. It doesn't.

"Hollis?" she asks softly.

"The last time I saw my mother, I was sixteen," I tell her.

It seems like enough to see how she reacts. Surprisingly, she reaches out and touches my arm.

"I'm sorry. That must be hard. What happened to her?" she asks.

"I don't know."

My heart sinks as I say the words out loud. *I don't know what happened to my mother.*

I could try to figure it out, I'm sure. One night, River looked her up but couldn't find anything. I figure she's in jail somewhere, rotting away for some misdeed.

"I was six when she lost custody of Harlee and me the first time," I say, staring at the wall ahead of me. "We left for school, and Child Protective Services picked us up around lunchtime. Apparently, our parents had a meth lab in the basement, and they got hauled off to jail as one does when things like that happen."

She squeaks a gasp. "I'm so sorry, Hollis."

I can feel Larissa's gaze on my cheek, but I don't look at her. I'm afraid of what I might see.

"My sister and I got split up," I say. "We stayed in touch for a few years, but after that, we lost contact. I have no idea what happened to her."

"I can't imagine. I wish I could … help. But … Hollis. I'm *so* sorry."

I nod. I get it. But there's nothing she can do.

"I bounced around from foster family to foster family," I continue for some strange reason. "In their defense, I wasn't an easy kid to take care of. I had a ton of energy and a chip on my shoulder, and I ran away from most of them at the first opportunity."

"That must have been awful for you," Larissa says. "I don't know what to say."

"There's nothing to say."

I look down at her and hold my breath, expecting to see pity. Instead, I see something else—something warm and kind and hopeful.

I don't know what to make of that, but it makes me want to keep talking.

"When I was fourteen, my mom got custody back," I say, my voice staying surprisingly steady. "She didn't get Harlee, just me. Dad was still in prison, so it was just the two of us."

My jaw clenches as I remember leaving the foster home I was in and moving back in with her. I didn't know her anymore and had only seen her a few times at visitation. She didn't look like the mom I recalled, and I didn't feel like I knew her—or her me—at all.

"We did okay for the first few months. But then shit got hard, and she lost her job, and we couldn't afford food. We were going to get evicted. So she got back into her old clique …" Tears sting the corners of my eyes. "And I sold my first bit of dope for her. I was sixteen."

"Hollis," Larissa whispers, her voice clearly in shock. "*Oh, my gosh.*"

I run my tongue over my teeth as I think about how badly all of that could've turned out.

"I know," I say. "She got picked up again a few months after, and I went back into foster care. Stayed with a couple named Philip and Kim, who were too nice to the kid I was back then."

"Thank God, you found them."

I nod. "Except they ended up leaving. Philip got transferred a few months before I turned eighteen, so I landed in a group home again until I graduated and could go down to Braxton."

I think of their warm home and the way they always had a ton of food in the fridge that you could just walk up to and take whatever you wanted. They never got mad at me when I pulled my shit—not mad like they should've.

"Are they in your life now?" she asks me.

I shake my head. "My car? That was Philip's. He gave it to me as a going-away present."

"So they just left you? Alone? With a car?"

"I wasn't theirs."

Her brows furrow. "I don't understand."

"They've tried to call me and write letters, but I just … I can't."

A lump forms in my throat as I remember the two people who have been more like a family to me than anyone and how much it hurts when I get a message from them. Because I know they went on with their lives, without me.

My brain automatically thinks of Judy and her proclamation that I was hers now. If only I wasn't leaving because she just might mean what she said.

I gaze into the distance. I've never told anyone these things. Never wanted to. Never thought it was necessary or that it mattered. But an unexpected lightness exists in my chest now that I've told Larissa some of my story.

I look at her and smile.

Even though tears well in her eyes, and I feel a little raw and a lot vulnerable, this is where I want to be right now.

She's nestled down in her blankets, her hair splayed against her pillows. She looks cozy and warm, and something about it pulls at me.

"My turn," I say. "Do you mind if I stay here tonight?"

She grins. "I hoped you would."

I hop up and turn off the light. Then I climb into bed with her.

And just like we've done it before, she curls up against me and falls asleep.

SIXTEEN
LARISSA

My eyes struggle to open.

The sun is bright. Too bright.

I stretch my arms over my head and twist my body to help me wake up. The haze in my head is real. The stream of jumbled images and memories makes it difficult to determine what is real and what is fiction.

I nestle down in my blankets again, cocooning myself in the soft folds of fabric. As soon as I start to drift back into a blissful sleep, I get a whiff of a man's cologne.

Hollis.

My heart spins to life.

He was here. He is here.

Oh, my god.

Thoughts of rooftop sex and dancing to "Holy" by Justin Bieber flood through my brain.

I sit up in bed. It's a clumsy, still-half-asleep motion. It's not pretty.

I pray Hollis isn't watching.

He's not.

He's gone.

All that's left is the scent of his leathery cologne.

Images replay through my mind on a never-ending spool. His boyish grin while I lured him to the dance floor last night by the end of his tie. The embarrassment in his cheeks when I did my best Britney impression and serenaded him with my rendition of "Make Me" on the dance floor. The way his laughter sounded so light and easy as he did the Dougie with my mom and me—a dance we learned years ago after having a couple too many mimosas with Coy on vacation in Los Angeles.

My head sends a shot of pain behind my eyes, and I wince. I vaguely remember drinking a delicious red wine. *How many glasses did I drink?*

I pull the blankets back and find a solitary white wrapper from a Ding Dong. My laughter is loud. I wince again, the sudden movement causing a shooting pain to rip across my forehead this time.

I climb out of bed and grab my robe. As I wrap myself up, I notice the chair I usually sit in is turned around and facing the window. There's a pencil sitting on the table beside it that's not usually there.

Furrowing my brow, I turn around and head to the hallway.

The house is eerily quiet, without a sign of Hollis at all. I peek into the living room as I pass, thinking maybe he felt weird sleeping with me or something and ended up on the couch—but nope.

I enter the kitchen and find no evidence of him in here either.

Leaning against the counter, I try to put all the pieces together and fill in the blanks.

I remember the wrapper in my bed and then remember him laying against my pillows with one of those little cakes in his hand. A bit of chocolate was on the corner of his mouth as he told me the story about his mom.

My heart sinks to my toes.

He's so much more burned, as he said, than I ever imagined. I figured he fought with his mom a lot, or she ran off the love of his life. Never in a million years did I imagine the pain she put him through.

I hate her. I don't know her, but my loathing for the woman runs deep. *How could she hurt someone like that, let alone a man so thoughtful and so kind? Her own son?*

"How did he turn out so strong?" I ask the kitchen.

I can't fathom having to deal with the things he had to deal with at this age, let alone as a child. To actually be alone in the world. Abandoned. *Used.*

My heart breaks for him and the sadness that ran so deep in his eyes. The pain was bottomless as he tried to avoid my gaze so I didn't see.

I make a cup of coffee. The ritual of it helps settle the misalignment of the morning. I switch over to good thoughts of Hollis because thinking of him with tears in his eyes makes me want to cry.

I wish he was here.

"He probably had something to do today," I say, working through my thoughts. "Or maybe he just didn't feel right being here this morning."

That's a real thing. I've felt that before when I had a quick hookup and wake up in his house. The need to leave is real.

I carry my cup through the house and realize that I'm not freaking out. Usually, when something goes awry with a guy or even appears to be going sideways, panic sets in. But I'm not now, and I'm not sure why.

Sitting on the couch, I tuck my legs under me. It's quite a revelation to feel this … free. Yet, at the same time, I've been spending time with Hollis. Sure, we're just friends, and this is nothing serious, but is spending time with a man supposed to be this easy?

It is when it's just a means to an end.

And the end is here.

I rest my cup on my knee as another realization hits me: our pact is over.

I helped him through dinner, and he made a show for my mom—an amazing one at that.

"Why can't real relationships be this easy?" I wonder aloud.

They never are. They're always filled with stress and compromise to the point when no one gets anything remotely like what they wanted in the first place. Once you attach yourself to someone else, their burdens somehow become yours.

"That's why they can't be easy. They're real-world. This thing with Hollis was just pretend." I smile. "It was fun."

I lean against the cushions and sigh a slow, steady breath. I've been looking forward to seeing him. The last couple of days came out of nowhere but have made me laugh and smile more than I have in a long damn time.

The bottom of my cup warms my leg a little too much, so I pick it up, taking a long sip and feeling the warmth fill my stomach.

"I need to find a guy like Hollis," I say. "Which is weird because he's totally my type but totally … *not*."

He's totally my type. From the broad shoulders to the way he makes my name sound seductive, Hollis Hudson is the kind of guy I hope to find one day. It's just perplexing that he also has all the qualities of the group of men who never fail to let me down.

I know, down deep, that you can't lump people together like that. I told Hollis that. But he's so different from the men I usually date that it's hard to fathom what it is about him that makes me feel totally different when we're together.

Because there is something about him that wasn't my type in the most wonderful way. Something that makes me feel confident and fun. Beautiful. I don't feel crazy for wanting to talk or to have goals of my own.

Just as long as I don't ask questions.

My amusement fades as I realize why he doesn't like to be prompted. He has many ghosts that I think he's ashamed of.

My bracelets dangle on my wrist. I set my cup down. Working carefully with the delicate clasp, I unfasten Siggy's gift. It was so thoughtful, and it's something I'd pick out for myself, but the one still wrapped around my arm is more special.

I hold it in the air and watch the little succulent sparkle in the light.

You said you liked rose gold jewelry. And you're going to school for something in landscape.

He listens. He listens to me.

Is that what's different?

"You're something else, Hollis," I say to an empty room.

I pick up my cup, and I take another drink.

Thank God he's leaving, or else I might be in some trouble.

But as the coffee splashes down my throat, I have to wonder —*am I in trouble already?*

Hollis

Sunlight bounces off the Savannah River. The water is dark and kind of moody as I watch it from a little sitting area I found. It's not far from Judy's—my original destination. But the sign on the door said she was closed today, so I walked on by until I found this place.

My brain has been on overdrive. Telling Larissa about my mom and Harlee, and Philip and Kim, put me into a weird frame of mind.

I lay beside Larissa as she slept. Memories I didn't know I still had came back to me in the dead of night. I remembered

Harlee screaming and trying to feed her a package of broken crackers I found in the cupboard. I recalled how our house always smelled like bleach. I heard my mom's voice, something I knew I remembered but intentionally blocked out, sing "When You Wish Upon A Star" while her voice broke and tears streamed down her cheeks.

My stomach knots as I remember it all again, and I wish so fucking much that things had been different.

But they weren't. All that shit—that fucked-up crap of a hand that I was dealt the day I was born—it's all a part of my makeup. It's ingrained into the fiber of my being.

I'll never escape it.

It's no wonder everyone walks away from me eventually. I'm poison.

"Don't you worry, Hollie Boy. I will always stay by your side, even when I'm so drunk and high that I can't feel my face. Mommy loves you. You're my person forever, Hollie. Forever."

I take out my phone and find River's number. He answers on the third ring.

"*Hollis*," he says, relief evident in his tone. "What's happening, buddy?"

"Do you know what I'm doing?"

"No, or else I wouldn't have asked."

I chuckle. "I'm looking at a fucking river."

"Is this some joke about my name because I've heard them all."

"I bet you have."

I run a hand down the side of my face. The stress in my back from sitting up most of the night eases just a bit.

"How's your mom?" I ask him.

A door squeaks in the background and then what I think are footsteps tap down a flight of stairs. Finally, he sighs. The sound is heavy and tired, and I know he's struggling.

"She's sick," he says as if that explains it all. "I just ... *fuck*."

"You know I'm sorry. I hate this for you. Is there something I can do?"

"Nah. I'm okay." He laughs. "I mean, I'm sure as hell not okay, but I'm making it."

"Ana with you?"

"No. She's with her folks back in Braxton. They flew in from Greece to be with her. Fucking miss her."

It's so hard thinking about River finding his person. His Kim to her Philip, the Judy to her Ronnie. It's not that I want that, but I can't begrudge my dude for finding his girl.

"Need me to Door Dash you some ramen or something?" I offer.

"There's no Door Dash here. And I hate ramen. You know that."

"Beggars can't be choosers," I joke.

"Good thing I'm not a beggar then."

We laugh. To an outside person listening in, it would sound like two friends having a light-hearted conversation about food. But it's not, and we both know it.

We both hear it.

Our voices are tired and riddled with anxiety. The words are gruffer than they usually are too.

"How's the blonde?" he asks.

"Larissa," I say, happy to get to her name. "She's good."

He scoffs. "Don't lie to me, Hudson."

"Nah, she really is good. *In every way*." I grin.

"There you go. You're coming back around now."

"You're such a fuck."

He laughs.

I look across the water again and feel the air against my face.

"I know what you're getting at," I tell him. "And she is good. We had fun last night."

He pauses. "But …"

"But it's done."

The words taste rotten as I spit them out and admit the finality of my time with Larissa. Sure, I could milk it out for a few more days while I'm in town, but what would be the point?

I'm a method to end the madness in her life, a screw in her toolbox, so to speak. That's it. *And that's fine.*

Why would I want more, anyway? What would be the point in trying to figure out how to see her again after I go back to school—if she even wanted to see me, that is? The reason I'm here in the first place is because I'm not at a Bowl game because I can't keep my shit together.

Why in the world would I even entertain the idea of juggling someone like Larissa when I can't keep myself in the air?

I had enough dropped passes this year to prove that.

"I'm going to be smart here for a second," River says. "This is a new skill of mine, so be patient."

I laugh at him.

"Watching my mom be sick has changed a lot of shit for me," he says, his voice void of any levity. "We went four years thinking football was life. We balled out, had fun—we lived a life, Hollis. But what do we have to show for it?"

"Not a National Championship this year."

"Exactly." He sighs. "Look, maybe this was the universe trying to tell us something. Maybe we … made complete asses out of ourselves on the field so we could look beyond the goalposts."

"Wow. What have you been doing up there in Vermont?"

"Listening to audiobooks, believe it or not."

"Huh. I'm not sure I like this version of you."

He snorts. "I'm not done. My brilliance continues."

"Great," I deadpan.

"Life isn't about anything we've been working for, man. It's not about statistics and ratings and scoreboards. Who cares about that shit?"

I wince. "Well, you did until your period of enlightenment."

He laughs. "What I'm trying to tell you is that what we had on the field was special because we had each other. It wasn't about being sports stars. Not really. It was about the huddle. The locker room. It was about The Truth Is Out There after a game and listening to Crazy Carl tell us every way we fucked up and laughing our asses off."

I nod, even though he can't see me. But I don't think it matters to him at this point.

"I realized it while I was sitting here with Mom. After a game, I called her. I wanted to share it with her, you know? I wanted her to be proud of me."

"She is. You know that."

"Dude, don't interrupt brilliance. You should be taking notes."

I laugh.

"I've sat here and watched my mom try not to *fucking die* and realized what's important. It's not anything tangible," he says.

"Ooh, big word."

"I know. It's impressive. Dammit, Hollis—don't sidetrack me!"

I can't help but laugh at him again. *God, I miss him.*

"Okay. I'm focusing here." He sighs.

"Nothing in this world matters unless you have someone around to share it with. How fun would winning have been if we didn't have each other? It makes all the hard shit you have to go through okay. We survived Three-A-Days and Hell Week and getting screamed at by Coach. Why? We had each other."

"Yeah …"

"That's what life is about. *It's about people, Hollis*. You, me, and Crew have had the world shoving that in our faces lately and we didn't get it." He takes a breath. "Life has been showing me and Crew that it's about the people in our lives through my mom getting sick and his pops passing away. And you've been focusing on the what's and how's of life and none of it makes any sense to you. *Because it's the wrong focus, man.*"

"That's deep," I say.

"It's the truth. Stop focusing on the Combine and getting your shit together and all that crap. Figure out who you're going to spend your time with and work from that angle. I'm telling you, man. This is where we're wrong. It's why we're struggling."

"Eh, I don't think I'm really struggling," I lie.

He scoffs. "You're struggling more than all of us. Like it or not."

This is why I called River and not Crew. I needed his raw and unedited truth.

But maybe I should've called Crew. He would've used lube.

I look at the sky and wish I could just fly away to an island somewhere by myself.

"I don't have a Vermont like you. There is no Ana. I don't have someone to take care of or a fucking farm that's a family treasure like Hollywood. I have me. And that's not as simple as it seems."

"I lived with you for four years. I'm pretty sure I know that."

I grin. "Then you know that being me is not conducive to attracting people who want to stick around."

"Promise me something," he says.

"Dude, no. What is this? You've been spending way too much time with women."

He laughs. "Trust me on this."

"Will you dedicate your first self-help book to me?"

"I give up." He yawns. "Okay. I gotta get going. Mom was up at like four this morning, and I need to try to take a quick nap before I run her to the doc in a couple of hours."

"Tell her I'm thinking of her."

"I will. Thanks, Hollis."

"Of course."

"Think about what I said," he says.

"Yes, Dr. Phil."

He snorts. "You're an asshole."

"Talk to you later."

"Bye."

I end the call and slip my phone back into my pocket.

If life was fair and things could be good, I'd like to see Larissa's face every day. But I can't do that to her. It *wouldn't* be fair.

I turn around to go to the hotel, but my phone buzzes in my pocket. I stop walking and pull it out, expecting a follow-up text from River.

It's not.

Larissa: Hey! I have a box of Ding Dongs over here and was thinking about getting a pizza. Know anyone who would like to hang out and watch a movie or something?

I walk again, my pace quickening. My fingers fly over the phone.

Me: I could find you someone.

Her response is immediate.

Larissa: I like football players.

Me: Shit. That narrows it down. I'm retired.

Larissa: Well, former players can work. I'm not *that* picky.

I can't help myself. I smile.

Me: Any other requirements?

Larissa: Nice abs.

Me: That definitely narrows down the field.

Larissa: An amazing voice.

Me: Eh, widens the field again.

Larissa: IT DOES NOT.

Me: LOL

Larissa: Fine. I'd prefer a guy who has amazing abs, buys perfect gifts (I haven't taken it off!), and has recent experience fucking me on a rooftop.

Immediately, my cock gets hard, and all thoughts of River's ridiculous theories are pushed to the wayside.

Me: I know a guy. What time should he be there?

Larissa: Around six-ish?

Me: I'll see you then.

Larissa: Oh, so it's you? <winks>

Me: If anyone else meets those requirements, I'd love for them to show up.

Larissa: See you tonight. <heart emoji>

I stare at her final text before pressing the button on the side of my phone.

What can it hurt to spend a little more time with her?

"I don't know," I say as I walk across the street, "but we're about to find out."

SEVENTEEN
LARISSA

I'm weak.

I knock the new box of Ding Dongs over, and they hit the counter with a thud.

"The things I'll do for a set of abs," I mutter to myself.

Even though I know that's not totally true—and it's definitely not even the start of why I texted Hollis earlier today—it's still embarrassing because it's rooted in truth.

I went around and around, trying to convince myself it was okay to invite him over.

He has nowhere else to go.

We're friends.

He's leaving town soon, so I should see him while I can.

He might be hungry.

That last one was the thing that put me over the edge. I could rationalize that.

I would be a bad person if I didn't invite him over, dammit!

I nearly talked myself out of it after talking to Bellamy. Her advice was to invite him over, answer the door naked, and then to ask him if he was hungry.

"I'm just being a good hostess," I affirm. "I'm doing the Lord's work here."

My laughter turns into a groan as I feel myself slipping. I've been fighting it—and doing a damn good job—but I'm a mortal.

Give me a smoking-hot man who has raw edges, a kind heart, and a vulnerability that needs protected, and I'm done. I'm such a sucker.

The doorbell rings, and I all but jog to the door.

"Hey," I say, pulling it open.

My excitement vanishes.

Standing on the other side isn't Hollis.

It's Sebastian.

"What are you doing here?" I ask.

"I came to check on you."

I look at him with total confusion. "For what?"

"I haven't seen you in a while."

"By design."

He looks over my shoulder and into my house. "Can I come in?"

I step outside and pull the door shut behind me. I don't give him the pleasure of a verbal answer.

"Please leave," I tell him.

He looks offended, which is a total joke. Sebastian doesn't get offended because he *doesn't care*. While that might have bothered me at one point, it doesn't now.

I glance down the road.

"You expecting someone?" he asks.

"That's really none of your business."

"I'm just trying to be friendly, Riss."

I roll my eyes so hard it hurts. "You don't do *friendly*, Sebastian. And to be perfectly honest, I wouldn't have answered the door if I had known it was you on the other side."

This bruises his ego. He crosses his arms over his chest.

"I came to ask you if you wanted to go to a New Year's Eve

party with me on Tybee Island," he says smugly. "But if you can't be nice, I won't ask."

What the actual fuck? He has a flipping girlfriend.

"Good. Take Catherine, your actual girlfriend. Now, leave and forget where I live, okay?"

"Larissa …"

He says the words like I'm an errant child, and it drives me nuts. I never realized the tone in which he talked to me until I had something else to compare it to.

Nothing about Sebastian makes me happy. Nothing makes me feel alive or funny or even entertaining—even if it's annoying. Standing on the porch next to a guy I spent way too much time invested in makes me sad for myself.

"Goodbye," I say.

But as I turn to go back inside, an engine rumbles down the street. I don't have to look to see who it is.

His car sounds like him—rough and smooth and a little grumpy when he doesn't get his way.

My eyes find his as he steps out of the driver's side door.

He might not be amused, but he *is* mouthwatering.

His jeans, white T-shirt with a Badgers logo on the front, and a blue-and-white flannel shirt are in stark contrast to Sebastian's brown sweater and loafers.

I take a step away from Sebastian for my own safety. If Sebastian says the wrong thing, I'm not sure how this is going to end.

Hollis flips his gaze to Sebastian as he nears the porch.

"What the fuck are you doing here?" Hollis bites out.

"We're having an adult conversation," Sebastian says.

My mouth hangs open. Sebastian either doesn't read the room, or he wants to die.

Hollis forgoes the stairs and jumps onto the porch in one swift leap. He stands close enough to Sebastian to make me a little concerned.

"Conversation is over," Hollis says. He works his jaw back and forth. "Head on out of here and don't come back."

Sebastian laughs. "I appreciate your opinion. I truly do. But this isn't your house."

"It's mine, asshole, and I've already asked you to leave a couple of times," I cut in.

"We can do this a couple of different ways," Hollis tells him. "You can walk out of here, or I can break your fucking legs, and you can crawl. You pick."

"Are you threatening me?" Sebastian asks.

"Definitely."

Sebastian tries to posture up against Hollis but quickly realizes that's not a good idea. He looks at me with a pitied look.

"This is what you want?" Sebastian looks at Hollis like the gum on the bottom of his shoe. "This piece of fraternity trash?"

I look at Hollis. He's watching me.

There's a doubt in his eyes as though he's not sure what I'm going to say.

In a matter of seconds, my emotions toward this man overwhelm me.

How can he be so alpha protective one moment yet unsure of himself the next?

I reach for his hand, and he gives it to me without hesitation. I pull myself against Hollis and rest my head against his chest. He wraps his arm around my side and holds me tight.

This isn't for show. He's not doing this to piss off Sebastian. His actions are too genuine, too authentic to be anything other than a concern for me.

"Yeah," I tell Sebastian. "This is my guy. He is exactly who I want."

Sebastian blows out a puff of air as he takes the steps hastily to the sidewalk. He's in his car in a flash.

We watch him drive away before we move a muscle.

"You know what's sad?" Hollis says.

I look up at him. "No. What?"

"Someone is gonna crack that motherfucker one of these days, and it's probably not going to get to be me."

I shake my head and extract myself from him. I ignore his cheeky grin as we walk back inside the house.

Garlic and oregano perfume the air as we enter the kitchen. I start toward the stove but am stopped by a large hand twirling me around.

Surprised, I go off-balance, but Hollis catches me in his arms. He's grinning a wide, cheek-splitting smile.

"Did you mean that?" he asks. "Or were you just fucking with him?"

I have no idea what he's talking about. "Huh?"

"Did you mean it? Did you mean it when you told Sebastian that I'm your guy?"

I return his smile. "I honestly just said it. I didn't think about it."

He attempts to bite back his smile, but he fails miserably. Even if he could have hidden it from me, he couldn't deny the shine in his eye.

I don't know what to call it.

Is he proud that I called him that? Does it make him happy? Does he find it ridiculous and think it's a part of the faux-mance we put on for Sebastian the first time?

I don't know.

But what I do know is that I would give anything to see this look on his face more often. *Daily.*

I shiver.

He leans forward and presses a sweet, chaste kiss to my lips. And then he lets me go.

"Hey!" I say, disappointed there wasn't more.

He laughs and swats my behind. "I gave you a little attention, but you distracted me with pizza. I smell it."

"So?"

"So feed me, and then maybe I'll give you a little more."

"*Fine*."

I head to the oven and take out the pizza. I get it cut and on plates while Hollis fumbles through the cabinets looking for glasses. I don't offer to cut in and tell him where they are because I quite like it that he's comfortable enough just to look himself.

"I need to go to the store, so I think our drink options are water and grape juice," I tell him.

"I drink water anyway."

"Really? You don't drink Coke?"

He shakes his head. "Coach had us on a strict diet regimen. It was tailored to each one of us. Pop was something I had to cut so I could keep my Ding Dongs."

I hand him a plate. "I'm glad you kept your Ding Dong."

He snorts and takes the pizza from me. "Why was Sebastian here?"

I shrug as we make our way into the living room. "Who knows? Probably just to screw with me. He likes thinking he has power over people, you know? He shows up here and I remember how much I miss him …" I roll my eyes as we sit on the couch. "His excuse was to invite me to Tybee for New Year's Eve. Can you believe that?"

"Yeah, I can. He's a dick."

"I agree." I start to take a bite of the pizza, but it's too hot. "Do you have any ex-girlfriends like that?"

He leans back on the couch. "Nah. I don't really have girlfriends."

"Really?"

He shrugs.

"May I ask why you don't, or is that going to get me a redirection?" I tease.

He half-smiles as he contemplates my request. I'm surprised he doesn't just redirect me without answering.

Progress.

"The truth?" he asks. "I can't be trusted to take care of another human. I'd be afraid to get a fucking dog."

"But you'd want a dog, right?"

"I'd love a dog. A black lab, actually. But I'd forget to feed it. I forget to feed myself half of the fucking time."

I grin. "You do realize that you'd be dating another human being that can feed herself, right?"

He knocks my knee with his. "You know what I mean."

I do. I know what he means. And I think I know a little more than that.

Pushing him on this is risky, but he's so cooperative and he responded so well—surprisingly well—to being my guy. *So maybe I risk it ...*

"You know what I think?" I ask.

"I think you're going to tell me."

"I think, silly boy, that you have trust issues."

He makes a face like I'm stupid and reaches for his pizza. Steam still rises from it in steady puffs, but he fills his mouth anyway.

"I think," I continue, picking my words carefully, "that you think that you can only trust your friends. I can't remember their names. Sorry."

"River and Crew."

"Yes. Them."

I turn on the couch so I'm facing him. I hesitate, drawing one knee to my chest.

He continues to chew, but he doesn't look away, and I have to wonder if he wants me to press him. *If not, wouldn't he change the subject?*

"I think you sell yourself short," I tell him.

"Oh, really?"

"Really," I say, smiling at him. I think back to what he's said about his mom and Philip and Kim. "I think … I think you think that people always give up on you."

His eyes go wary. "That's a lot of thinking."

"It is, huh?"

Holding my breath, I wait for him to respond. He sets his plate down and grabs his glass of water. He takes an intentionally long drink.

He swallows and sets the glass next to the plate.

"You wanna know what I think?" he asks.

Suddenly, I'm nervous.

"No," I say.

"Ah, the pretty girl doesn't like it when the script is turned on her, does she?" He settles against the couch. "It's not fun, huh?"

I shake my head and wonder where he's going with this. "No, but I respect that you want to get to know me better."

He makes a face. "I already know this. I'm telling you."

"Oh."

He laughs. "I think you pick guys that you think won't work out, so you don't have to settle down."

"What? You're crazy," I say. "You're wrong. *So wrong.*"

He doesn't laugh. He just sits still and watches me.

I squirm under his gaze. "What?"

"Am I wrong?"

"Yes. You're wrong."

He shrugs.

His refusal to elaborate is killing me.

That's not what I do. Not at all.

He's crazy.

"One of us is good at this and that one of us isn't you," I say, picking up my plate.

"Why else would a smart woman like you pick someone like Sebastian? Or me," he adds. "It doesn't make sense. The only thing it can be is that you know both of us are fuck-ups. You'll have an out if you want it. You just have to wait for it."

"*Or*," I say, feeling my cheeks heat, "I pick a certain type of guy and it's not a good match for me. I can't help what I'm attracted to."

He takes my plate out of my hands and sets it on the table.

"I wasn't done," I tell him.

When he faces me again, he's grinning. "Did you just admit you're attracted to me?"

"Well, like that's new news."

He's satisfied. "I really like this you today. I just want to make that clear."

I lean back on the couch and gaze up at him. "I really like the playful you today. Just to be clear."

"We better figure out what put us in such a good mood."

"Oh, I already know what it was," I tease.

He quirks a brow. "You do?"

"Uh-huh. It was all the … *talking*."

His face falls. "I thought it was the sex."

"Close second."

"Damn."

His eyes hood as he takes me in. He stands up and hovers over me.

"There is one thing you could do to make the sex be number one," I tell him.

"What's that?"

"Show me those abs, baby."

He bursts out laughing. Animation sweeps across his face, and it makes me laugh too.

"If you insist …" He shrugs off his flannel.

And then, inch by inch in a Magic Mike-esque move, he peels his T-shirt off in the slowest way possible.

With each inch it rises up his tanned midsection, a new block of muscle is exposed. The lines are defined and appear to have been crafted by the hand of God. The muscles lining his sides are just as clear, and the higher up his shirt goes, the broader his body gets.

My eyes widen, and I let them. I don't even pretend not to be impressed. Downplaying something that was clearly chiseled by an angel seems like a disgrace.

Finally, the shirt comes all the way off, and he throws it at my face.

I giggle. "Wow. That's worth the wait."

He flexes, making me giggle louder.

"Can I touch it?" I ask. "Or, better yet, can I lick it?"

"I have an idea."

"What's that—ah!"

He sweeps me up in his arms in one quick move. I throw an arm around his shoulder to steady myself and nearly melt when my fingertips sweep the edge of his muscled shoulder.

"You can touch me or lick me—whatever you want," he says, carrying me toward my bedroom. "But only if I can lick you first."

I look into his relaxed, playful eyes and grin. "Deal."

EIGHTEEN
HOLLIS

Me: Miss me?

I set my phone on my stomach and grab the remote. I flip through the channels as I wait for Crew or River to respond.

There's a show about a guy hunting for a monster in a river. A lot of shows about cooking, which I could probably get into, but Judy's box of snacks is long gone. The most interesting thing is an old Western movie that has such poor audio that I can't get into it. But I need to get into something because my brain won't stop thinking.

"I think you think that no one would ever stick out the hard times with you. That you'd never be the first pick."

The girl has my number. *How?* I don't know. But it sure feels like she and River are on the same page.

That's scary.

"What is it with everyone on my ass about this right now?" I ask aloud. "And why is no one texting me back?"

I hop to the floor and press out a few push-ups. The movement helps move things through my head.

They're both right in that I think—*that I know*—that people don't stick around when shit gets hard. But they're both wrong in that they think it's something I can fix.

It's a flaw in the system of my life. I didn't design it this way.

When your mom quits on you, there's a deeper problem than what an attitude adjustment can fix.

Would I like for it to be untrue? Abso-fucking-lutely. I wish I was a normal person like River or Crew or Larissa and could just decide, *Yeah, I'm gonna flip this switch and live a normal happy life with people who adore me.* But that just doesn't work in my world.

My phone buzzes, and I scramble to my feet.

Crew: Not yet. <winks> How are you?

Me: Good, actually.

Crew: Wow. Did you pop a little kid's balloon or something?

Me: You know, I've forgotten how NOT funny you really are.

Crew: I'm just kidding. What's going on? Big plans for New Year's Eve?

When I planned on coming here and just hanging out until the Catching-A-Cares banquet, I figured I'd spend the holiday in this room alone. And while that might be true at this moment, it's not going to be true tonight. Larissa gave me no out. She demanded I accompany her to this party, telling me I'd already told Boone I would go—which I believe isn't true.

Oh, well. I would've gone without her bringing Boone into it.

The party at Larissa's aunt's house is apparently a big fucking deal. She was going on and on about it when I left her house this morning. But, hey—at least she wasn't asking me questions for once.

Me: I do, actually. I'm going to a party.

Crew: Good for you, man.

Me: What are you up to?

Crew: Recuperating. Making life choices. The fun stuff.

Me: Ouch.

Crew: Did you make any decisions about things?

Me: No.

I think about leaving in a couple of days.

It's not the leaving part that bothers me. It's what it entails.

I love campus life. I always have. It's like the big family I never had. There's always something going on and someone around to do something with.

Wanna act like a complete idiot? There's a person. Need a workout buddy? No problem. Looking for a guy who has your homework paper done a week early? Someone knows someone —don't panic.

But the thought of going back to campus doesn't sit right in my stomach. I have to do it. When I took the scholarship, I promised Coach that I would graduate with a diploma, and I'll be damned if I don't honor that agreement. Besides, all those classes for four years should get me something.

I'm good with going back. I just wish I wasn't so far away from here.

Which is fucking stupid.

Me: How are you doing about Pops? You okay?

Crew: Yeah. I mean, I'm making it. Talk to River today?

Me: No. You?

Crew: Not yet. I'm going to try to call him later.

Me: Cool.

I glance at the clock.

Me: If I don't talk to you, Happy New Year, Hollywood.

Crew: Back at ya, Hollis.

I lock my screen and get to my feet.

My suitcase is on the other queen-sized bed in my room. I sort through what I brought to figure out what to wear to Larissa's aunt's house. It's mostly a bunch of T-shirts and flannels, but I do spot a black button-up shirt.

I pull it out. It's not too wrinkled, and there's an iron I saw by the door that I could use to fix it up.

I second-guess my choice and look back at my clothes.

Shit.

I reach for my phone and find Larissa's number.

"Hey," she answers immediately. Her voice is bright and cheery. "What's happening, handsome?"

I look at myself in the mirror and laugh.

I'm such a tool.

"Nothing," I say, shaking my head at how stupid I'm acting. "I have a question."

"Finally!"

I snort.

She laughs. "I've been waiting for this moment. Go for it."

"Can I wear jeans to this thing?"

She bursts out laughing. "Clearly, you haven't seen your ass in jeans, or you wouldn't be asking me this question."

Her flattery feels good, which is weird because it's usually unwanted. But, coming from her, it feels like it means something. It feels … honest.

"So that's a yes?" I ask.

"Yes. You can come in anything you want, and it'll be fine. I promise."

I walk to the window.

I haven't seen her since I left her house this morning and I both love and hate the way I feel about it. She had to go help put the finishing touches on the party, which I understand. But I'm bored.

And I miss her.

That does not bode well for me, I know.

But instead of focusing on that, I'm trying to roll with it. Enjoy it. *Enjoy her.*

"Did everything go okay today at your aunt's?" I ask.

"I just got home to get ready."

"Should it take you long?"

"No. I picked everything out this morning after you left."

I grin. "What do you have to do? Shower and get dressed?"

The thought of her naked and wet sets my blood aflame. I adjust my cock, groaning at the contact.

"Yeah. It shouldn't take me long," she says.

I glance at the clock again and do some quick math.

"What time do you have to be there?" I ask her.

"Let's see, it's six now," she says. "Everyone will show up around eight or eight thirty, I bet. As long as I'm there by nine, it'll be fine. What time are you planning on coming?"

I grab jeans, shirt, and keys and head for the door. "Right now."

"Already?"

"Look," I say, opening the hotel room door and walking into the hallway, "if you're planning on being in the shower and I'm just here by myself—"

"I'll go unlock the door."

I laugh. "That's my girl."

And I might just mean that. Maybe.

NINETEEN
HOLLIS

"I hate wet hair," Larissa says as she climbs into bed next to me.

I slide an arm under her and pull her into my body. She curls up next to me and smiles against my chest.

"Wet anything on you is good, beautiful," I tell her.

She hums against me as her eyes flutter closed.

I settle back into her pillows and close my eyes too.

I could get used to this.

The words rattle through my brain.

My eyes open, and I feel the burst of energy that always comes when I get too comfortable in a situation. I learned in a football lecture once that the shock of energy is my Fight or Flight instinct. It happens when you feel like your life might be in danger.

I catch my breath before it gets out of control and settle myself.

You are fine. You are good.

I look down at Riss.

You are more than good.

I run my fingers through her hair. She's so attractive. But the thing I see when I look at her isn't her beauty at first. It's the aura around her, the genuineness that exudes out of her pores. It's her bright smile and the way she reaches for me like she wants to be as close as she can to me.

Like now.

A warmth spreads through my body, and I pull her closer.

This whole thing blindsided me. When I came here, I expected to spend my days sitting on the beach or checking out the tourist traps. Never in a million years did I expect to be lying in a woman's bed.

And acknowledging that I don't want to leave.

I sigh, closing my eyes and trying to slow myself down.

This thing between us happened so fast—like a tornado in the summer.

Could this thing actually work out between us?

I want to laugh at myself—at the possibility that Larissa Mason would want anything to do with me for an extended time. Why would she?

But the way she feels in my arms and the way she looks at me gives me a little … hope.

I don't even know if it's safe to hope. Every time I've wished for something, it bit me in the ass. The last time I almost believed that things were going to work out, I watched Philip and Kim's car pull down the street without me.

Maybe this could be different? Maybe my luck has somehow changed? Perhaps I'm not the same person I was, and my past won't follow me now.

"What are you thinking about?" she whispers sleepily.

It's like she can read my mind.

"That shower sex is the best sex with you. Not that I don't love it all," I tell her. "But I *really* loved it in there."

She grins. "I liked the rooftop sex."

"Did you now?"

"Yeah. There's something about the first time that's special."

I open my mouth to tell her that I can see her point when I

realize—she might have first times with other men at some point. If I leave and this doesn't work out, then she definitely will.

I want to climb out of my skin at the thought. The sensation of needing to move sweeps over me again but, this time, I oblige it.

Rolling her over onto her back—ignoring her protest—I position myself so that I'm hovering over her.

She looks up at me like I'm some kind of saint.

Sweet, confused girl.

I smile. "How about we try out after-shower sex and see where it ranks?"

Her knees fall to the side as she raises her hips. "Good idea."

I start to move towards her but stop.

"I don't have a condom," I say. "Shit."

She nibbles her bottom lip. "I'm on the pill. Actually, I have the shot and it's good for a very long time."

"I'm clean. I have physicals constantly, and I always use protection." I swallow hard. "Like, always. This kind of freaks me out."

"Then don't do it."

I look into her eyes and feel something stir inside me. It's not a need to get off or to prove my prowess.

I just want to be close to her.

"You okay with it?" I ask her.

She grins shyly. "Yes."

Instead of sinking into her, I kiss her. It takes her by surprise. Hell, it does me too.

She grips the sides of my face and kisses me gently. Her lips work on mine, telling them a story that I can't quite make out.

I slip my cock between her legs and press into her soft body. She moans into my mouth.

Her hands slip down my chest, around my sides, and to my back. Her hips rock as she pushes on me to go harder.

I'm all for going hard. I love it hard with her. I can't get enough of feeling Larissa want *me* like that.

But there's something about this moment that makes me want something different.

Something probably insane.

Something I've never wanted before.

"Hey," I say, breaking our kiss.

She looks up at me.

"Can we take this one slow?" I ask her, a little unsure of what I mean.

Her features soften, and her smile stretches across her face. "Yeah."

She locks her legs around my ass and pulls my face to hers again.

We kiss more than we fuck. We touch more than we come. We laugh and tickle and take our time.

I'm not sure what to call this, but it isn't fucking. It isn't sex. But it is the best.

Because it's with her.

TWENTY
HOLLIS

"Who is going to be here again?" I ask.

Larissa looks at me from the passenger's seat. She has the mirror pulled down from the visor and a tube of lipstick in her hand.

"Everyone," she answers.

I hold a hand out and look at her like she's crazy. "What the hell does that mean?"

"It means," she says, running the tube around her lips, "that everyone I know will be here. Okay. Maybe not *everyone*." She smacks her lips together and folds the mirror back up. "But most of them."

I lean back in my seat and try to rationalize how many people that might be. It might be a few hundred if everyone brings someone and you count the stragglers sneaking in for free beer on campus.

"Give me a quick rundown," I tell her.

She shoves her lipstick in her purse and settles back in her seat. "Okay. Well, Aunt Siggy and Uncle Rodney. My dad. Siggy and Rodney's kids—Holt, Oliver, Wade, Coy, and Boone."

"Holy shit, that's a lot of kids."

"It's just five."

I balk. "That's a lot of kids, Riss."

She smiles at me. "How many kids do you want?"

"Zero."

"Hollis!"

"What?" I ask, leaning away from her. "They seem like a pain in the ass."

Kids have never been on my radar. I stay fully-wrapped up during sex and have walked out of situations that seem sketchy. A sketchy chick cannot be hot enough to risk getting pregnant.

I do not want kids.

But I can see Larissa as a mother and that fucks with me a little bit on a level I don't want to indulge at the moment.

"Well, I want like six," she says, staring ahead.

She says it very matter-of-factly, but a hint of something in her voice has me reaching across the console and grabbing her thigh. I squeeze gently, applying just enough pressure that has her smacking my hand.

She doesn't push it away. But she doesn't look at me either.

"Tell me about your cousins," I say to keep her interacting with me. "Do I need to watch out for any of them?"

A grin ghosts her lips. "Holt and Oliver run a real estate investment company. Holt is my buddy. He's the one I go to when I need help convincing my parents of something. Oliver is … Oliver." She laughs. "He's more of a jokester but still super smart. He's a good mix of them all, I think."

That all sounds doable.

"Wade is serious. He's an architect. He just works … and that's it. He has no life. Boone is the wild one. You met him."

I nod.

"He's my best friend, besides Bellamy. It used to be me, Bells, Boone, and Coy, but then …" She holds her hands out. "Whatever. I don't know. But I'm close with Boone. Coy is off touring the world most of the time now so we don't see him as much. I'm excited he'll be here tonight, though. He flew in just for the night."

I furrow my brow. "Is he military or something?"

She bursts out laughing.

"I … Is something funny?" I ask.

"*Hollis*." She says my name as a complete sentence. "Coy is Kelvin McCoy."

I snap my face to her. "The country music guy?"

She nods with a look of amusement on her face.

"Wait. Your cousin is Kelvin McCoy. No shit?"

"No shit."

What the actual fuck?

I withdraw my hand from her leg and follow my GPS's instructions to turn right. Up ahead, the road is lined with cars on both sides.

"Mason family hack," she says, sitting up in her seat. "Pull up to the driveway. It'll be blocked off, but we'll tell the guy it's me, and he'll let me through."

"Nice."

I do as instructed. A man stops us on the road. A rather large man with a suit on leans into the car.

"Hey, Nate!" she says. "Can we get through, please?"

"Hey, Larissa. Sure thing."

He steps back from the car, and we're allowed to proceed up a driveway made to look like cobblestones.

"That guy looks like he could throw down."

She winces. "I bet he can. He owns a bar called The Gold Room. I think being able to hold your own kind of goes with the territory."

We proceed up the tree-lined drive. The house in front of us is even more impressive than the Landry's. It appears to be three stories, all brick, with a manicured lawn that's lit up by little hanging lanterns in the trees.

It looks like a movie set. There are no two ways about it.

"This is pretty, huh?" she asks.

"Pretty *fucking incredible*. Holy shit, Riss."

She grins. "This is my favorite place in the world."

"I thought it was with me," I say as I park my car behind a Range Rover.

"You're totally a close second."

I shake my head, knowing she's full of shit.

She doesn't wait for me to open her door, but she's so excited to get inside that I can't blame her. She reminds me of how I feel on the first day of football practice. I can't deny her that kind of joy.

An arch has been erected out of golden-colored lights. Larissa takes my hand as we approach it.

"They don't spare any expenses, do they?" I crack.

"No. This is my aunt's claim to fame."

We walk through the lights to see what appears to be icicles dripping from the top. It's incredible, and I wish I had this kind of money lying around to put to my claim to fame.

Not that I know what that would even be. But still.

We enter through an oversized wooden door, and it's party chaos in the most sophisticated way. There's music playing through speakers hidden from view. Balloons in golds and silvers coat the ceiling with little ribbon pieces extending down and floating just a few feet overhead. The house is crowded with people wearing everything from suits and dresses like Jack's event to jeans and T-shirts.

"What do you think?" Larissa asks.

"It's … something."

"Come on. Let's find my family."

I suck in a breath and allow her to lead me through the throngs of people. We're stopped every few steps, and I'm introduced to someone new. It's not until I hear someone yell Larissa's name that I put a face with a name.

Kelvin McCoy, the guy I listen to all the time while I'm

going over the playbook, stands in front of me with his arms wrapped around my girl. He holds a cup of beer in one hand and grins at me over Larissa's head.

"Hey," he says to me. "You must be the famous Hollis Hudson."

Larissa ducks out from under his arms.

"Hollis, this is my cousin Coy. Coy, this is Hollis."

Coy shakes my hand and pulls me into a man-hug.

"It's nice to meet you," he says. "I've heard a lot about you."

"Really?"

"Yeah. Boone keeps me pretty up-to-date on the family. And Mom told me that Riss was pretty crazy over some dude—ouch!" he says as Larissa sticks an elbow in his side. "I probably shouldn't have said that," he jokes.

"You think?" Larissa threatens to elbow him again. "Behave. Please."

Coy smirks. "If I behave, can we go get Bells?"

Larissa rolls her eyes. "No. Leave her alone."

"She isn't coming?" I ask.

Larissa levels her gaze to me. "When she said she wouldn't come if Coy was home, she meant it."

I look at Coy. He's flashing me a shit-eating grin.

"All right. I gotta go say hi to some more people. Only home for about eighteen hours, so I gotta make the best of it," Coy says.

"It was nice to meet you," I say.

"You, too. I'll catch up with you guys before you leave." He runs his hand on top of Larissa's head, much to her dismay. "See ya, Riss."

I open my mouth to comment on just meeting a rock star when another man comes up to Larissa's side and plants a kiss on the top of her head.

What the hell? I open my mouth to make some shit clear when the man laughs.

"How are you, baby girl?" he asks.

Larissa laughs at whatever my face does. "Hollis, please meet my father, Howard."

I make a face like I just made a mistake. Howard laughs right along with me.

"How are you?" he asks, shaking my hand.

"Good, except I think I just made an ass out of myself."

He smiles widely. "Hell, no. I like it. It shows you know how special this little girl is."

Larissa beams. I think my cheeks turn red.

"I hear you play football," he says.

"Yeah," I say, trying to move past my fuckup. "Tight end."

"I was a linebacker through my sophomore year at Kent State. Found out I had spinal stenosis, and that ended my football career," he says. "But, hell—I did just fine in life without football. There could be a worse ending to this story."

I nod. "That's true. Absolutely."

"If I would've known you were coming, I would've looked you up. I feel a little rude not knowing your stats."

I laugh. "Trust me—this was a shit year. I'm happy you haven't seen them."

"We all have those years." He takes a drink of his beer. "What brings you to Savannah?"

Larissa steps into our line of sight. She grins at me. She looks … *proud.*

Of me.

"Hollis won an award for Lincoln Landry's charity," she says, standing tall. "Isn't that amazing?"

Howard looks at me with a raised brow. "Is that right?"

"It's no big deal," I tell him, trying to gloss over the whole thing. "I—"

"The hell it isn't," Howard says, cutting me off. "I know those Landry boys, and they don't do anything half-assed. If they say you're deserving of something, then you are. What's it for?"

I bite my bottom lip and wish I could just disappear. I don't want this kind of attention. It feels as though it cheapens it—as though it cheapens *me*.

"It's just for some volunteer work. It's not a big deal. Honest," I say, reaching for Larissa.

It's an automatic reaction. Before I can catch myself, she stands next to me and wraps her arm around my waist. Instantly, my nerves calm. I think Howard notices.

He grins. "I'm gonna tell you what—I don't know where my daughter found you, but she needs to spend more time there, and away from those rats my ex-wife hooks her up with."

"Daddy!"

Howard blows out a breath. "It's the truth, Larissa. I love you, and I know your mother is doing what she thinks is best, but she's out of her damn mind if she thinks you should be with a guy like Sebastian Townsend."

"Your daughter should definitely listen to her dad," I tell him, gripping Larissa's waist.

Howard looks amused. "You've met him, I assume?"

"I about knocked his head off yesterday."

His laugh is loud and boisterous, and now I know where Larissa gets that from. He's incredibly genuine, which shouldn't surprise me.

"I mean, I don't know Sebastian that well," I say, "but he has no business being around her." I nod my head to Larissa. "He is not a good guy."

"He's a bastard. That's what he is, and I couldn't be happier that she's not with him anymore." Howard takes a drink. "I like you. You're the first one I've liked in a long time."

Larissa laughs. "Who else did you like?"

He thinks. "You're right. Hollis is the first."

His compliment feels good. He's complimenting me—not my route or the way I caught a pass or my smile. I can't wipe the smile off my face.

"I'm going to get another drink," he says, resting his hand on my shoulder as he walks by. "Nice to meet you, Hollis. Hope to see you around."

"Likewise, sir," I say.

As soon as he's out of earshot, Larissa spins around to face me.

"Oh, my gosh," she gushes. "You just charmed my dad!"

"So?"

"So? So that's … *impossible*."

I look at him over my shoulder. He stands next to a man who heavily resembles him and I'm guessing that's her uncle Rodney.

"It wasn't that hard," I say, turning back around. "Really."

Her face is lit up like the icicle lights dripping from everything nailed down.

"Let's go find my aunt Siggy." She reaches up and runs her hand through her hair.

I can't help but notice the bracelet I bought her on her wrist. That feels just as good as Howard's niceties.

"Let's go find her," I say.

TWENTY-ONE
LARISSA

"Where are you going?" Boone asks. "Fifteen minutes until the ball drops."

He points at a big projection screen hung in the dining room where the news is covering Times Square.

It's a tradition in the Mason family to all watch the ball drop together. It's something you just can't miss. And I don't want to miss it except I can't find my man.

"Have you seen Hollis?" I ask him. "I haven't seen him in a half hour or so."

Boone smiles. "The last time I saw him, he was sitting at the piano upstairs with Coy."

"Really?"

He nods.

I make my way to the stairs. After avoiding a spilled drink, I finally make it to the top. Despite the music playing overhead, I can hear the faint notes of a piano coming from the library.

I pad down the hallway and peek around the corner. And, just as Boone said, Coy and Hollis sit at Siggy's baby grand piano.

"What about this?" Coy says. He presses the keys in quick succession and sings a refrain that isn't quite finished.

"Hey," I say once he stops playing. "It's almost ball drop time."

Hollis's eyes find mine. They're so alert and … *happy.*

My heart fills, and I give him a smile. When it's returned, I want to run to him and wrap myself around him.

"Your boy here has a great ear," Coy says. "I've been fucking around with this melody for a month now, and Hollis just sat down and fixed it up in ten minutes." He looks at Hollis. "What the fuck, man?"

Hollis shrugs it off like he does everything.

I march across the room and rest my arms over his shoulders. "He's pretty great," I say, setting my chin on top of his head.

Coy nods his head in agreement. "I'm gonna go get a beer and find my mom. She'll have my ass if I come home and don't watch the ball with her." He gets to his feet. "I'm not joking, Hollis—we need to have a writing session soon."

"Yeah. Anytime," he says as if he's in disbelief.

Coy flashes me a smile before he disappears around the corner.

"So," I say, sitting next to him on the piano bench. "Sounds like you've had a productive night."

He laughs, running a hand down his face. "I can't believe I just helped Kelvin McCoy write a song. I mean, we didn't finish it, but he actually took my fucking suggestions."

"Because you're talented."

He snorts. "I think he must be drunk."

"Hollis," I say. "Stop. You never give yourself any credit."

"It's just … hard to believe."

"Why? Why is it any harder to believe that you could help Coy than some random dude in Los Angeles?"

He watches me carefully, the shine of the moment still there. "Because I'm me. I don't know what I'm doing, Riss. I just gave him my opinion."

"So it comes more naturally to you. It's awesome. Another

hidden talent you can use for the next ambush question-and-answer session," I joke.

He laughs, pulling me into his side. He kisses the top of my head.

"I like this with you," he says softly. "Do you think that's okay?"

"I think that's very okay. That makes me happy."

He kisses my head again. This time, I feel his smile pressed against it too.

"You know that it's okay to have hope, right?" I ask him. "It's okay to want to have things … and people … in your life."

I say it gently because I don't want to startle him and make him retreat behind his shield. This vulnerable side of him—or the fact that he's allowing himself to show it—is new. And I don't think he's quite sure how to manage it.

"That's what River told me," he says softly.

"I think I like River."

"You would. He's a good guy. He'd give you the shirt off his back."

I giggle. "I'd much rather have the shirt off yours if I get to see those abs again."

He snorts and shakes his head. "What am I going to do with you?"

"I have suggestions."

He takes my hand and gets to his feet. I stand too.

I look up into his face. Instead of seeing a wall that's keeping me out, I think I get a glimpse behind the curtain. His features are a little softer and his gaze not quite as severe. His touch is a little sweeter as he runs a hand down my cheek.

My breathing gets shallow as I try to remember not to hold it in.

"Things feel different when I'm with you," he whispers. "It's the craziest shit ever."

"I'm glad."

I nod, giving him a smile. I know this is hard for him to admit and I need to let him work this out on his own.

Because I've already worked it out. He came into my life like a whirlwind and flipped every script I had.

When I look into his eyes, I can see … a future. Together. The kind of life that Siggy and Rodney have.

There would be a lot to figure out. I know that. But I want to figure it out. There's time to do that.

If only he wants to, too.

I force a swallow. "Do you feel it too?"

"I don't know what I feel, beautiful. I know that being around you makes me want to get up in the morning. It makes everything funnier and more enjoyable." He strokes my cheek with his thumb. "I know I look forward to seeing you. *Naked*."

I laugh softly.

He grins too. "I don't know … Maybe there's something to be said for new years and new beginnings, right? Maybe?"

"Maybe."

My heart swells in my chest. The room completely stills and all the sounds from below fade away. I just take in this guy that's standing here with me and hope against all hope that it is a new beginning. For both of us. *Together*.

"Riss …" he says.

But before he can finish, Boone blasts my name from downstairs.

"Riss! Get down here!" he yells.

Hollis grins. He bends down and kisses me softly. I try to deepen it, but he pulls back and chuckles.

"Later, naughty girl. We have to get down there for the ball drop. I can't fuck it all up now."

I groan as he leads me to the staircase and down it.

We gather with my family in the dining room. The room is packed with bodies and air horns and confetti primed to be tossed. We tuck ourselves in a corner next to a giant aloe vera plant.

Hollis stands behind me with his arms over my shoulders. The ball begins to drop down the pole and everyone starts to cheer.

The room fills with shouts and premature horns and I take a moment to breathe.

"Hey," Hollis whispers in my ear.

I look up at him.

He smiles the sweetest, softest smile I've ever seen and it melts my heart.

The room bursts into the countdown.

5!

4!

3!

2!

1!

"Auld Lang Syne" plays over the entertainment system as everyone toots horns and shakes noisemakers.

Hollis grabs my face in his hands and kisses me.

It starts soft and sweet but gets deeper and harder as the seconds sweep by. My knees go weak from the taste of his mouth—cake mixed with beer mixed with *Hollis*—and the happiness at having him here.

And having him happy.

He pulls back, panting, and laughs. "Happy New Year, baby."

I bite my lip and try not to show him how affected I am by him. "Happy New Year, Hollis."

Colored confetti falls onto our heads and Hollis wipes a piece off of my eyelashes. "You are something, you know that?"

"I've heard that before."

He laughs as Boone walks by shouting, "Happy New Year!"

Hollis starts to say something else when my aunt Siggy's traditional first song of the year starts to play. The harps and flutes float happily through the entire house and probably the yard because Aunt Siggy lives and dies by setting the year with this anthem.

"Want to get some champagne?" I ask.

His eyes dart around the room. I look to see what he's looking at, but nothing looks amiss.

"The food will be changing to breakfast-y stuff soon, so if you want any more pizza, we should grab … it now …" My voice trails off. "Hollis?"

His shoulders are stiff, his eyes a muddied mix of expressions.

"What song is this?" he asks, gripping the back of his neck with his hand. "I can barely hear it."

"Oh this?" I laugh. "This is Aunt Siggy's New Year's theme song. She says it's to remind everyone of their dreams and to wish on stars and … all that jazz. It's the creative in her."

He nods and looks around, clearly uneasy.

"Hey," I say, touching his shoulder. "Are you okay?"

He nods again. It's accompanied by a forced swallow. "I need to get some air. Okay?"

"Yeah," I stammer, confused. "Want me to come with you?"

"No. I'll be back."

He all but storms out of the dining room and disappears in the mix.

My back hits the wall as I try to figure out what in the hell just happened.

Siggy comes up to me. Her smile slides off her face as she takes me in.

"Hey, Riss. You okay?"

"I think so?" It comes out more like a question than an answer, but it's the best that I can give her. "Something just happened with Hollis, and I don't know what it was."

She looks around. "Where'd he go?"

I shrug.

"Give him a few minutes. Holidays can be a roller coaster for some people." She kisses my cheek. "Happy New Year, my favorite niece."

"Happy New Year, Aunt Siggy."

She tosses me a wink and moves to a circle of her friends.

I stand in place with the knot that's twisting so tight in my stomach that it pains me to breathe. Something is wrong. I know it.

Tears prickle the corners of my eyes as I replay the emotion in his from just a few minutes ago. *Was it fear? Anger? Sadness?* I don't know.

And that kills me.

I slip through the house, looking for him. I avoid every set of eyes and every attempt at conversation. Once I'm sure he's not inside, I walk to the front porch.

The lawn is dark unless you're under the twinkling lights, so if he's out there, I'll never find him.

I venture down the tunnel. When I come to the other end, I see him sitting inside his car.

The engine is off, and the heat from his breath has fogged up the windows a little bit. His head hangs, and I wonder if he's texting someone or just dozing off.

He doesn't look up as I walk toward him. He doesn't look up at all until I lift my door handle. His head jerks up, and he looks surprised to see me.

"Hey," I say, climbing inside. The air is cold, and I shiver. "Are you okay?"

The happiness in his eyes from earlier is gone. It's replaced with a heavy dose of dark and hard and desolate.

I don't know how he carries all of that around.

My heart breaks for the beautiful man in front of me.

"I'm not feeling great. I think that shrimp didn't sit well with me," he says. "I can leave my car here, and I'll call an Uber."

"What?"

"I want to go, but I know that you—"

"Hey." I touch him on his arm. His gaze falls to my hand. "If you're leaving, I'm leaving."

"You don't have to do that."

I smile softly. "I know. But we came together, and we leave together. Besides," I say, trying to make him laugh, "having you in the car to myself is my favorite time to interrogate you."

He almost grins. "You're a pain in the ass."

"I know." I wink at him. "Let's go."

I reach back and grab my seat belt.

"Don't you need to go in and tell them goodbye?" He looks toward the house. "They'll miss you."

"They can text me." I lean across the console and press a kiss on his cheek. "Now get this car started because I'm freezing."

Relief washes across his face, and he starts the car. We head home in silence. I don't think I'll be seeing the light in his eyes anytime soon. Something just switched off.

But what?

TWENTY-TWO
HOLLIS

I should've stayed with her.

I sit in the chair in the corner of my hotel room, still dressed in the clothes I wore to Siggy's house. I don't think I've moved a muscle.

The sun came up a few hours ago. Even the sunrise was disappointing. It's like it was prepping me that the new year will suck and not to get my hopes up.

Not to be wishing on any fucking stars.

I wipe my hand down my face.

For a moment, I almost bought into it. There was a period of time last night when things felt different. Like maybe River and Larissa were right, and a guy like me could manage to have people in his life and create something that rose from the bullshit and … wasn't terrible.

That was my mistake.

"Thanks for the reminder, Mom," I spit out as I press down on my right shoulder until it pops back into place. "Thanks for reminding me of who I am before I pull someone else into our curse."

The feelings inside me that the stupid song rustled up are

ones I've avoided nearly my entire life. But now they're here, on the surface, and they're fucking with me at a time in my life when things were finally starting to turn around.

Or I convinced myself they were.

It just goes to show that maybe they aren't supposed to turn around for me.

All of that nonsense River was saying is a bunch of hocus-pocus, something some quack doctor spewed into an audiobook to get rich. It's not real.

I put my head in my hands. My temples throb.

You did a really good job at faking your relationship with her. That's why she bought into it. She told you herself that she always falls for the wrong guys. You are her type—the type that doesn't work out.

My breath is shaky.

It wouldn't have lasted anyway.

How could it?

You had to save her from her own undoing.

I force a swallow.

Her perfume is still on my shirt. It's the only reason I haven't taken it off. Every time I've started to, my heart lodges in my throat, and my hands fall to my sides.

If I have to give myself a break somewhere, it's going to be here. The scent will fade away at some point, so I might as well soak it in while it still exists.

I groan, bending forward and putting my head in my hands.

It was such a dick move to take her home and then go back to my hotel this morning. She didn't expect it. She didn't like it. But, to her credit, she didn't make a big deal out of it.

She hasn't called or texted. But I wouldn't have either if I were her.

Suddenly, I have to move. I have to go. I have to do.

I jump to my feet and head for the door.

The elevator is slow as I wait for it and even slower as it

takes me to the ground floor. The lobby is relatively empty as I stride across it.

The air is warmer than I expect. I don't give it too much thought.

I just walk.

I don't know where I'm going. I just know I can't sit in that room anymore.

My feet march down the sidewalk. I try to numb my mind by humming a song, but it ends up being the one that I helped Coy with last night, and that doesn't help.

It makes things worse. I hate being fucking alone, but I need it. I need to be by myself.

But then I find myself in front of Judy's pink sign … that says she's closed. I peer inside to see her putting those little jars of honey on a shelf.

Relief washes over me at the sight of her and I peck against the glass—*rap! rap! rap!*—until she turns around. Her face lights up when she sees me.

She hustles as much as an old woman can hustle toward the door. With a quick snap, it's unlocked.

"Well, how'd I get so lucky to see you on New Year's Day?" she asks, kissing my cheek.

I grin. "I was hoping you had more of those apple fritters you put in my box."

"You know I do. Come on, boy, and tell me what's on your mind."

I follow her toward the back of the building. "Who said anything was on my mind?"

"Am I wrong then?"

I slump into the same booth I occupied the last time I was here. "Well, no."

"Okay, then. Spill."

She carries a plate and a mug to the table. Two apple fritters and a steaming cup of coffee are placed in front of me. Then she slides into the opposite seat.

I don't really want the fritters. As a matter of fact, the thought of eating them makes me want to vomit. I nibble at one not to be rude.

"Is this about your girlfriend?" she asks.

I consider the question. "No. It's about me, I think."

She lays her hands on the table with her palms up. Her skin is wrinkly and worn from a life of obvious hard work.

"Well, let's figure it out," she says. "What's going on?"

I blow out a breath.

I don't even know what to tell her or where to start.

Things got complicated so fast. *How did that happen?*

"Hollis?"

"I had to walk away from a girl I really like if I'm being honest."

Admitting it out loud feels like a weight is off my shoulders. But it's also accompanied by a pain, *a loneliness* that's deeper and darker than anything I've ever felt in my life.

"You don't seem too happy about it," she says gently.

I shrug. "Sometimes you have to do what you gotta do."

"That's what they say." She leans forward. "You know what I say?"

"What?"

"I say that's what people say who don't want to really think about it."

I chuckle sadly. "You'd be right. I don't want to think about it."

I sit back in my chair to put a little distance between us. I need space. Air.

Advice.

Because I don't know if I can live like this without some help.

I avoid getting close to people so this doesn't happen. It's not like I don't know the pain of losing someone you think might care about you. And even though this is different—that I'm the one walking away—it was necessary.

Hearing that song reminded me of what, and who, I am. I've been a chameleon my whole life. I've had to be to survive. But being surrounded by a family like the Masons with a woman like Larissa in my arms? I wasn't supposed to be there. I could only keep up that charade for so long.

Eventually, they'd see me for who I am. A guy with nothing to offer, with no plans or an idea of where to even start. They'd get tired of dealing with me, of having to make excuses for me, and it would hurt a hell of a lot worse for them to walk away from me than for me to do it.

I'm saving us all trouble, really.

Even if it's the most painful thing I've ever done.

"What happened?" Judy asks.

"You should see her life," I tell her. "It's fucking incredible. She has money, and fancy shit, and her cousin is famous. They're the kind of people who probably have bonfires and sit around singing 'Kumbayah.'"

"What's her name, sweet boy?"

"Larissa Mason."

"Mm-hmm."

I let the back of my head hit the booth.

"So, what's the problem? I'm not seeing it," she says.

"Because you don't know me well enough to see it either. Look, Grandma Judy," I say, shaking my head, "I don't belong in this world down here."

"Where do you belong then?"

I shrug. "I don't know."

She reaches across the table and pats my hand. There's a sadness in her eyes for me.

"It would be really easy for me to sit here and tell you to have faith in yourself and her," Judy says. "And that's the truth. You should. But you aren't gonna listen to that, are you?"

My foot taps against the floor as my eyes sting. That fucking song about the stars plays over and over in my head. I can't escape it. It just becomes too much.

"Faith is lies," I say. "What am I supposed to do? Have faith that Larissa sees me differently than I am. When push comes to shove, I'm me and I can't get around that."

"Maybe she doesn't see you like you see yourself. Maybe she sees you like I do."

I appreciate her smile, but it makes me sadder.

"Do you know how hard it is to know that no one wants you?" I ask her.

Her eyes go wide, but she doesn't say anything.

"I'm sure you don't because you're a great person. But I'm going to tell you that I'm not like that. I'm not the guy that people keep around. And that's cool. I've accepted it about myself. But that doesn't mean it doesn't hurt like a motherfucker."

"Oh, honey."

My chest burns as I spew my truth, something I've never done out loud before. It's freeing and cathartic and, before I know it, my mouth is running again.

"I don't want to go through that again," I say, more animated this time. "It hurts so fucking bad, and you just gotta keep going. You have to get up the next morning and go to class or to work or whatever it is and know the whole time that you're just out there by yourself. You wonder if everyone is looking at you—like can they see the stain on your soul?"

"Hollis, stop that."

"Why? It's true." My jaw clenches. "I'm like a pet that is left on the side of the road when the family moves, Judy. And that's fine. But it's a whole hell of a lot easier to just stay alone than to watch that car drive off."

"So, we're moving, Hollis. I got a job offer in Detroit. Kim

will make some calls, but it's probably not legal to take you with us, and you'll be eighteen soon enough anyway ..."

My eyes burn with a mixture of anger and pain, but I hide it from the only lady who's ever accepted me.

"I can't imagine what it would feel like to watch Riss leave me," I say, my voice wobbly. "I'm sure I wouldn't survive it."

"Hollis, honey, listen to your grandma," she says. "Every door that has closed on you wasn't your door. The good Lord isn't going to let you walk into a room that's not the room for you."

I wipe my face with the back of my hand.

"Think about it," she says. "If all of those people tucked you up under their arm and took you with them, would you be here and falling in love with Larissa?"

"No, but ... I ..."

In love with Larissa.

Panic streaks through me as I shake my head. "No, Judy. No, no, no. It's not like that."

"I think it might be."

"You're wrong this time."

She shrugs. "Maybe. I'm human. But I know for a fact with my hand up that you are right where you're supposed to be. You just don't want to accept it."

"Because it's not true."

She pats my hand again. "Sweetie, it's okay to be scared. Especially if people have given you little reason to have hope in humanity. But those aren't your people. God had to push them away so you could make it down here to your grandma Judy and Miss Larissa. Let us love you through this. Don't push us all away."

I wish. I wish so badly that she was right, and that this is where I belong. That I could come in here and have breakfast with Grandma Judy on the weekends and bring Larissa with me to meet her.

That I didn't have to push them all away.

But all of that is a fantasy, a dream that won't come true. Dreams don't.

No matter how many stars I wish on.

Because I've tried that too. All that's out there are dark skies.

TWENTY-THREE
LARISSA

Patience is not my forte.

I dump my oatmeal down the garbage disposal.

I glance at my phone for the millionth time since Hollis dropped me off almost twelve hours ago.

What happened?

My emotions have gone through the wringer since he kissed me like his life depended on it and then waited for me to lock the door.

He left in a flash. And unlike the last time I felt like our goodbye was incomplete—he didn't come back.

I sink against the counter.

My heart is bruised because I wanted to spend the first night of the year with him. I wanted him to have fun. I'd hoped we could start the year off in an amazing way with karaoke with Coy and the water gun fights that always happen before dawn.

He didn't get to experience all those things, and I think he'd really have liked them.

But even more than that—my nerves are frayed.

He closed off more dramatically than the last time I saw him shut down. *I hate it.* I don't think it was me. I hope it wasn't. But

I don't know what set him off, and most of all, I'm terrified he won't let me back in.

My throat constricts, my saliva hot as I try to stay calm. And look at my phone again.

The longer I stare at the screen, the more worried I get. The panic feeds off my fear and my desperate need to contact him.

I can't take it anymore. I have to do something.

With my phone in my hand feeling like a brick, I press Bellamy's number.

"How are you even awake?" she says with a laugh. "You all didn't wrap up that party until well after dawn."

"Not me. I was home before one."

I hear her blankets moving around in the background. "Why? What happened?"

"Bells …" I force the lump that appeared out of nowhere away. "I don't know what happened."

"Starting from the beginning is usually a solid idea."

I ignore her sarcasm. "Things were just …" I remember him sitting with Coy and how he chatted my dad up like they were buddies. The ease in the way he walked and how the little lines between his eyes vanished. "Things were great. Really great. And then they weren't. I don't know why. He just said he didn't feel well and wanted to go. He dropped me off around one this morning, and … here we are."

"Well, I'm going to need a little more to help you. Want me to come over?"

I shake my head. "No. Please don't. I just need to figure this out." I press my fingertips to my temple.

"Where is Hollis?"

"I don't know, honestly. His hotel room, I guess. I hope."

"You haven't heard from him at all?"

"No. He's … complicated. If you push him too much, he shuts down. Well, he usually ends up entertaining me and playing along, but last night was different, Bells."

"So you thought he needed some space?"

"Yeah," I say through the burn in my throat.

She sighs. "Well, it's almost noon, so I think you've accomplished your mission."

"Yeah," I say again because that's all I have.

Silence descends between us.

The cabinet bites into my behind. I press off it and pace around the kitchen.

"Are you waiting on me to tell you what to do?" she asks.

"You do every other time in my life, so …"

She laughs. "Sitting at home and stewing about it isn't going to do you any good. It's not going to help him either."

"But what if he doesn't want to talk to me?"

"Then you go home. Look, if he's as complicated as you say he is, that stems from somewhere, and quite frankly, you haven't known him long enough for it to be you at the root."

"Okay," I say, my spirits a little brighter. "That helps."

"He might even need you. I'm guessing he's not used to asking people for help."

I bet she's right.

He told me he's been abandoned by everyone in his life. He probably doesn't know how to lean on someone.

I make a mad dash to my bedroom to get dressed.

"I hate to say this," I tell my best friend. "So don't let this go to your head, but you're a genius."

"It's been said."

"And you're so humble," I say.

"That's … never been said."

We laugh together.

I dig through my closet and pull out a pair of sweatpants and an oversized sweatshirt.

Nothing like starting the New Year off in style.

I grin.

But if things go according to plan, I'll spend it cuddling with Hollis, and in that case, I won't need clothes anyway.

"I gotta go, Bells."

"Go get your man, baby girl."

"Never call me that again."

"Yeah. They did that in a movie I was watching last night while I was home. *Alone*. While y'all were out having fun at the neighbor's house."

"A party you were invited to," I point out.

She scoffs. "I'm sorry I don't party with Satan."

I burst out laughing as I pull the sweatpants on. "A little dramatic, don't you think?"

"Not even close. Now go and call me when you get back. Or if it's gonna be a while, and you're doing the make-up dirty-dirty, just text me and let me know it's all fixed."

The idea of making up with Hollis makes me smile. "Will do."

"Byeeeee."

"Bye, Bells."

I slip the sweatshirt over my head and throw my hair in a messy bun that looks more homeless than chic, but whatever.

I grab my keys and my purse and go.

I PULL into the parking lot of the hotel across from Paddy's. It takes a whole minute to find Hollis's black Mustang.

There is a spot two spaces down from his, and I pull in and park.

I climb out and make my way through the sea of cars until I hit the sidewalk. It's a pretty morning, and birds chirp happily overhead. It gives me a spring in my step as I try to find my guy and help him through whatever is going on.

He won't like it. That I'm sure. But I know he'll come around. He gives in to me eventually. He has, anyway.

The thought makes me smile as I round the corner of the building. I come up with a plan to persuade the desk attendant to give me his room number—the one little piece of the puzzle I don't have figured out.

The lobby is modern and clean with orange and bright green accents that feel very Savannah. I make my way toward the reception desk when my attention is drawn behind me like a magnet.

I turn on my heel and come eye-to-eye with Hollis.

"Hey," I say, trying to hide my surprise at how shitty he looks.

He's wearing the same clothes as last night. The area beneath his eyes is dark, as if he didn't sleep, and his hair is more of a wreck than usual.

The lines are heavy between his thick eyebrows.

Whatever was wrong last night is still wrong. That much is clear.

"What are you doing here?" he asks me.

"I came to see you. You didn't call."

He runs a hand through his hair and looks around the lobby. I get the distinct impression he's not looking for someone or something. He's just not wanting to look at me.

A sense of doom settles in my stomach. It's heavy, and my body shakes, physically recoiling its presence.

"Hollis? What's going on?"

He looks at the ceiling. The skin on his throat is red as though his internal irritation is seeping out of his body.

"Did I do something?" I ask although I'm clueless as to what it could be.

He levels his head but closes his eyes. "No, Riss. Of course not."

"Then what's going on."

With a sigh that causes his whole body to sag, he opens his eyes. “I wish you would’ve called first.”

“I wish you would’ve called too.”

“Fair enough,” he mumbles. “Let’s … We can’t do this here. Come on.”

Can’t do this here. What?

He turns toward the elevators. He does not grab my hand.

The rock in my stomach gets heavier and heavier with each step I take behind him. I scramble through last night and try to make sense of this.

We enter the elevator in silence. I reach for his shoulder because my touch usually settles him, but he leans against the wall and avoids my hand.

My breathing gets more rapid as I fight to stay calm. Tears prickle my eyes even though nothing has even happened.

Maybe it has nothing to do with me. Maybe it has nothing to do with us.

With us.

Shit, Larissa.

My senses go into hyperdrive as we walk down a short hallway, and he opens a door. There’s nothing friendly or warm about the process. It feels more like a death knell.

I want to bolt, to turn around and leave and pretend I never came. I want to get in my car and go home and tell myself he’ll come over later.

But as the door clicks shut behind me and he turns around to face me, I know that’s not going to happen.

“Hollis?” I ask despite the compression in my chest making it hard to breathe. “What’s happening?”

“I …” He sighs. “I have the Landry thing tomorrow, and then I’m going to head to Vermont and check on River.”

He’s going through the motions of telling me goodbye. He’s just not saying it.

“Why?” It’s all I can say, all I can ask.

"His mom is—"

"Dammit, Hollis. I know his mom is sick, and you know I'm not asking why you're going to see your friend." I take a step closer to him. "Why are you leaving?"

"To go see River."

"That's bullshit, and you know it," I tell him, my voice rising.

He might need to check on his friend, but that's not why he's leaving. We both know that. But the only other reason he could be avoiding me—which he clearly is—is that *he doesn't want to be with me.*

It's a shot directly to the heart that I'd opened up for him. My body tightens as if I was actually hit with a bullet. And, to make it worse, he was choosing to avoid me rather than even saying goodbye.

"You don't have to want to be here with me," I tell him, "but you could at least tell me the truth. Don't I deserve that much?"

Tears wet my eyes. It doesn't go unnoticed.

"Riss …" He says my name softly, but he doesn't make any movements toward me.

I see where this is going. I feel the start of the pain that will overwhelm me soon. It rips through my chest, shredding my heart into a million pieces.

"What did I do?" I ask him, my voice breaking. "Everything was fine, and then …"

"Everything was. Everything is. It's just not ..."

"It's not what?"

He watches me warily. But as I look deeper into those eyes I love so much, I see it. The shield, the guard, the switch he flips to keep himself safe is coming down.

"Maybe I can come back and see you this summer," he says, his voice weak. But it's not an offer. Not really. It's one of his infamous tries to redirect the conversation.

I laugh, but this time it's tinged with anger. He hears it, too, because he takes a step back.

"That's a weak attempt at deflection," I say. "You can do much better."

"How is it deflecting? I'm offering to come and see you!"

"It's deflecting because it avoids the reason you're leaving *and it is not River*," I say as he opens his mouth to repeat his false argument. "What do you want from me? To just be like, '*Oh, okay, he might be back in June*'?"

He holds his hands out to his sides. "What else do *you* want?"

"Oh, I don't know. Maybe for you to be the man I know and love."

The words flow past my lips freely before I can catch them and scoop them back up. They hang in the air between us like an unwanted visitor.

His eyes are as wide as his shoulders as he takes me in, shaking his head. "No, Larissa. Come on. You don't love me."

I don't know where that word choice came from. It's not one I use loosely. But I said it, and now, on the other side, I don't regret it.

I mean it.

The man has taught me more in a few days than all the men I've ever dated combined. He's taught me that it's okay to be me. He's made me feel confident and gorgeous. I've witnessed loyalty and know what it's like to have a guy around whose eyes don't troll on a room for other beautiful women. While in my presence. Not even beautiful Bellamy. He stood up for me to Sebastian and made an effort to talk to my family. He listened to me ramble about my day and worked through his hang-ups to open up to a woman who desperately wanted to get to know him.

The thought of not telling him about my day tomorrow makes me want to cry. Considering that I won't know if he's happy or what he's working on feels like a fraying rope in my chest.

I'll never be able to put all of those strands back together.

"I do love you," I tell him, my heart breaking. I've never felt this before. I've never felt as treasured as I have with Hollis. Yet, he was going to walk away without even facing me. "I get that you were leaving Savannah. I've known that from the beginning, and I haven't asked you for any promises. Or any reciprocation of feelings." I sniffle, my lip trembling. "But you weren't even going to say goodbye."

Tears stream down my cheeks, and I don't even try to stop them. I'm trying to fight my insecurities that, once again, someone will leave me—does this stem from my mom's pain from when my dad left?—but this hurts more because I gave away my heart.

"Don't cry," he begs.

"Why not? Because it makes it harder for you to face reality? That you're walking away from someone who loves you?"

He groans. "I didn't ask for this. I didn't want this."

"We don't ask for a lot of stuff in our lives, Hollis, but we have to deal with it."

"You don't think I know that?" His voice rises. "Look at all the shit I have to deal with. I think I deal pretty fucking well, if you ask me."

Something about his tone pisses me off. I jam a finger in his direction.

"You're right," I tell him. "You will deal with this pretty fucking well too because you'll just shove it in the back of your mind and not think about it. You'll just pretend I don't exist just as you pretend Philip and Kim don't love you. You just—"

"Watch it, Riss."

"Or what?" I say, my voice rising. "You'll leave? Because you already are, and if you're going to leave, then I'm going to make sure you do it and know what you're leaving behind."

He growls through the air, tugging at his hair.

"Ever since I was a little girl, I've wanted some man to love me madly," I say, my tone softening. "I wanted a safe place to create a little world where I could garden and make dinners and raise kids."

Images of Bellamy's grandparents filter through my mind. They made love look so easy. They fought. They forgave. They loved. They showed me that love can sustain a relationship. It can sustain a marriage when both people are committed to put in the work. Giving up wasn't an option.

It makes my tears fall again.

"I wanted someone to look at me like I was the most important thing in the world to him. That would tell the whole universe that I was his girl," I say, wiping my cheeks. "That's all. I didn't want money or cars or fame. I just wanted to find my best friend and to create a beautiful corner of the world just for us."

My words stall in my throat.

Hollis stands in front of me. His arms hang at his sides.

"And I found you," I say, the words so muffled that I don't know if he can hear me. "And you don't want me."

"That's not it," he says quickly. "I swear that's not it."

"Then what is it?"

He looks me in the eye. I think he's trying to put up a front and make me think he believes his own bullshit, but it doesn't work.

"You have to find the person in your life that you can share stuff with," he says. "Find the door you should walk through. And I'm not that guy. *I'm not,*" he says again as though saying it twice will make it more believable. "I have nothing to share with you. *And eventually, you'd realize that.*"

I cover my face with my hands and cry. I cry for me, for him, for a life we could've figured out. Together.

I'm sure of it. I'm sure we could've made something work. It's too good between us to have failed.

Only it did.

The realest thing I've ever experienced is over.

He doesn't come to me, and he doesn't reach out. But I don't reach for him either. Why make things harder?

I get myself under control the best I can and look up at him through blurry eyes. I take in the last glimpse of Hollis Hudson that I'll probably ever have and commit it to memory.

"Eventually, you'll realize there are people in the world who love you," I whisper. "And you pushed them all away. Just remember that I was one of them."

He just looks at me, and I can't take it.

I turn on my heel and leave the only man I've ever loved behind. I'm walking away at what I had stupidly believed might be my slice of happiness. And even though my heart aches to an unfathomable level, I'm also hurting for Hollis.

That man is filled with so much goodness, strength of character, loyalty, and … well, love. I'm so afraid he'll always be alone because he refuses to see all that. He won't accept it.

It's not right. It's so terrible.

But there is absolutely nothing I can do.

TWENTY-FOUR
HOLLIS

My luggage is gathered and on the other bed.

As soon as the sun comes up, I'm going to get up and drive to the ocean. I haven't had a day sitting on the sand in three or four years. Hopefully, the salty air will clear my head, and I can show up to the Catching-A-Care thing without wanting to hurl.

Then I'll come back here, grab my shit, and go back to campus.

I roll over onto my side. A spring I can't escape stabs me in the hip.

Even the bed is pissed at me.

"I hate you, too," I tell it.

It cares about as much as anyone does when I dislike them.

This was the longest day of my life. The afternoon melted into the evening, and the evening got dark and lasted forever. The nighttime has worn on and on. I've just laid here and sulked.

It's not my fault things are this way. I'm just really glad I understand the reality of shit so I can act accordingly.

Could I have fucked around with Larissa? For sure.

Would that have been the right choice? Nah.

Do I have to pay the price for trying to do the right thing? Of course.

And I will. I will pay the price because I love her.

My body stills against the unyielding spring. My breathing stops. I mull that word in my mind. I sit with it. I feel the vibrations of it from head to toe.

"Do I?" I ask aloud, as if the fucking spring will back off and squeak out an answer.

I don't know if I do or not. I don't know what love means, really.

I also don't know if it matters.

The only thing I can compare this to is Crew and River. And that's not an exact comparison. I'd take a bullet for those guys. I've taken massive hits to protect them on the field more times than I can count. I'll show up for them every time they need me.

Larissa's laughter plays through my mind, and I can't help the smile that graces my lips. I can still smell her on my shirt. I remember the softness of her skin and the twinkle in her eye when she taught me that stupid dance at Jack's party.

I'd jump in front of a bullet for her, no questions asked. I couldn't imagine living with myself if I didn't. And even though she probably hates me right now and will never speak to me again, if she called and needed me tonight? I'd go.

But it's more than that. It's a softness in the core of my body when it comes to her. It's the way time flies when we're together. It's that things are more optimistic when she's around. Life is more fun with jokes on another level when they come from her. She also saw me—the real me. The me behind all the crap I shove out there to keep people from looking.

I smile sadly.

She didn't take no for an answer, crazy woman.

She could see my pain and wanted to be my balm.

How did she do that? Why?

I don't want kids, but if I did, I'd want them with her. I'd trust her to take care of them and love them. But I won't be a burden to her. I refuse.

Even if it kills me in the meantime.

I glance at the clock next to the bed and check the time. It's ten minutes past four in the morning.

"I can't sit here anymore," I say, getting up and turning on the light. It's bright, making me squint. I can barely see to type out my text.

Me: Anyone up?

I wait for a full ten minutes to no avail. So I brush my teeth and then grab my wallet and room key.

I switch off the light and head to the beach and away from everything that reminds me of Larissa.

Fuck this.

TWENTY-FIVE
LARISSA

"I blame you," I say, looking at Bellamy.

She's stretched out on my sofa with a Nerds Rope in her hand. She twirls it around while she watches me accuse her of ruining my life.

"You should've had my back. You should've told me not to get involved with Hollis," I tell her. "You let me down, Bells. Bad best friend."

She snorts. "Yeah. That's a different tune than the night he had you on the rooftop, and you were … I was basically the greatest best friend in the universe that night."

"What? How? Please. Explain your logic."

"Because you would've written off all men if it weren't for me." She chomps off the end of her candy. "I made you see the light."

"You pushed me into the light."

"And into how many orgasms? *Please.* I'll wait for you to thank me later."

I take a pillow off the chair beside me and throw it at her. It has a little more pizazz than I intended, but maybe getting walloped will do her some good.

She giggles and presses the pillow to her chest as she continues to eat her candy.

"Don't take this the wrong way," she says. "But you *actually* look like a raccoon today."

"Bells, you're pushing it."

She just shrugs.

I settle back in my chair and tug my blanket around me.

My entire body feels achy yet numb. It's the weirdest sensation. It's like I'm numb to anything but the complete sadness that starts in my chest and radiates outward until every piece of me succumbs to the pain.

I miss him. Dammit, I miss him. I miss being able to hear his voice if I call and seeing a text here and there. To think I'll never hear from him again feels like I've fallen into a hole that I can never escape.

It would have to be an escape because Hollis completely captured me.

And I let him.

"Cut yourself some slack," Bellamy says. "You took a chance, and it didn't work out."

"But why couldn't it? Why couldn't our relationship have been real and worked out?"

"How would I know? Men have the dumbest excuses for things."

"I wasn't asking you. It was rhetorical."

She makes a face. "Fine. But do you think it even matters? Will it change anything?"

"I have nothing to share with you. And eventually, you'd realize that."

His words echo in my brain. I know he believes that to be true. It's sad that a man like him would believe the least about himself because of how people have treated him in the past. But that's his truth.

But it's not *the* truth. And even if it was and I wanted him anyway, isn't that my choice to make?

"Get your phone," Bellamy says, snapping me back to reality.

I look down and see it glowing on the coffee table.

My heart skips in my chest as I lunge for the device, hoping against hope that it's Hollis.

I don't even care what he wants or if he just wants to come by and get his T-shirt that I put on as soon as I got home. He can even call to tell me I'm mean. I don't care. I just want to hear his voice.

But it's not him. Not even close.

I groan, getting comfy again. "Hi, Mom."

"Hey, sweetie. I wanted to see if you had fun last night at Siggy's."

I lean my head back and fake cry.

"What's the matter?" she asks.

"Just … bad timing, Mom."

"*Okay*."

"Is Hollis there? Should I let you go?" she asks. "I don't want to interrupt."

I sigh. "You're not interrupting, and he's not here. Just Bellamy."

"Just Bellamy," Bellamy mocks me. "Like I'm chopped liver."

I ignore her. "What's up with you?"

"I'm actually doing laundry. Can you believe that? Laundry on New Year's Day."

"Life goes on."

I frown, realizing how true my words are and how much I hate them. I don't want them to go on.

They'll never go on the same way they've gone on over the past week.

It was a taste of something that I'll probably never experience again—something fun and playful and feel-good. There were no expectations between Hollis and me. Just a pact to pretend to have a relationship that I ended up believing could be real.

The tears come again from nowhere. They're silent and wet and hot as they slide down my cheeks. Bellamy watches me from the couch.

"Are you crying, honey?" Mom asks. "Oh, Riss. What's the matter?"

"Well," I say, my voice shaking, "apparently, Hollis and I are done."

"Oh. Why?"

"Do you want the bullshit answer he gave me or the real one?"

"Bullshit first."

"Well, he thinks he has nothing to offer me."

"I saw him. I talked to him. I danced with him, for crying out loud. That's not true."

"I know."

"So what's the truth, then?"

I think of his sweet smile—the shy one I only got to see a few times. I remember the moment of true happiness at the piano and the soulfulness of his voice singing Adele.

"The truth is … he doesn't know that it's okay to be happy. He doesn't know how to trust people."

"*Oh, honey.*"

"There's nothing I can do," I say, feeling helpless. "I confronted him. I went to him. And he just pushed me away."

The phone clicks, and I know I'm on speakerphone again. I roll my eyes at Bellamy.

"What's your next step?" Mom asks.

"I don't know. Tacos?"

"Larissa!"

"What? What the hell am I supposed to do, *Mom*? I can't force him to want me."

A faucet turns on, and I can hear a glass or a kettle being filled up. And then, finally, she takes me off speakerphone.

"You're not giving up that easy, are you?" she asks me.

"Don't start."

"What's that supposed to mean?"

"It means I'm not going to chase him down and beg him to be with me. And for heaven's sake, don't you even think about trying to set me up with someone else!"

She gasps. "Why would I do something like that?"

"Are you serious?" I deadpan. "Tell me you're kidding."

"No, I'm not kidding. I only set you up with men who I think you might like so that you can find your soul mate. I don't want you to wait too long to find him. It turns out, you didn't need me for that at all."

I move around in my chair to try to get comfortable.

"You have to go after that boy, Riss. He's *The One*."

My eyes well up with tears. "And do what? Cry? Beg? I've already done both."

Her voice drops. "Have you learned anything from me?"

I don't know what she means by that question, so I don't answer her. There are so many directions it could take.

"Larissa, darling, listen to me. You have to fight for love. If your heart is hurting, and I know it is, that means something is worth your time to fix it."

"But I can't make him listen to me!"

She sighs. "I'm going to tell you something I've never told you. Okay? And I don't want to talk about it. It's private, and it causes me a lot of pain."

"*Mom …*"

I sit up in my chair, my heart racing. I have no idea where this is going or if I even want it to go there.

"When your father left me, he had his reasons. They weren't

great, but he did what he thought he had to do in order for all of us to be happy," she says, her voice unnaturally even. "But the reason we got a divorce? That's my fault."

This is news to me. I've never known what caused their breakup, but now? I don't know if I want to know. I have too much to process the way it is.

"I don't know if I can deal with this right now," I tell her.

"Larissa, I didn't fight for us."

It's a simple sentence, all of six words. But something about it, about the way she says it takes my breath away.

"Mom …"

"I didn't. There was some pride involved, I guess. A lot of it was me being hardheaded and refusing to compromise with him on a few important things. I just let him go because it was easier than working through it and being patient. I cut the ties and moved on … and I've regretted that every day since."

I still, processing this unusually raw and honest statement from my mother.

"I love Jack. He's wonderful, and I wouldn't trade him for the world. But there's something sweet about the idea of having lived with your father and raising you that makes me sad that I didn't try."

"I don't know how to feel about this."

"It's not for you to feel anything. It's for you to learn." She sighs. "I met your father when I was young. I was in my early twenties, and I feel like that was such a magical time. That's why I'm always trying to get you to meet people because I want you to experience that spark, that connection with someone you could grow and change and build something with."

My lip quivers.

I know what she wants for me. I want it too. And I know I had it, if only for a few days.

"I met that person, Mom."

"I know you did. That's why you have to go get him."

"What if he doesn't want me?"

"Oh, he wants you," Bellamy chimes in from the couch.

I ignore her again.

"He might fight it. If he really doesn't know how to trust people, you might have to teach him. And if he thinks it's not okay to be happy, then you show him how to smile. Because I saw him look at you, and he was smiling, Larissa. It's hard not to smile when you're around."

I sniffle, not sure what to do now.

Is she right? Should I show him I won't give up on him? On us? Would it make a difference?

Bellamy gets up and walks by me. She whispers something that I can't make out. I don't ask her to repeat it, and I don't follow her because it's probably something about snacks.

"He's leaving tonight, I think," I tell my mother. "I think it's too late."

"It's never too late. But you need a plan."

I rest my head on the back of the chair. "But do I? Mom, I'm not sure it matters. His mind is made up."

"Is it? Or are you just scared to try?"

My head throbs, pain pulsing through my temples, and I just can't do it anymore.

"I'm going to shut my phone off for a while." I tell her. "I just … I need to think and not look at it every three minutes to see if he's called. Because he won't. I know it."

"I understand. Just have some faith, okay?"

"I'll try. I love you, Mom."

"And I love you, baby girl."

I hang up the phone.

TWENTY-SIX
HOLLIS

There is sand in my shoe.

Each step I take feels like I'm walking on tiny little pebbles. It takes my already foul mood and worsens it.

The sun and the salt didn't help. Everywhere I turned, there was a reminder of Larissa.

A blonde in a bikini the same green color as the dress Riss wore to Jack's event.

There was a succulent in an oversized terra-cotta pot by the lifeguard's shack.

A woman was walking with a black Labrador and a little boy was tossing a football up in the air, as if the universe was taunting me with what could've been.

Is it going to be like this when I get home?

My suitcase is in the trunk of my car. Check-out has been completed at the hotel. Grandma Judy's shop was closed, but I shoved a piece of paper under the door and thanked her for everything.

I've sat in this room for a half of an hour and waited to be called to the podium. The Landry's have created a fun environment backstage and I just can't enjoy it.

I think I'm broken.

Maybe broken-hearted.

"Hey, Hollis, my man," Lincoln Landry says, coming into the room. He shakes my hand but then pulls me into a man-hug. "How are you?"

"Excited to be here," I say with zero enthusiasm.

He quirks a brow. "Don't pass out from all that excitement or anything."

"I know. I'm sorry." I suck in a deep breath. "It's been a long week."

"That's what I heard. Hey, while I have you here, can you do me a favor?"

Can I do him a favor?

I want to tell him that I'm the guy you call to fuck everything all up, not save the day. *But how do you say no to him? You don't.*

"Of course," I say. "Whatever you want."

He grips my shoulder. "Danielle has a special guest here this evening. She sat her down with some cookies in the back and then vanished. I don't know if Dani thought I was the entertainment committee around here tonight or what, but you know, I have to pretend to be a professional. I need to be with the people." He motions toward the stage. "Will you help me out?"

I'm so, so confused. But it's Lincoln, so of course I'm going to say yes.

"Uh, sure. What do you want me to do?" I ask.

He looks relieved. "Thanks, Hollis. Just, um, go into the blue room. Did you see the area where the refreshments are?"

I nod. I saw it but didn't partake. I didn't want to hurl.

"Just head back there." He gives me a wide, million-dollar smile. "I'll have someone come and get you before it's your turn. I'll talk to you afterward, okay?"

"Yeah, sure. Um, Lincoln, but I …" But he's already gone. "Well, shit."

I take a deep breath and pull out my phone.

There are no missed calls or messages. I don't know why I hoped there would be one. I wouldn't reach out to me again, either.

"This is it," I tell myself as I enter the hallway. "This is the start of the rest of your life. It could've gone one direction, but you chose this. Now you get to live with it."

The path less traveled has never felt truer.

I hum a few bars of the refrain that Coy and I were playing together. It's an attempt to distract myself, but what it really does is remind me that my world was very different not long ago.

I was at Siggy's drinking craft beer, making music with one of the hottest musicians in the world … and I had the girl of my dreams smiling at me.

I want to cry. I want to slide my back down the wall and just collapse on the floor and cry.

Is this what it feels like to actually want to be with someone? Why would anyone want to feel this way? It's bullshit.

I straighten my tie and pause outside of the refreshments room. The other award winners are gathered at the far end of the hall. We laughed and shot the shit earlier. They're pretty good guys.

They wave and shout for me to join them.

"I'll be there in a second," I tell them.

Loosening my shoulders, I step inside the room.

And then I stop.

"Grandma Judy?" I ask, bewildered. "I … What are you doing here?"

She's wearing a pale blue and white dress with black grandmotherly shoes that look like bricks. She sits, smiling, as I walk toward her.

"Am I not allowed here?" She laughs. "Come give me a hug, you naughty boy."

I press my tie to my chest and bend down. She wraps her

arms around my neck and kisses my cheek. I'm taken aback by how natural it feels to interact with her like this.

She pulls back and fixes my hair.

"Did you come to make sure I don't look like a mess?" I ask her, sitting beside her.

"Heavens, no. I don't think you could look like a mess if you tried." She bumps my shoulder with hers. "And I think you know that. And I think that's a part of your problem."

"Before we get to my so-called problems, how the hell did you find me here?"

"Hollis, honey, Savannah is a small town. I've known the Landry kids since they were pups. They used to come in and get donuts on Saturday mornings. Barrett, the eldest Landry boy, worked for me one summer to pay his dad back for wrecking his car."

I grin.

"They're good kids. All of them. Barrett was governor of Georgia. Can you believe that?"

"Nope," I say and then laugh. "Judy, I have no idea who you're talking about, but I'm happy they make you happy."

She pats my leg. "Well, anyway, that's how I found you."

I nod my head and sit in silence. She doesn't speak, just lets me have a moment to wrap my brain around this day.

Finally, she sighs. "Can we talk about your problems now?"

"Is that why you came all the way over here?"

"No. It was to see your sweet little face. But I figure I should lend an ear since I'm here."

I sink back against my chair. "There's been no change in anything."

"Meaning you haven't fixed things with Larissa."

I look at her out of the corner of my eye. "I assume you know her too."

"I might."

"Now who is the rascal?"

She looks proud of herself. She makes a face and reaches up, fluffing her hair.

I laugh.

"Okay, enough playing," she tells me. "I tried to give you time to come to your senses. Now we're going to be serious."

I get to my feet, wiping my sweaty palms down my pant legs.

I'm in shock. *This has to be shock.* This wonderful lady that didn't know me a week ago came here to see me.

I feel ... less alone.

Still, I can't let her presence undermine what is necessary.

I have to leave. Move forward. *Accept the loss, hit the locker room, and get ready for another game tomorrow.*

"I'm going to be fine," I say. "I'm going to go home, and I'm going to get back to my life that feels a hell of a lot better than this, by the way."

"Well, it's a damn good thing that most people don't subscribe to that theory, or the human population would be extinct."

I quirk a brow. "Excuse me?"

"Have you ever thought about pushing something the size of a watermelon out of a hole the size of a pea?"

I make a face. "No. I haven't. But I get where you're going with this, and I don't appreciate the visual." I shake my head. "I'm never having kids for sure now."

"Oh, it's not like you have to do the work."

"But, like, I'll be the cause of that. Why doesn't anyone tell kids that in high school? You wanna ruin that pus—*never mind*."

She snorts. "I'm old but not dead, Hollis. I know what you were going to say."

"Good. Then I don't have to say it."

"If women lived by your motto, we'd never give birth. Humanity would be wiped out. But we don't. Do you want to know why?" she asks.

"Because you like to have sex?"

"Because, smart-ass, we know that you have to go through some pain to enjoy the pleasure."

My lips twitch. "Grandma Judy, I'm letting that one sit right there. I'm not going to touch it."

"You won't when you imagine a watermelon coming out of it," she says smugly.

My jaw drops. "Judy!"

"That was good, huh? See? I still have it together up here." She taps the side of her head. "I'm quick."

"Yeah. Let's just gently transition this conversation out of the bedroom, okay?"

She smiles. "Then I'll get to the point."

"Please do."

Judy takes a deep breath. "The best things in life require work. Sometimes that means pain. You play football. Doesn't a win taste a little sweeter after you make a comeback? Or when you score the last shot of the game that you weren't supposed to hit?"

"Um, point made but it's football. Not basketball. And that thing you just said? It doesn't really track."

She runs a hand through the air like it doesn't make a difference. "It's the same with having kids. You have to endure the worst pain of your life before you have them. It's like … sometimes you can't have the best things if you don't prove you want it. Why would God bless you if you just walk around with your hand out like a spoiled child?"

I sit down beside her. My body calms, and my brain slows down from the race it's been running all day.

She leans toward me, her voice low and pain-filled. "The worst time of my life—the time I wasn't sure I could make it—is when I lost my Ronnie. Our house just burned down, and one of our sons had passed away from colon cancer." Her voice breaks. "And he collapsed in my living room, and I couldn't do anything for him. I called the paramedics, and they came, but he was gone. Took his last breaths in my arms."

Fuck.

She takes a handkerchief from her purse and dabs her eye.

"Hey, now," I say, pulling her into me. "Don't cry. One of us has to be tough today."

Judy chuckles and sits back up. She sniffles.

"It still hurts," she tells me. "Every day, I think about him. I miss him so much that I think I'll lose my mind someday over it. I work at this age because, if I don't stay busy, I sit at home and cry."

"*Judy*," I say, my heart breaking.

"But I wouldn't trade it. Not a single day of it. I'd live for another hundred years and miss him like this if I had to give up the years we had together." She smiles sadly at me. "We weren't put on this earth to be alone, sweet boy."

"Yeah . . ."

My spirits sink. She makes so much sense, but it's so much of a risk. There's too much of a risk.

"You have so much love to give," she says, looking me earnestly in the eye. "And you have a big old hole right here," she says, patting my chest with her old, wrinkly hand, "for someone to fill up. Now, I have every intention of helping scoop some love in there for you. But I'm a slow scooper."

I laugh, holding her hand to me. "You scoop just fine."

"So does someone else I know."

I blow out a breath as she withdraws her hand.

"Look, you're going to be miserable either way," she says, speaking frankly. "And I guarantee you that Larissa is as distraught as you are. So be miserable together. It's better than being miserable alone. And if it doesn't work out, then it wasn't the door for you." She leans toward me and whispers. "But I'm pretty sure it is."

We look up as a head pops around the door. A bald man walks in.

"I'm sorry to interrupt. But, Judy, Lincoln asked me to take you to your seat. Hollis, are you ready?" he asks.

I nod.

Judy gets to her feet with my assistance. She motions for me to bend down. When I do, she kisses my cheek again, squeezing the other side of my face in the process.

"Don't be scared," she whispers. "Grandma is with you."

She lets go of me and walks out with the usher.

I take in a deep breath and feel my heart start to pound.

So much of what she said made sense. Victory is so much sweeter when you have to work for it.

But is that what this is with Larissa? Me working for it?

I pace around the room, mulling over what Judy said.

What if I fuck it all up? What if she walks away when she sees how messed up I am? What if she can't handle me when I can't sleep for days at a time because I have nightmares? Will she be embarrassed when we go places, and I never have anyone in the stands for me?

Warmth fills me when I realize that Judy will be out there today.

Someone will be here for me.

I scrub a hand down my face. Panic starts to set in.

I would never want Larissa to think I wasn't there for her.

But ... you're not, Hudson. She's in pain right now—pain that you caused by being a total jerk—and she's alone.

And you made her alone. You pushed her away.

Sweat dots my brows as I pace the room. I dig my phone out of my pocket and find her number. I don't know how this will work out, or if she'll even talk to me. Maybe she'll say she's had enough of me, but I have to try. She has to know that I love her.

My stomach drops.

The phone rings—once, twice, three times.

"Pick up," I plead. "Pick up, Riss."

The line clicks. "This is Larissa. I'm sorry I'm not availab—"

Her voice is a balm and buckshot.

I end the call.

Me: Riss, if you're avoiding me, I get it. I understand. Please answer.

I wait for a response.

Nothing.

"Hollis," the usher says, reappearing out of nowhere. "We're just about ready."

"I'm coming. Yeah. Sorry." I walk toward the door.

Me: I'm so sorry. I was a dick.

"This way, please," the usher tells me.

I don't want to be here. I need to find her. I have to fix this.

I can't walk away from her.

Judy is right. Larissa is everything.

I want her to be mine.

She is mine.

Damn it.

We approach the large black curtains that separate the back of the stage with the audience out front. Someone drones on about their experiences, and I tune them out.

I punch her number again.

My foot taps against the floor as I listen to the line ring.

Pick up, Riss. Pick up, baby.

My stomach churns.

I'm so sorry.

"Hollis Hudson!" Lincoln's voice saying my name in the mic grabs my attention.

Shit.

The line picks up, and my heart jumps in my chest. "This is Larissa. I'm sorry I'm not available. Please leave a message after the tone, and I will return your call as soon as possible. Thanks!"

Beep.

The usher touches my elbow. "Go on," he whispers.

I nod and turn back to the phone. "Riss, baby, it's Hollis. I bet you fucking hate me, and I deserve it, but please, please talk to me. Let me explain or try to explain. Shit, I don't know. I gotta go on stage now, but … I love you. Okay? *Fuck.* I'll call you back."

The curtains are parted for me, and I have no time to reflect on my message.

I walk up the steps to a round of applause.

TWENTY-SEVEN
HOLLIS

I pass Lincoln on the way to the microphone. He smiles, giving me a knowing look.

Ignoring the way my stomach clenches as if it's preparing me for a hard block on game day, I reach the podium.

My hand goes into my pocket, and I silence my phone, hoping like crazy that if Larissa calls, she'll understand why I didn't answer. But as I take the piece of paper with the notes for my speech out of my other pocket, I realize I can't not see my phone screen. I'll be distracted the whole time and wondering if she has texted me back. So, I put it on the podium next to the scratch paper that Judy left in the goodie box for me. I read again the words she wrote along the top of the paper.

To my chosen and newest grandson,
You are always welcome at my table.
Love, Grandma Judy

I take a deep breath.

No texts.

I adjust the microphone.

The lights above me are hot. The podium is a little low for my taste. The microphone is loud and screeches as it bounces on its stand, and I reach up and steady it.

I clear my throat.

"I'd like to first thank the Catching-A-Cares Foundation for the opportunity to be here. At first, I didn't believe it and was … slightly uncooperative," I say, getting a chuckle from the crowd. "But their patience and kindness have been unmatched. So, I'd like to thank them for that. And to Mr. and Mrs. Landry for personally welcoming me to Georgia. I appreciate you both so much."

Applause helps drown out the voice in my head that reminds me that Larissa was with me that night.

No texts.

I clear my throat again. "Many of you might know me from my time spent on the football field. Although, if you could forget this past season, I'd be grateful."

The crowd laughs at what they think is a joke. It's not.

No texts.

My heart constricts.

Come on, Riss.

"What many of you don't know is that I arrived in Georgia straight out of foster care. The system took me in when I didn't have anyone and made sure I had a safe place to sleep at night. Because of the families who were willing to open their doors to a wild boy, I had enough stability in my life to find football."

I suck in a deep breath.

"Football gave me the outlet I needed to stay out of trouble. It allowed me a safe place to spend my time and to release the aggression I had built up inside me. It gave me structure and coaches that pushed me to succeed when no one else did."

I glance down.

No texts.

"Thanks to the commitment from the men and women in the foster care program as well as the Union High School Football Program, Coach Herbert made a promise to a guy who was as rough around the edges as you can get. He never gave up on me."

My voice breaks at the end.

I sniffle and try to keep myself under control.

No texts.

"I had a hard start in life. But the men and women who gave their time—many of them selflessly and without pay—kept me from being a statistic. They literally changed my life. And that's how I Caught-A-Care," I say, using the tagline for the nonprofit.

The audience breaks out into applause again.

I blow out a breath and grab both sides of the podium.

"I don't have any more notes," I say. "Yet my speech feels incomplete … and I know why. Because my story isn't over."

I clear my throat again.

No texts.

Really, Larissa. Please …

"I was sitting by the ocean this morning and wondering what the rest of my life looks like now that football is over. And I realized that, for some reason, I'd assumed that I was on my own now. That just because I'm an adult by every indicator meant that no one cares. But that's not true."

I press my thumb on Judy's name.

"I would like to go on record and say that, while many of us here remember to support children—myself included, there are many adults who need support too. And when a Care is passed our way, we need to … scoop it up and do our part."

My voice breaks again, and I kick myself.

I slide my hands down my pants, my heart thundering in my chest.

"So, in addition to the many families and coaches that

helped raise me, I'd like to thank the handful of people who helped teach this young man about family and love recently." I smile sadly. "They welcomed me into their homes and their lives and showed me what it was like to truly be accepted, flaws and traumas and all. Not because someone told them they had to or because I can catch a ball reasonably well … most of the time."

The crowd chuckles again, making me smile.

"But they chose to … *maybe love me*," I say, having to bow my head to make my throat stop constricting so hard. I clear my throat. "So, to my new grandma Judy, thank you. Your love means more to me than you'll ever know."

I look up into the crowd to find her.

"And to a family that will probably never speak to me again, but will forever be … a part …"

I lean forward as if that will help me see better.

What the …?

Judy sits on the end in her blue and white dress. She gives me a bright smile and points to her right.

Sitting next to her is, I think, Larissa's aunt, Siggy.

My gaze keeps moving down the line.

Boone waves when my eyes land on him.

Then sits Bellamy. She gives me the biggest, silliest wink.

And then, next to her, with tears streaming down her face, is Larissa.

My body lunges to the side before I catch myself.

"Where is your phone?" I ask before I can stop myself.

The crowd laughs.

She holds her hands out like she doesn't know.

Blood pumps through my veins and, while I'm incredibly thankful to the Landrys for being here, I want nothing more than to not be.

I fiddle with the paper, not able to take my eyes off Riss.

"I …" I laugh and look into the crowd.

And for the first time ever, there are people here … for me. *With me.*

Whatever I thought it might feel like to look into a crowd and see someone there for you—I had no fucking clue, but it's better. *It's so much better.*

"Thank you to the Catching-A-Cares Foundation," I say. "Thank you so much."

When I turn around, Lincoln is walking my way. He winks.

"Go get her," he whispers.

I laugh. "I'm on it."

I jog down the stairs and along the side of the room.

Lincoln thanks everyone for coming and instructs them on where to donate, but I'm not registering any of it. I walk as quickly as I can across the back of the room and see Larissa and her family exiting the row.

"Riss," I say, jogging up to her.

Her eyes are clouded with tears. "Hollis, I—"

I grab her face and kiss her with everything I have.

"Let's try to keep this PG-13," Bellamy says as she walks by. "People are watching."

I pull back and rest my forehead on Larissa's.

"Let 'em watch," I say, looking into her pretty eyes. "I was calling you. And texting you. Where's your phone?"

"I turned it off, and now I can't find it," she says.

"I'm sorry. I was stupid and—"

"I know."

Siggy stands beside us. "Hollis, we are so proud of you."

"Yes, honey, we are," Judy says, standing beside Siggy.

I release Larissa's face but grab her hand instead and pull her into my side.

"Thank you all for coming. I mean, I guess you are here to see me." My stomach drops. "But you might not be. I—"

"Of course, we're here for you," Siggy says. "I think you're family now. Right, Riss?"

I look down to see her smiling up at me.

"Well, he can try not to be, but I'll just have to keep pestering him with questions until he gets tired of me and agrees."

I grin at her. "I love you."

Her eyes grow wide.

"I told you in a voice message, which was probably the total wrong way to do that, but it just came out," I say with a shrug. "And I should've said it on stage so you could've gotten your public declaration you were telling me you always wanted, but this will have to do."

She smiles so wide that the corners of her lips touch her eyes. "I love you too."

"Well, I love food, and I'm starving," Boone says. "Can we grab some food and continue this little love fest elsewhere?"

"I'll call Hillary's House and have them deliver," Siggy says. "Everyone, come to my house. Judy, would you like to come?"

Judy clutches her pearls. "Why, yes. I think that would be nice."

"Fabulous." Siggy smiles. "We'll see you all there." She grabs Judy's arm gently and helps her out.

Boone slaps my back, drawing my attention away from Siggy and Judy. "Hey, man. Good work on the field and off. I'm glad Riss found a decent guy for once."

"Well, you can stop worrying because I'm where it stops for her."

She stills beside me. "You are?"

I look down into her eyes and know it's true. I can fight it, but it won't matter.

All the doors that closed up to this point were so that I would walk through this one. And I'm jumping in headfirst.

"I am." I nuzzle my cheek against the side of her head. "We're going to need another pact."

"Oohh, you're right." She grins against my side. "What should this one include?"

"Me and you forever."

She wraps both arms around me. "That's a relationship pact I'll be happy to sign."

The end

EPILOGUE #1

Hollis

The swing goes back and forth. It's a lazy movement, completely inconsiderate of time.

Larissa lies longways with her head on my lap. I brush her hair out of her face as I keep us swaying in the breeze.

The lasagna Siggy ordered for an early dinner was amazing, and I ate more than any guy should ever eat in front of a girl's family. It was nice to have my appetite back.

I look down at my girl. Her eyes are closed. She looks content, and I want to keep it that way.

No matter what.

"Can I ask you something?" I ask.

"Mm-hmm."

"How did you know I was there? And how did you get everyone to go with you?"

She grins. "Well, Boone and Bellamy and I were going to go anyway. Or we were before you decided to be a jerk."

"Fair enough."

She opens her eyes. They're sparkling. "I had kind of called it off because I didn't think you wanted us there. That and I was really mad. And hurt."

I wince.

"But Judy called Lincoln and told him she wanted to go and that he needed to get ahold of me."

"She did?"

Larissa nods.

"Huh."

I gaze across the lawn behind Siggy's house at the trees dotting the landscape—giant southern oaks covered in Spanish moss that dusts the ground at some points. There are bushes with deep purple flowers along both sides of a path that leads from the porch steps and over a hill.

Judy's actions on my behalf surprise me. I don't know why. She's a meddling and territorial lady, and I shouldn't be shocked to find out she exerted her will over anything, let alone my problems.

How did I get so lucky to stumble into her little shop that day?

I look down to see Larissa watching me.

How did I get so lucky to find her?

She climbs off my lap and moseys down the steps. She shoves her hands in the pockets of her wine-colored dress and gazes down the pathway.

I get off the porch and go to her.

"Can I ask you something else?" I say.

She laughs. "Look at who's the one full of questions now."

"It's paybacks." I stand behind her and wrap my arms around her front, locking my hands at her belly button. She holds on to my hands, her succulent bracelet tickling my skin. "Why did you come today? Why did you still show up after I pushed you away?"

She stills in my arms. "Because I love you, and you needed me."

My throat tightens as I hold this woman.

She came because I needed her. Even though I never told her.

I don't know what to say to that.

"I'll always be here for you. So will my family." She lifts her chin and looks up at me. "You have so many people who love you. If you will just let us."

Something happens inside me, a shift that I didn't think would ever happen. It's like a number of puzzle pieces click together. I can hear the snap as they form one picture.

"I love you," I tell her. "I don't know what that means. I'm not promising you I'm not going to make mistakes because, well, I'm Hollis Hudson, and I'm kind of known for that."

She laughs.

"But I'll love you with everything I have," I tell her. "And I'll never leave you alone to try to figure things out by yourself. You have me."

"And you have me. And if you decide you don't want me, I'll come and show you that I'm not going anywhere. I choose you, baby."

I grin. "I choose you, too. Every time, beautiful girl. Every time. No matter what."

She spins around in my arms and faces me. "What do we do about you going back to school?"

I groan, wondering why the world has to constantly throw speed bumps in my way.

"I have an idea," she says.

"Shoot, Shooter."

"I have a semester left too. And Braxton is not that far from here. What? Three hours?"

"Yeah. About that."

She plays with the buttons on my shirt. "So we both finish our degrees because that's important. And we make a deal that we see each other at least every two weeks. Whoever can travel the easiest, that's the person who goes. But it's non-negotiable."

"Can I come every weekend if I can? I don't think I have classes on Monday or Friday. I could probably swing a lot of long weekends either way."

Her face brightens. "Perfect."

A grin toys against my lips. "Let's see how this goes. Let's be open to change. But whatever happens, we stick together. We're teammates."

"How about family? Teammates make me think of sweaty socks and stinky shoes."

I laugh, pressing my lips against her forehead.

We'll be family someday. For real. I promise you.

"Now," she says, looking up at me warily, "I have something to tell you, and you can't get mad."

"What? What did you do?"

My brows pull together as I wonder what in the world she could've done in twenty-four hours to make me that mad.

She bites her lip. "Promise you won't be mad first."

"Do you want me to lie to you? Because if you say the name Sebastian or some dumb shit like that, I promise nothing."

She giggles. "It's nothing like that. I promise."

I consider this. "I promise, but I include an addendum that if I do get mad that it will be in response to whatever you've done. Same scale."

"I accept."

"Now, what is it?"

She makes a face. "I found a poem you wrote the night you stayed and then left before I woke up. It might be a poem or lyrics or just thoughts that seem to kind of flow …"

I remember writing that. It was about watching her sleep and how it felt like the purest, sweetest moment I'd ever felt. It was just a bunch of thoughts that kind of rambled and I couldn't sleep.

I just forgot to take it.

"It was under my chair," she says. "And I gave it to Coy. Well, I didn't give it to him. I took a screenshot and sent it to him."

She bites her teeth together and waits for my reaction.

I feel a bit violated that my thoughts were shared outside of me, but I'm the one who forgot to take it with me. And I know, without a doubt, that she meant well.

"Okay," I say. "I'm not mad. I'm not thrilled, but I'm not mad."

She squeals. "Good, because Coy wants you to call him. He wants to buy it from you, but there are contracts and stuff that you'll have to sign because he wants to record it—"

"What?"

My eyes about fall out of my head.

"I know, right?" She beams. "You are so talented. Coy thinks so too. He will be home in a few days again—something happened, I don't know—and he wants to sit down with you and talk to you about maybe actually writing some stuff for him."

I don't know what to say. I just stand there like an idiot and wonder if it's a dream. Because it feels like it.

"See what happens when you don't block your blessings?" she asks. "Good things happen."

I pull her to me and kiss her again.

Good things happen, indeed.

EPILOGUE #2

Three months later ...

Hollis

Me: My abs are a little worse for the wear, but they still look better than yours.

It takes a minute before my texts blow up.

River: For the love of God.

Crew: Do you just sit around and think about your abs?

Me: Sometimes. Don't you?

Crew: Never.

River: Honestly? Yeah. Sometimes. But I don't think about texting you about it.

Me: How are the audiobooks coming?

River: Oh, I have more genius to share. Call me later. This time, it's about fish.

Crew: Why do I feel like I missed something?

Me: Consider yourself lucky, Hollywood.

Crew: Done.

Larissa lies asleep next to me. She brought new sheets and blankets to the house, and I think she used Lysol on everything before she touched it. But, hey—whatever it takes to get her to visit me on the weekends that I can't get to Savannah.

Me: Having dinner with Coach next week. He wants to know my plans post-graduation. I think he's going to offer me a job this summer working with the receivers.

Crew: Why? You can't catch.

River: Burn!

Crew: Kidding. That's awesome, Hollis.

Me: I'm going to turn it down. I'm not going to the Combine either. Turns out that I played ball for the people and not the game.

River: Sounds genius-level thought process.

I laugh.

Crew: So what are you going to do then?

Me: I'm going to graduate and then I'm going to work with Kelvin McCoy and write some music.

River: THAT IS SICK.

Crew: Oh, wow.

Me: I might suck at it. I'm nervous. But it should be fun.

River: It'll definitely be fun.

Me: Okay, well, that's all I had to say.

Crew: You are so random.

Me: Again, you asked for random check-ins.

River: This is true, Hollywood.

Crew: Check-in made. Good night.

River: Later.

Me: Night.

I lean against the pillows and sigh.

Tossing and turning, I try to sleep, but I can't. Not even with Larissa beside me. I'm in a funk again where my brain just spins all night and wonders about everything from the *Titanic* to my sister.

I haven't heard back from Child Protective Services about Harlee. My old case manager said she'd try to track her down but didn't know how possible that would be. That was two days ago. It's as though now I've found my peace—my future—I need to reconcile with my past too.

It's time Harlee had a big brother again. Someone to show up for her. Someone in her corner to love her unconditionally.

Someone like me.

I climb out of bed and sneak out of the room. Maybe if I finish the last thing on my to-do list, I'll be able to sleep.

Crew's desk is in the corner of the living room. I sit down at it. The notebook I left on top is still there, and I open it.

I find the first blank piece of paper and pick up a pen.

Dear Philip and Kim,

Hey, guys. I know it's been a while. I just wanted to check in and let you know I'm doing great now …

A NOTE FROM THE AUTHOR

Dear Reader,

Thank you for reading The Relationship Pact. I hope you enjoyed Hollis and Larissa's story.

If you want to keep reading about these football players, you're in luck. The Kings of Football series contains two more standalone stories by two other amazing authors. In the next few pages, you can take a peek at Ilsa Madden-Mills' The Revenge Pact and Meghan Quinn's The Romantic Pact.

Also, **if you want more Coy and Bellamy, their novel is out now**! It's called Reputation and you can read the first chapter if you keep swiping.

Please consider this your official invitation to my reader groups, Books by Adriana Locke (Facebook) and All Locked Up (Goodreads). I'd love to see you there!

Thank you again for reading. I'd be thrilled if you would consider leaving a review for The Relationship Pact.

Keep reading for all the books.

With love,

Adriana

THE REVENGE PACT

Excerpt from *The Revenge Pact (Kings of Football)* by Ilsa Madden-Mills
The Revenge Pact

River

"Why is the elevator so slow?" she mutters.

"Tell me three things you're grateful for," I say.

She does a double take. "Is this where I'm like your…pet project? Don't feel sorry for me."

Rainbow, sorry is the *last* thing I feel for you.

I want you under me.

Deep and hard.

There aren't enough minutes in the day for how long I want to fuck you.

She blows out a breath. "Fine. I can see you aren't going to budge. One, June is still around. Sam is keeping her low key.

Two, I finished my paper, and three, I got off work to go on the ski trip."

"How are things with Donovan?"

Her throat bobs. "I-I can't talk to you about him. I mean, yeah, um, it…doesn't feel right, you know, to him." A sigh escapes her lips.

Right. He's her boyfriend and *my* frat brother.

The door opens and she slips out, her arm brushing against my chest. I follow, sucking down the electricity between us. "I just wanted to check in—"

"I know what this is, why you're being nice to me—"

"Yeah? Tell me, because I can't figure it out," I snap, annoyed she won't open up while the other side is pissed at myself for asking. "Trust me, I wish I didn't…" I stop, my jaw clenching.

She stops at the door to class and turns to face me. Her expression torn, she takes a deep breath. "Your paper. I'm sorry I can't help you, I really am. I love helping others, but I don't think it's a good idea for us…" She licks her lips, her gaze avoiding mine. "There's something about you and me—" She halts and looks down at her feet. "Anyway, I know a few students who tutor athletes. Let me give you their names—"

"No one but you, Anastasia."

"What? Why?"

Instinct takes over and I back her against the wall, towering over her. I tilt her chin up, and she doesn't speak or move, just breathing fast, as my hand slides around to her nape. A hum of heat goes through my body as my hands tangle in her hair.

"River…what…" Pink rises on her cheeks as her lashes flutter.

Fuck.

Every time, I'm pushing a little more, the dark side of me winning. Monday. Her apartment. Now.

I could kiss her right now, but it's wrong, immensely so, I'm being bad, so bad, but one touch and my dick is a steel pipe, damn, what would it be like to have her in my arms…

She gazes up at me, her eyes flaring, the gold around her pupils darkening. She swallows as goose bumps appear on her neck.

A primal sound builds in my throat.

Anger.

Frustration.

Loyalty.

Dammit. I shouldn't be this close, shouldn't touch her—

"I'll wait." I grind my teeth and step back.

Her lips part, a small puff of air coming out. She looks at my mouth. "For what?"

The lethal side of me, the one itching to play this game no matter the consequences, tries to take over and speak the truth. I shove it down.

You, I say in my head.

Leaving her there, I sweep past her and go to my seat.

Five fucking rows back.

To find out what happens with River and Ana, click HERE.

THE ROMANTIC PACT

Excerpt from *The Romantic Pact (Kings of Football)* by Meghan Quinn
The Romantic Pact

Crew

"Hazel?" I ask, my heart tripping at the sight of an old friend.

Her warm, caramel-colored eyes snap to mine, her face registering shock. "Crew?" A small smile pulls at her lips. She checks her seat number and then her ticket again and smiles even larger. "Would you look at that? Seems as though we're seatmates."

"Holy shit," I say as she takes a seat and beams at me.

"How are you, Hollywood?"

"Better now." I wrap my arms around her and pull her into a hug.

Hazel Allen.

Born and raised in the neighboring house to Pops's farm, this outgoing ball of sugar and spice was a staple of my childhood ever since I can remember. Her grandpa, Thomas, was best friends with Pops, and she worked on the farm from a very young age. Whenever I visited, she always made fun of me and my latest West Coast style as she strutted around in overalls, a tank top, and rubber boots. Her hair was always tied up on the top of her head, with a rolled-up bandanna around the crown to hold back any stray hairs.

Down to earth, fun, and a jokester, Hazel was one of my best friends growing up.

Pen pals.

Long-distance friends.

And of course, each other's first kiss.

When we pull away, Hazel lifts her hand to my face and presses her palm to my cheek. "God, you just keep getting more and more handsome."

I chuckle.

"And this scruff. Now you're really looking like your DILF of a dad."

"Can you not refer to my dad as a DILF? It really creeps me the fuck out."

"Ahh, but he is a hot piece of dad ass. Sorry." She shrugs, sets her backpack on the floor, then turns in her seat to face me. "When my Grandpa told me about this trip, I had an inkling you might be my traveling partner, but I wasn't sure." She takes my hand in hers. "God, I'm so glad it's you."

"The feeling is mutual, Haze," I say, taking in her rosy, freckled cheeks and the way her hair softly falls over her forehead. *Thank you, Pops.* How easy it will be to travel with one of my best friends.

God, when was the last time I saw her? I think it's been a few years, to be honest. Once college started, I kind of lost contact with everyone. Training, studying game videos, and perfecting my throw took over.

Eyes softening, she asks, "How have you been? I saw your season . . ." She winces.

"Yeah," I huff out, staring down at the way her small hand fits in mine, the callouses on her fingers from all the hard work on the farm reminding me just how different our lives are, despite a lot of the variables being the same. "Wasn't my best show on the field. Just wasn't in it mentally."

"I can understand that." She squeezes my hand and then says, "But we're not here to talk about all of your interceptions, and I mean all of them . . ." When I glance up at her, she's smiling a Julia Roberts smile. I poke her side and she laughs, her head falling back as she pushes my hand away.

"How have you been, Hazel?" God, I've missed this girl.

"Oh, you know, just living the life out on the farm. Got caught up in some mourning, ate way too much pumpkin pie this past fall. Did you get your fair share of pumpkin spice lattes?" She nudges me. "I know what a basic bitch you are."

I laugh. "Yeah, I had a few."

"A few? I remember senior year in high school when you were drinking one a day. At least, that's what you wrote to me. Then again, it has been three years . . ."

"Has it?" I ask, knowing damn well it's been three years since I've seen her. Three years since . . . hell, three years since I ran from her.

Want to find out exactly why Crew ran away from Hazel? Oo, it's a doozy. Keep reading here: https://amzn.to/2HLdH60

Want to see why Bellamy hates Coy? You're in luck! REPUTATION, their enemies-to-lovers story comes out on January 5th. You can preorder it HERE.

Can't wait? Swipe to the next page to read Chapter One.

CHAPTER ONE: REPUTATION

Coy Mason & Bellamy Davenport's Story

Coy

"You're not doing anything stupid, are you?"

"Not yet," I say, slurping the milk off my spoon. "But I just got here. Give me time."

My eldest brother, Holt, half-laughs, half-groans through the phone.

The groan is there because he knows me enough to be afraid I'm serious. The laugh is there because, as much as he hates it, he's entertained by my antics.

Somewhat, anyway.

I scoop up another spoonful of fruity cereal and shove it into my mouth. Ice-cold milk dribbles down my chin, and I swipe it away with the back of my hand.

"At least you decided to stay with Mom and Dad," Holt says. "Maybe that'll keep you out of trouble."

"Yeah, because that's worked out so well in the past."

"Good point."

I lean against the counter. The edge of the marble is cold and bites into my hip. I wish for a split second that I had bothered to put a shirt on when I woke up twenty minutes ago.

"I almost rented a house on Tybee Island," I say, "but figured I might as well save the cash. Besides, Mom cleans my room and makes food just how I like it. I can't really go wrong here."

"You realize you're in your mid-twenties now and have money of your own, right?"

"Your point, old man?"

Holt chuckles. "I'm simply pointing out that you're capable of procuring food and housing on your own."

"I procured them on my own." I scrape the little flakes of cereal off the side of the bowl. "I called Mom myself … which was an easy choice when I got hit with how much it was going to cost on Tybee. Do you know what places are going for down there? Hell, Holt. I might quit performing and buy rental homcs."

"Great idea. I'm sure Wade would help you."

"Very funny," I say, making a face.

Out of all of my brothers, Wade is the last one I want to deal with. About anything. Not that any of them are particularly a barrel of fun—except my youngest brother, Boone—but Wade and I rarely see eye to eye on anything. If I'm music and mayhem, he's silence and spreadsheets. I'm not even sure how we have the same genetics.

"Be nice, Coy," Holt says.

"What? You think that Wade and I could do anything together? He has a resting dick face and a repulsion for strip clubs. Yeah. I think not."

Holt struggles to hide his laughter. He succeeds … barely.

"I'm just happy to hear you're managing your money well," Holt says. "Even if you can't manage your women."

"Hey now," I say, dunking the spoon into the bowl again with a little more force than necessary. "Keep your jealousy in check.

I can't help it that I'm a rock star and make women lose their damn minds."

"Rock star?" Holt's laughter fills the line with no attempt at restraint. "That's a stretch."

I smile. "Okay. You're right. I believe the last headline I saw called me a *country music sensation*. If it makes you feel better to call me that, I'm good with it."

"Well, the last headline *I* saw said something about you fleeing Los Angeles with your tail between your legs."

Fucker.

I fill my mouth with cereal before a bunch of verbal diarrhea comes spewing out.

My tail between my legs.

What-the fuck-ever.

My stomach churns the children's cereal as Willa Welch and a particular day last week comes to mind.

The pretty blond actress is better at her job than anyone understands. Hell, I'm not even sure what's real and what's not when it comes to her.

The only thing I am certain of is, somehow, I was automatically the bad guy in the press.

Again.

I swallow hard before taking another bite.

My brain plays the incident back again. The way the boutique door sounded when it closed behind us. The sun's bright rays as we strolled down the street. The way she pivoted out of nowhere and looked like she was going to cry.

My confusion. The bag—the one holding the overpriced shirt with the semi-witty saying on it that I'd just bought her as a token of good faith—coming straight for my head. My shock. The shrill of her voice followed by the swarm of paparazzi who ate the dramatics up like starving hyenas.

I've only been caught off guard a few times in my life, but this was one of them. My first thought was that our shared agent,

Meadow, had concocted this fight for Willa and me just like she created our fake relationship. It seemed crazy but so did the original premise.

"*You need to clean up this bad-boy image you have, Coy. Willa needs to dirty hers up some to get the roles she wants. It's perfection,*" my agent said.

I was quite satisfied with my reputation but whatever. I just wanted the cash, and if being a nice guy would get me more opportunities, I was in. Besides, all I had to do was pretend with Willa.

All of it was bullshit.

One of us forgot that.

That one of us wasn't me.

It all came to a screeching halt—along with a dozen cars—on Sunset Boulevard. I can't remember what I said, but I was silenced by Willa throwing her coffee in my face as the grand finale. Thankfully, it was iced.

"Are you listening to me?" Holt asks.

"I did get the hell out of LA," I say, annoyed. "But the only thing between my legs was my giant—"

"Okay, okay." Holt's sigh is tinged with amusement. "When are you planning on going back?"

"Not sure. I swore a blood oath to Meadow that I'd stay under the radar until she works her PR magic. I'm supposed to relax and write music—two of the three things I do best."

My brother snorts. "I don't even want to know the third thing."

"Your call, but I could probably give you a few pointers."

Holt seamlessly changes the subject to some business deal he's working on, but I find it hard to follow along. My attention span is already short, thanks to the reminder of Willa.

The back of my neck tenses as I work through the asinine events leading up to me being in Savannah.

My jaw pulses as I try to calm down. It's a load of crap that

I'm banished to my parents' house while she's allowed to stay home and cry to the press. For what? Nothing I did.

Why am I always the bad guy? I mean, granted, I usually am, but why is it a foregone conclusion that I screwed up?

It doesn't sit well with me, but I can't do anything about it except be pissed.

"You can go with us if you want," Holt says.

"Where?"

"You weren't listening, were you?"

"Kind of," I admit. "Not really."

He goes on again, repeating the offer to go with him … somewhere. But my attention is redirected.

The sound of footsteps rings through the kitchen. My mother breezes through the doorway in what looks like a lazy stroll, but it's not. I can see the wheels turning in her head as she glances my way and floats me an easy smile.

My mother makes *everything* look easy. She never used a cleaning service or bought dinner out very often for our family of seven. She managed the house, her five sons, a husband with a penchant for gin martinis and poker, and was still on the board of directors for various Savannah programs. Everyone thinks my brothers got their drive from our father, but it was really Mom. She's the queen around here.

She points at the phone with a perfectly painted red fingernail. "Is that important?" she whispers.

"Nah. It's just Holt," I say around a mouthful of cereal.

"Don't talk with your mouth full," she admonishes before letting my error go. "I have an appointment in twenty minutes and will be home around six. Your father should be home slightly before me."

"Got it."

"Can you take the trash out for me, please?" she asks as casually as if she's asking me what I want for dinner—a question she did not ask.

My spoon pauses midway to my mouth. Milk drips off the sides and hits the counter.

"Did you just ask me to take out the trash?" I ask.

"Yes, Coy, I did." She slides a water bottle into her oversized black leather bag. "Is that a problem?"

She glances at me over her shoulder with *that look* in her eye. It's a quiet challenge, a silent invitation to press the issue.

"Mom," I say, not really wanting to press the issue but unable to help myself. "Really?"

She stops at the door leading to the garage. "Really what?"

"I had the number one song on the radio for eight weeks two months ago, and …"

She opens the garage door as she simultaneously pins me to my seat with a firm gaze. After a long, awkward few seconds, her face breaks out into a victorious smile.

"Do it before I get home, please. Love you, Coy. Tell Holt I love him too."

The door snaps closed behind her.

"Well, I'll be damned," I mutter.

"Better get that trash taken out," Holt says with a laugh. "I'll let ya go. I have a meeting with Oliver in a few anyway."

"Tell my favorite brother I said hi."

"I'll remember that the next time you call me needing a favor."

"Well, you could be my favorite if you come over here and take out the trash for me," I joke.

"Hard no. I pay someone to take mine out. Besides," he says with what I'm sure is a shit-eating grin, "it might do you some good to remember where you came from."

I look around the kitchen. The counters are a white granite and set off a dark-colored Viking range. Sub-Zero freezer drawers and a blast chiller are hidden in the cabinets. A crystal chandelier hangs arrogantly overhead.

"Yeah," I say, my voice full of sarcasm. "Better remember my roots."

"That's not what I mean, asshole."

I feign shock. "Asshole? That's it. I'm going to have to bump another brother over you on the favorites list."

"So what you're saying is that Oliver and Boone are ahead of me, and Wade is last?"

"Well, yeah, basically."

Holt laughs. "I gotta go. Call me later."

"Bye."

"See ya."

I end the call and slide my phone across the counter. It narrowly misses the splashes of milk dotting the surface around my cereal bowl.

A loud, unnecessary growl rumbles through the air as I stretch my arms overhead. The clock says it's late in the afternoon, but my brain lobbies to go back to bed. I try to bargain with myself that I got into town late and didn't get to bed until well into the early morning hours. But truth be told, I wouldn't have been to bed before three in the morning anyway.

I march to the cabinet where I think the trash bags are kept. There's a broom and a mop and a basket full of batteries. It raises a lot of questions that I force out of my mind.

I'm about to give up anyway when a slight rasp on the door leading to the side yard distracts me.

"Who is that?" I mumble as the faint knocking sounds again.

My family would use the garage door. If any salespeople manage to get by the neighborhood's gated entry, they'd knock on the front door. The only people who would use the side door would be my dad if he's coming in from grilling out … so twice a year at best, and this isn't one of those two occasions.

I run my hands down my jeans—the same ones I slept in last night—and head to the door. There's an outline of someone shorter than me by a good bit through the thin cream-colored curtain.

"Hang on," I say, fiddling with the lock.

It takes a few seconds to figure out the fancy new combination lock that wasn't here the last time I visited. Lucky for me, my parents' choice of numbers was predictable.

I open the door.

"Hello—fuck!" I shout as I'm hit in the side of the face.

Hard.

It feels like I was smashed by a large man or attacked by a swarm of bees. My eyes go blurry from the pain radiating through the side of my face.

"Oh, my gosh! I'm so sorry," a voice squeals in front of me.

"Did I kill him?" another voice asks from farther away.

"No," the person in front of me says. "Just … sit down, Bree. Please. Right there. Sit still."

I struggle through the wetness building in my eyes to see. I work my jaw back and forth to try to loosen the stiffness already settling in my face.

Finally, I get my bearings and open my eyes.

Through the blurry haze, I think I see heaven. And a little piece of hell.

Purchase HERE.

BOOKS BY ADRIANA LOCKE

The Exception Series

The Exception

The Connection

The Perception

Landry Family Series

Sway

Swing

Switch

Swear

Swink

Sweet—coming soon

The Gibson Boys Series

Crank

Craft

Cross

Crave

Crazy

Dogwood Lane Series

Tumble

Tangle

Trouble

Mason Family Series

Restraint

Reputation

Reckless

Honey Creek Series

Like You Love Me

Cherry Falls

608 Alpha Avenue

907 For Keeps Way

Standalone Novels

Sacrifice

Wherever It Leads

Written in the Scars

Lucky Number Eleven

Battle of Sexes

The Relationship Pact

For an email every time Adriana has a new release, sign up for an alert here: http://bit.ly/AmazonAlertAddy or text the word adriana to 21000

ACKNOWLEDGMENTS

I would like to take a moment and acknowledge the incredible people that have supported me and stood by my side as I wrote this book.

No one comes before the Creator. Thank you for your infinite blessings and patience as I learn to be the person you designed.

My husband, Saul, is my everything. You're my best friend. I love you.

My children, Alexander, Aristotle, Achilles, and Ajax are the reason behind everything I do. I'm your mother before I'm anything.

My parents are with me in spirit every day. I could not be the person I am had I not been born to them.

Peggy and Rob are the people that pick up all the pieces I drop. I love you two more than I could ever express.

Meghan Quinn and Ilsa Madden-Mills are truly the best teammates in this process. I adore you both and am humbled to work with you.

Kari March is my first friend in this world. She sets an example in professionalism and friendship.

Tiffany Remy is my right hand. Without her, everything falls apart. We did it again.

Mandi Beck is the Bellamy to my Larissa. She's the best friend a girl could want.

S.L. Scott makes my life better. I'm beyond lucky to call her one of my best friends in the world.

Jen Costa and Susan Raynor are the original beta readers that have been with me since my first book. I can't do this without you.

Jenn Wolfel answered my plea for help. Your insight made this book better. Thank you.

Anjelica Grace was my cheerleader and sounding board. I'm in awe of your insight and can't wait to repay the favor.

Kristi Lynn picked up the phone when I needed her. Thank you for going on this journey with me.

Chelle Sloan is my go-to for all things sports. She probably regretted that this time. Thank you for always being willing to help me out.

My editors, Marion and Jenny, are true professionals in every sense of the word. Thank you for being all you are to me and the book community.

Michele Ficht never turns me down when I ask her to proof-read. I'm so honored to work with you and for your friendship.

Letitia Hasser's patience and kindness blew me away when designing this cover. I adore you.

Tiffany Black, of T.E. Black Designs, helped create gorgeous images for this launch. I'm in awe of her talent.

Candi Kane PR never fails to impress. Thank you, Candi, for always being what I need.

Jenn Watson with Social Butterfly PR has astounded me with her kindness. You are amazing.

Ebbie Moresco, Kaitie Reister, and Stephanie Gibson keep the wheels turning. You three make my life better—and not just because of what you do for me. Because of your friendship.

A huge hug goes out to all the bloggers that shout about my books. You help make it possible for me to keep writing. Thank you doesn't seem sufficient, but it's all I have.

And, last but not least, thank you to every reader that picks up my book. I know you have a million choices and I'm honored you chose mine. I hope you found a couple of hours of entertainment inside these pages and that this story made you smile. Sending you all my love.

ABOUT THE AUTHOR

USA Today Bestselling author Adriana Locke lives and breathes books. After years of slightly obsessive relationships with the flawed bad boys created by other authors, Adriana created her own.

She resides in the Midwest with her husband, sons, two dogs, two cats, and a bird. She spends a large amount of time playing with her kids, drinking coffee, and cooking. You can find her outside if the weather's nice and there's always a piece of candy in her pocket.

Besides cinnamon gummy bears, boxing, and random quotes, her next favorite thing is chatting with readers. She'd love to hear from you!

Join her reader group and talk all the bookish things by clicking here.

www.adrianalocke.com

Made in the USA
Middletown, DE
20 March 2021

35914170R00176